ALL FOR THE TASKMASTER

by

MICHAEL O'CONNOR

CHIMERA

All Chimera books are distributed by Turnaround Distribution, Unit 3, Olympia Trading Estate, Coburg Road, London N22 6TZ

All for Her Master published by
Chimera Publishing Ltd
PO Box 152
Waterlooville
Hants
PO8 9FS

Printed and bound in Great Britain by
Cox & Wyman Ltd, Reading.

The right of Michael O'Connor to be identified as author of this book has been asserted
in accordance with section 77 and 78 of the Copyrights Designs and Patents Act 1988

ALL FOR HER MASTER

Michael O'Connor

The coarse young man did not seem at all concerned by the prospect of being caught in the room. He stroked and prodded Constance, all the while crudely continuing to compliment her physical attributes. Eventually, much to her relief, his attention was diverted to the board game on the table.

'I wonder what this is all about,' he mused, leaning over to carefully study it. 'Better not touch anything, just to be on the safe side. Wouldn't want to get on the wrong side of your master.' He turned back to Constance. 'I wonder how long he'll be gone for. Long enough for me to have a little fun with you, eh?'

She whimpered and vigorously shook her head.

He grinned. 'If I didn't know better, I'd think you couldn't wait to get rid of me. Know what? I think I'll take a chance and live dangerously. If your master does come back before I'm finished with you, we'll just have to hope he understands. I'm sure you won't object to me taking out your gag, will you?'

She hesitated, then shook her head.

He reached for the strap at the back of her head. 'I didn't think so. You don't have to worry. I won't hurt you. Just a quick blow-job an' I'll be on my way. Okay?'

Chapter One

Constance Brooking surveyed her reflection in the full-length wall mirror and permitted herself a slight smile. Blushing she might well be, but she looked nothing like any woman who had ever walked up a church aisle to the strains of *Here Comes the Bride*.

A great deal of thought had gone into the costume for the biggest day of her life, though none of it had been hers. Up to an hour ago, she had not even known what she would be wearing. Her master had only promised it would be nothing she would have ever stocked in her boutique.

How right he had been.

Her wedding dress resembled some fashion designer's S/M fantasy brought to life in gleaming chains and strong, shiny black rubber, letting the firm globes of Constance's breasts spill over the top. They were tightly wrapped in a light silver chain, criss-crossed several times around her shoulders and held in place by a padlock attached to the back of her iron collar. A silver bullet was clamped to both nipples. Her buttocks, tightly clenched by the tightness of her dress and covered in body oil, were also bare. She teetered unsteadily on the high spike heels of her glossy black leather thigh boots. A six-inch wide chain joined them together at the ankles.

This was the day of the slave princess and Constance had never before had such attention lavished upon her. Two bridesmaids, identically attired in transparent gowns of loosely fitting white silk that flowed to their ankles, had been assigned to her preparations. They had first bathed her, then massaged her all over with scented oils. Then, while one had brushed her hair, the other had lovingly manicured her pubis. Only then had she been allowed to see her outfit.

'Right, time to tie your hands,' said the plump blonde half of the duo.

Constance obediently raised her arms and intertwined her fingers at the back of her neck.

'The perfect bride in bondage,' the bridesmaid said with a smile, securing her wrists in the handcuffs chained to her collar.

'This is definitely not how I envisaged my wedding day,' said Constance.

'You look beautiful,' the red-haired bridesmaid assured her. 'I wish I had been hitched to my master in such style. Unfortunately, we had to make do with a registry office.'

'We've already been married in a registry office,' Constance reminded her. 'What's happening now is just... Well, I don't quite know what you'd call it.'

'The really significant ceremony,' said Barbara. 'You've been joined as husband and wife. Now you're to become slave and master. This is what you really want, isn't it?'

'It's what I've always wanted,' Constance replied. 'I just don't know what to expect when I step outside that door. Can't you at least give me a hint?'

'And risk a public thrashing from our masters?' Barbara shook her head emphatically. 'It's time we put on your veil and let you find out for yourself what awaits you.'

'Wait – I need a cigarette,' Constance pleaded.

'Nervous?' the second bridesmaid asked.

'Terrified,' she replied. 'Besides, it's the prerogative of the bride to be a few minutes late.'

'As long as you don't mind not being able to sit down for the meal.' Barbara took a cigarette from a packet on the dressing table and placed it between Constance's roseate glossed lips. The red-haired bridesmaid lit it and held it between her fingers, as the bride-to-be smoked gratefully.

'If we keep them waiting much longer, we'll all have our backsides reddened,' Barbara said anxiously.

Constance exhaled a cloud of smoke. 'Would we have it any other way? Okay, I'm ready.'

Five minutes later, the heavy oak door swung slowly open and all heads in the huge room beyond turned towards the bride. With her heavy black silk veil in place, only Constance's blue eyes remained visible. Momentarily forgetting that her boots were chained together, she took a nervous step forward and almost collapsed in an undignified heap on the treacherously polished red rubber carpet.

She hurriedly composed herself and began shuffling awkwardly towards the altar, which seemed to be miles away. The makeshift construction was draped in rich red velvet and laid out with a coiled whip and a small black cushion in the centre. Before it stood her husband of three days. What meant far more to them both was that he was about to become her lifelong master. Her bridesmaids remained in the doorway behind her, trying to keep their anxiety concealed. If they had overlooked even the slightest detail of her preparations, they would be severely punished by their masters.

Constance kept her eyes fixed straight ahead, ignoring the camcorder that followed her every move. Masters standing sentinel-like, in uniforms of rubber and black leather, lined her path on either side. Their female slaves knelt at their feet, as befitted their subservient role. Not for the first time, Constance found herself wondering just what manner of humiliation she was letting herself in for. As long as she managed not to trip, she told herself that she would be fine.

The long tongue of a whip snaked through the air, the sound of its crack on tender flesh like a rifle shot breaking the silence. Constance yelped and stumbled, feeling a line of white-hot fire streak across her buttocks. A cruel smile crossed the face of the tall man who had delivered the lash.

She regained her balance and continued her shuffle towards the altar. Casting anxious glances from left to right, she noticed whips gripped in the hands of several more men. Knowing it would be both inappropriate and pointless to beg for mercy, she braced herself for the inevitable. Though it seemed a lifetime since she had been a stranger to the sting of a master's whip, this was one occasion when it was far from welcome.

A few agonising yards further on, she saw a bearded master to her left grin in anticipation. Standing opposite him was a familiar figure in black leather. Having taken a few steps past the two men, she could not resist an anxious backward glance. Two whips hissed as one, their lashes exploding across her buttocks. With a shriek that echoed off the white walls of the high-ceilinged room, Constance fell to her knees. A signal from the dark-suited man at the altar brought her bridesmaids rushing to her assistance.

'You're doing fine,' Barbara whispered as they helped her to her feet.

'Grin and bear it,' her companion added. 'Not every bride has the privilege of being whipped to the altar.'

8

Constance sighed. 'What a lucky lady I am.'

As she resumed her tortuous trek in bondage, several dozen whips beat a loud bridal refrain on the rubber carpet. Whenever a lash licked her buttocks, a high-pitched cry issued from beneath her sombre veil. By the time she reached the altar, several minutes and a further humiliating tumble later, her rear cheeks were liberally streaked with the flaming signature of the whip.

The next part of the ceremony had been carefully rehearsed beforehand, courtesy of the bridesmaids. Should Constance make any mistakes now, they would be held responsible and suitably punished.

She lowered herself to her knees on the black satin-covered cushion at her master's feet. As she gazed lovingly up into his eyes, a second man took up position behind her.

'Is it your wish to be taken as the slave of this man before whom you kneel?' he enquired in a loud voice, pressing the burnished ash of a cane firmly against her throbbing buttocks.

'It is,' she replied, without hesitation.

He looked at the man towering over her. 'And is it your wish to have this woman as your slave?'

'It most certainly is,' he answered.

'Slave, recite the oath of subservience to your master,' the other man told her.

Constance cleared her throat, then repeated the phrase she had been studiously learning for the past several days. 'Master, I humbly offer myself to you. I would be honoured if you would take me as your slave. I promise to love, honour and obey you, for better or worse, for pleasure or pain, in bondage and submission, till death us do part.'

Following a momentary pause, her master spoke. 'I

accept you as my slave and do hereby declare that I will love, train and discipline you, by whip or by cane, with reason or without, however I may please, for as long as I wish.'

The assembled congregation greeted the exchange of vows with a resounding forty-eight whip salute on the rubber carpet. Constance's master clipped a leash to her collar, led her on her knees to the altar and directed her to rise. As she bent over the altar, she began to tremble. She knew what was coming next and dreaded it as she had never dreaded anything in her entire life. But it was much too late for second thoughts. In consenting to become her master's wife and slave, she accepted all the pain and indignity the latter entailed.

She rested her chin on the cushion on top of the altar. The red-haired bridesmaid stood in front of her and placed both hands firmly on her shoulders. The blonde unhooked the chain that joined her boots together, then pushed her feet wide apart. An iron manacle on a short chain, bolted to the floor, was fitted around either ankle, ensuring she would be unable to move her legs. The rubber of her wedding dress was stretched to bursting point, but it had served its purpose. With a gleaming razor blade, her master sliced it open from her backside to her ankles. Barbara drew apart the folds like a pair of curtains, leaving Constance's recently shaven pink pubis lewdly exposed. The entire assembly of masters and slaves gathered around, all eager for a grandstand view of the highlight of the occasion. Crouched on one knee, directly behind Constance, the man with the camcorder was in prime position.

'You have the ring?' enquired her master.

The man who was serving as vicar for the sado-ceremony produced a small red box from his jacket pocket and opened it. Inside was a slender gold ring. Having glanced at it, her master then took a slightly larger black box from his own pocket. Constance did not need to look to know what was inside. She had to bite her lower lip to suppress a whimper as he withdrew a long silver needle and held it aloft for all to see.

Chapter Two

Rich, dynamic and unattached – that was Constance Brooking. But the latter she had ceased to regard as an achievement. It was not that she wanted the traditional ball-and-chain of husband and kids. Motherhood held marginally less appeal than a clitoridectomy. Constance's ever more urgent need was for a man in the masterful mould – one who would know how to release the submissive slut straining within her. Until recently, all her energies had been devoted to making Brooking's Boutique a resounding success. Now, it was time to expend that same energy on her love-life.

With her combination of exceptional beauty and supreme self-confidence, Constance was too intimidating for most men. Those who did dare to get close invariably left her disappointed. She had begun to believe that all men were bland clones, when it came to the bedroom – devotees of tedious seduction routines and equally lack-lustre love-making technique. When she yearned to be treated like a whore, they treated her like a princess. Even the dominant ones became wimps before they had fully satisfied her.

It was a pirate radio station, of all things, that finally restored her faith in the existence of real men. She found S/M-FM in the early hours of a Sunday morning as she tossed and turned in her bed, once again cursing the shortcomings of the male gender. Her increasingly desperate search for Mr Right had led her to answer a personal ad in a listings magazine. Several subsequent telephone conversations with the man who had placed the ad – a 35-year-old recently divorced 'entrepreneur' named Damon – had given her cause for optimism. He was friendly and talkative, his Mancunian accent displaying a refreshingly rough edge. By the time a first meeting had been arranged, Constance was already fantasising about being ravished by a burly giant with rough hands and a nice line in coital expletives.

Her expectations rendered the reality even more disappointing. She had arrived at the appointed bar at the appointed time, casually yet eye-catchingly dressed in cowboy boots, skin-tight black denim jeans, a cleavage-hugging black satin vest and a white jacket. Her naturally blonde hair had hung loosely about her shoulders, framing a face with high cheekbones and a creamy complexion that rendered make-up redundant.

Ten minutes later, Damon had arrived. Though they had not exchanged photographs, she had known that it was him the instant he entered the bar. He had been almost exactly as she had pictured him: craggily attractive and broad-shouldered, like a rugby player in an open-necked white shirt and bouncer's suit. He had cast a glance in her direction and their eyes had met briefly as he made his way to the bar. Constance had remained at her corner table, sipping her drink and trying to look nonchalant. Once he had been served, she had expected him to approach. Instead, he had glanced nervously in her direction again, before gulping down half his pint of beer in the manner of a man dying of thirst.

During the next half-hour he had consumed a further three pints, while continuing to throw frequent glances in her direction. Watching him, Constance had become ever more irritated. The masterful man she had spent all week looking forward to meeting was behaving like a teenager, tanking himself up with Dutch courage. Well, she was damned if she was going to make the first move. She had been tempted to get up and leave, but decided instead to wait and see what sufficient beer would eventually embolden him to do.

Finally, at the end of a prolonged leer in her direction, he had spoken to the bartender, who had then approached her table and informed her that the gentleman at the bar wished to buy her a drink.

'Tell him it's no wonder so many women are lesbians,' she had replied acidly.

She did not wait for the response of the inebriated lonely-heart, simply leaving the bar and going home.

Too frustrated to get to sleep that evening, Constance finally got out of bed. She went downstairs, poured herself a glass of wine, then returned to the bedroom. The easy-listening music from her favourite radio station was beginning to annoy rather than soothe. Sitting on the edge of the bed, she began turning the dial, more to distract herself than in the hope of finding more stimulating listening. Having skipped over a further half-dozen banal music stations, she heard a soft-accented male voice that grabbed her attention immediately.

'A great many women enjoy being dominated,' the presenter was saying. 'That may sound sexist – Neanderthal, even – but we enlightened folk know better, don't we? There are women listening right now – strong, confident and successful women – who nevertheless enjoy being dominated. They are sick to death of politically correct so-called new men, who are so afraid of taking the upper hand that they may as well be

14

castrated. It's time for a little honesty to hit the airwaves, my liberated friends. Thousands of ladies who crave the crack of a cane, or the smack of a firm hand on their bare backsides, are being denied the right to express their submissive nature by these limp-dicked wimps. That is not equality, my friends. That is not respect. What that is, is a shameful reflection on the state of nineties man.'

Constance could scarcely believe what she was hearing. Such talk was unheard of on the national airwaves, even at two in the morning.

'Ladies, don't just listen passively,' the presenter continued. 'This is your forum and this show is dedicated to the joys of female submission. Demand your rights on the only liberated radio station in the UK. Share your fantasies and desires with your masters at S/M-FM, in total confidence. That is my command. Obey me now!'

There was a sound like a whiplash, followed by a high-pitched squeal that could have been pain or pleasure, then he gave out a telephone number. As he proceeded to read a chapter from an explicit S/M book entitled *Number One Slave*, Constance grew convinced that she was listening to some form of weird nocturnal phone-in. After he had finished reading, the presenter took a call from a nervous-sounding woman who gave her name as 'LC'.

'My master commanded me to call you,' she said hesitantly. 'We listen to you every Saturday night and really enjoy the show. It's high time slaves and masters were given a voice on the airwaves.'

'I like a woman who knows how to grovel,' the presenter replied. 'What is it you wish to say to our listeners?'

'With your permission, I should like to tell you of a

game my master and I play,' LC answered.

'Permission granted.' At the silence that followed, he snapped, 'Well, come on. Speak up, or I shall instruct your master to cane you on air.'

She took a deep breath, then resumed speaking, in a faltering voice. 'My master has developed a computer game called "Password". To play it, he keys in a secret word. It can be any word, as long as it contains the letters S and M. I then press a letter key and the computer selects a command for me to carry out. It might be something simple, like kissing my master's boots for sixty seconds, or something much more degrading.'

'Such as?' the presenter prompted.

'I might... uh, for instance, have to hop around the room on one leg for two minutes, while screwing myself with a cucumber,' the woman answered. 'Or perhaps I would be commanded to stick a finger up my bottom and tap-dance for a minute. That one happened the last time we played. The game continues until I correctly spell out the word my master has entered.'

'Sounds like fun,' the presenter enthused. 'You are a very lucky slave to have such a creative master. Would you like to send a message to the many submissive women I know are listening at this very moment?'

'Uh, yes, okay,' she replied. 'I have been my master's slave for several years now, and we could not be happier. We love one another dearly and I am never forced to do anything against my will. I have a good job, lots of friends and a great social life, but when my master and I are alone, I am a different woman. To love and serve a man in this way is the most beautiful and fulfilling thing in the world. To any woman listening I would say, don't be afraid.'

At that moment Constance felt as though the caller

were speaking to her personally. She was still certain she was listening to some kind of bizarre X-rated play and the voice was that of an actress. But when the presenter, who called himself 'KT', repeated the telephone number of S/M-FM, she decided there was only one way to find out for sure.

Her call was answered by a woman with the maternal tones of a middle-aged agony aunt, who identified herself as 'G'. She did not ask Constance for her name and Constance would not have dreamt of volunteering it.

'This cannot be a real radio station,' Constance said.

'Oh, S/M-FM is very real, believe me,' the woman assured her. 'We're on air every weekend, from midnight to four a.m. Sub/dom community radio is what we're all about. You're a first-time listener, I can tell.'

'How ever did you manage to get a licence?' Constance demanded.

'We didn't,' G replied. 'You've heard of pirate radio, I assume? Well, we're as unlicensed as you could possibly get. It's when submissive women ring in that it all seems worthwhile. Would you like me to put you on air? You won't be asked to give your name, or any information that could identify you.'

'Why not?' said Constance, her heart beating faster. 'After the night I've had, I could do with a cheap thrill.'

A few moments later she heard the voice of KT welcoming her to his show.

'I still think this must be some kind of wind-up,' she began.

'You have your radio on in the background,' he replied. 'You hear your own voice from the speakers. Do you really think a so-called respectable station would be allowed to broadcast a show like this?'

'Perhaps not,' she conceded.

'Now that you are on air, do you have anything you wish to tell our listeners?' he demanded gently. 'Perhaps you'd like to reveal some of the kinky games you play with your master.'

'I don't have a master,' she replied, without thinking.

'No master?' His tone was sympathetic. 'But you would like to have one, wouldn't you? Why else would you be calling? Tell you what, why don't I be your master? We can play a little game right here on air. Doesn't that sound appealing, my poor lonely little virgin?'

'I'm no virgin,' she snapped.

'A fiery young woman who needs to be taken firmly in hand, then,' KT added. 'Well, are you game to be my slave of the air-waves, or would you rather we discussed politics?'

His arrogance infuriated and excited Constance, in equal measure. He was probably some dirty old man with a radio transmitter rigged up in his basement, seeking on-air cheap thrills. Nevertheless, it could not hurt to play along with him. 'Okay, I'll be your slave,' she agreed. 'What do I do?'

'Whatever I tell you,' he answered. 'Are you in your bedroom?'

She confirmed that she was.

'What are you wearing?'

'Just my knickers.'

'Describe them.'

'Lacy pink. Not much of them.'

'Take them off.'

Constance smiled. 'Whatever you say.'

'Address me as "master",' he said firmly. 'And don't be tempted to disobey my instructions just because I can't see you. I don't take kindly to cheating at games.'

'Yes, master,' she heard herself breathe as she reached with her free hand for the waistband of her panties. She had not intended to obey his instructions, but the firmness of his tone was sufficient to make her change her mind.

When she was naked he instructed her to kneel by the bed. She complied without hesitation.

'Now, I am going to hear your confession,' he said. 'You have a secret fantasy you wish to share with me. Don't be shy. I'm your master, tall and domineering. Close your eyes and I'm there in your bedroom with you, standing behind you, cane in hand. Would you like to feel my cane across your bare backside, whacking those soft, tender cheeks?'

'No, master,' she gasped, shutting her eyes.

'Then speak to me,' he told her. 'Bare your frustrated soul, just as you've bared your body. There can be no secrets between us. Understood?'

It took a few moments of further stern persuasion for Constance to summon a favourite fantasy from the recesses of her mind. She spoke haltingly as she began confessing, her voice sounding to her own ears like that of a shy young girl, rather than an assertive woman. 'I have this fantasy of visiting a... some kind of kinky club, where everybody is dressed in leather and rubber. I've read about such places in magazines, but never had the guts to visit one. Anyway, this place I'm thinking about has a darkroom at the back. It's pitch black in there, just like being blindfolded.

'I'm wearing a very short black leather dress and a mask, so that nobody will recognise me. I step into the darkroom and the door is bolted shut behind me. I don't know what to expect. It's terrifying, yet very exciting as well. There are a lot of people in there. Nobody speaks, but I can hear their heavy breathing. I'm feeling my way around. Someone grabs me and I cry out.

'The next thing I know there are hands all over me, peeling off my dress and groping me all over. I try to fight them off, but all these rough, horny men know exactly what I want. They strip me naked and push me to the ground. I don't know how many there are, but they're like a pack of wild animals, thinking about nothing but their own pleasure. They all have me, three or four at a time. They don't even know what I look like and they don't care. All I am to them is a slave, to be taken and humiliated until they've fully satisfied themselves. They could be young men, old men, handsome or ugly. I never see their faces: I just feel their hands and their cocks. When they've finished with me they throw me out of the darkroom, like a used condom.'

'You enjoyed telling me that story, didn't you?' KT said when she had finished.

'Yes, master,' she responded, having managed to lose herself completely in her fantasy.

'I enjoyed hearing it,' he continued. 'In fact, I should like to reward you for sharing it and for becoming a devotee of S/M-FM. There is a club just like the one you mentioned, where you can turn your fantasy into reality. Would you like to become a member – a truly liberated woman?'

Constance wasn't sure. Relating an anonymous masturbation fantasy over the phone was one thing, but turning it into reality might be a step too far. For all she knew, the voice on the other end of the line could be that of a psychopathic pervert. Then again, as he knew absolutely nothing about her, it could not hurt to say yes, even if she had no intention of actually visiting the place.

'Masturbate!'

The word cut like a hot sword through her reverie.

'What?' she cried.

'Play with yourself,' he told her. 'You're still my slave and I know how much sharing your dirty little story with me has turned you on – so do as I say.'

Almost dreamily, Constance allowed her free hand to drift down between her thighs, to cup the downy, hot mound of her sex.

'Tell me what you're thinking,' he commanded as she slipped a finger between her slick labia.

'I... I want you, master,' she gasped, thrusting her finger deeper. 'I want your hard cock inside me, taking me, making me come – ohhhhhh, yesssss, your big, hard, juicy cock in me...'

As she frigged herself to a rapid climax, KT urged her to describe in detail what he was doing to her. Immediately afterwards, as she returned to her senses, she was shocked by the complete lack of inhibition which had seized her. It was one thing to lose herself so completely in the grip of passion with a man, but she had never dreamt she could do it for a disembodied voice, especially with any number of people listening in. Even then, she did not put down the receiver.

'I think I've found a genuinely submissive lady,' KT said triumphantly. 'The name of the club is The Master's Masque. I'll put you back to G and she'll give you all the details, along with your own private password, which you'll need to gain admission. It's going to be my pleasure to guide you on your path to fulfilment as a slave, mystery woman.'

Chapter Three

The club was located in South London, which meant Constance could not use distance as an excuse for not going the following Thursday night. Although she was normally a very decisive person, she was plagued by doubts in the days following her call to S/M-FM. Dare she take the plunge, or should she forget ever having heard of the club?

She could think of a dozen reasons not to go, the principal one being the potential danger. At the same time it was the most compelling reason to proceed with her visit. Whatever happened, she was unlikely to encounter anything like her pathetic blind date from the previous Saturday night. In the end she knew she would never be able to forgive herself if she didn't at least check it out.

She pressed the buzzer on the black iron door to the basement club and glanced nervously round as she awaited a response.

'Password,' a gruff male voice demanded.

'Virginal,' Constance replied nervously.

A moment passed, then a bolt was drawn and the door was opened. Taking a deep breath, she stepped into the unknown.

Just as in her fantasy, The Master's Masque was a place for fetishists to parade their outrageous selves, a Mecca for masters and their submissive other halves. Rubber, leather and uniforms of every conceivable persuasion were the order of the night.

Constance entertained little hope of chancing upon the man of her dreams. She was there as a voyeur, window-shopping for cheap fantasies in a market of exotic creatures. Though she had never been timid by nature, something about the ambience of The Master's Masque intimidated her.

She also felt vulnerable in her provocatively low-cut dress of skin-tight black satin, with a slit running from the spiked heels of her shoes to the tops of her thighs, leaving the full length of her seamed black silk stockings and an inch of creamy thigh on display. She reasoned that her customary sharp suits and designer dresses would have made her look far more out of place in the club. She hid her eyes behind dark glasses, like a rock star in fear of being recognised.

She half-expected to be set upon and ravished on sight, but the assembled masters were quite content to ogle her from a safe distance — at least for the time being. As she made her way to the bar, glancing nervously round, she found herself wondering how many of the hundred or so people present had heard her broadcast her fantasy and masturbate over the air-waves the previous weekend. The call had whetted her appetite for illicit thrills and the thought that even one of these men might realise who she was caused a delicious thrill to run through her body.

The barmaid was a tall and strikingly attractive redhead in her early twenties. Her pert breasts were bare and a heavy gold padlock dangled from a steel clip on either nipple. In the full-length mirror behind the bar, Constance could see that all she wore below waist level were scarlet high heels and a pair of matching rubber tights, with cutouts through which the milky moons of her buttocks peeped. She tried not to stare as she ordered a glass of red wine.

'This one's on the house,' the barmaid said with a smile when she had poured Constance's drink. 'We like to make our new members feel welcome.'

'How did you know I was a new member?' Constance demanded.

'We spoke the other night,' the redhead replied. 'I'm G..'

Constance almost spilt her drink. So much for anonymity. At least in the dim light her blush might not be seen. 'Who else knows who I am?' she asked.

'Nobody knows who you are,' the girl answered. 'You're a mystery woman who called S/M-FM and shared a beautiful fantasy with our listeners. Let's give you a name. What are your initials?'

'CB.'

'Okay, you are now CB – code-name Virginal.'

'This is all very cloak-and-dagger,' said Constance.

'It's more fun that way,' G replied. 'Besides, the majority of our members are respectable pillars of the community. There's a big, unenlightened world out there that sees people like us as some kind of threat. The first time is always a bit nerve-wracking, but you'll soon be feeling right at home. Excuse me, I must get back to work.'

Constance took her drink to an unoccupied table nearby and seated herself on a cold iron chair. Creature comforts were obviously not a priority of The Master's Masque. In the centre of the table was a glossy magazine entitled *The Masque*. Below the blood red gothic-lettered heading was a picture of a blonde girl with huge breasts, whose features were concealed beneath a purple rubber face-mask. She was kneeling by a chair, her arms stretched above her head and her wrists chained together. Her prominent breasts were tightly wrapped in thick rope which left only the tips exposed. Another rope was wrapped around her lower body, from her hips to her knees. A master clad in black leather towered over her, brandishing a riding crop in his gloved right fist. His right boot was planted on the chair and his slave was licking the pointed toe through the mouth-slit of her mask.

Intrigued, Constance picked up the magazine and began leafing through it. The photographs and drawings on the glossy pages depicted masters and slaves in a variety of bizarre and erotic scenarios. The captions underneath claimed that all participants were members of The Master's Masque and many of the pictures had been taken in the club.

Constance could not help imagining herself as one of the helplessly trussed models, willingly submitting to the will of a domineering master, in the presence of an appreciative audience. In the back of the magazine were three pages of personal ads – many with photographs – from masters and couples seeking slaves for all manner of games, as well as from submissive women seeking to be dominated. It was a glimpse into a world she had only hitherto been informed about by occasional spicy newspaper stories. With every passing moment she grew more excited by the prospect of discovering the truth for herself.

'Fancy seeing a live show?' The soft voice interrupted her flight of fantasy. G was standing by her table, a knowing smile crossing her purple-painted lips. 'There's a show about to get underway in one of the play-rooms at the back,' G explained. 'I think you'd find it enlightening.'

'What kind of show?' asked Constance.

'Close encounters of the S/M kind,' G answered. 'It's much more exciting when you see it happening for real.'

It was an invitation Constance was in no mood to resist. She followed the tall slave to a black velvet padded door to the left of the bar.

'Enjoy,' said G, sliding open the heavy door and ushering her through.

The room beyond was in near total darkness, which rendered the sight on the spot-lit circular stage in the centre all the more striking. A pair of blindfolded and naked girls stood back-to-back on the podium, bound tightly together by thongs of thick leather around their shins, thighs and waists. Above their heads was a horizontal iron bar suspended from a pair of heavy chains, to which their wrists and upper arms were lashed. Their legs were spread wide apart and held in place by two chrome spreader bars manacled to their ankles. Fastened around their heads was a double harness of studded black leather, hanging by a chain from the overhead bar. The thick straps snugly constricted their foreheads and chins. Scrawled in red lipstick across the midriff of the plump blonde was the word 'pleasure'. 'Pain' was written on her black-haired companion in bondage. Small round red labels dotted the breasts of both.

Constance found herself drawn to the tableau, like a moth to a flame. She tried to imagine how the two women must be feeling at that moment, so utterly helpless and lewdly exposed before the eyes of dozens of people. Before tonight she would have thought otherwise, but she had no doubt that they were willing victims of whatever perverse ritual was underway. The mystery was their motivation in succumbing to such a public indignity

A moustachioed master in a low-peaked leather cap, black shirt, jodhpurs and knee-high jackboots mounted the podium. Both bound women visibly tensed when he cracked the riding crop in his right hand against his calf.

'Now that our two lovely slaves are in place, we can begin our game,' he boomed. 'These two beauties have no idea what manner of pain and humiliation lies in store for them over the next sixty minutes, but doesn't every slave love surprises? We're fortunate to have them at our mercy, so let's not spare them.

'The game we are about to play is called *Pleasure and Pain* – two things guaranteed to test the endurance of our slaves. When I give the signal, their masters will come up and begin subjecting them to the two P's. Whichever slave first makes a sound shall earn for the other either sixty seconds of the most exquisite pleasure and for herself sixty seconds of pain, or the other way round. She won't know which until a sticker is removed from her breasts. If it's black underneath, pain is the penalty. If it's white, the reward is pleasure. So masters, don't keep your eager slaves waiting any longer.'

The master of ceremonies stepped aside as two other men mounted the podium and took their places before their respective slaves. At the sound of a shrill whistle the man standing before the blonde produced from beneath his black leather jacket a feather duster, and his companion a sleek black vibrator.

The bound blonde squirmed in an agony of discomfort as the feather duster set to work, tickling the sensitive spots under her armpits and around her waist. The other master glided the thrumming crown of the vibrator over the puckering folds of the brunette's dark thatched sex.

She bit her lower lip in order to contain a whimper of pleasure.

The masters teased and tormented their slaves with well-practised and fiendish expertise, manipulating them to the point where they could not help crying out. After several minutes of sustained tickle torture, the blonde finally uttered a small cry. Her master peeled a label from her left breast and held it up for the audience to see. The sticky surface was black, which meant that the other slave was condemned to sixty seconds of pain. Her delighted master produced a small silver chain with a steel clip on either end. She squealed as the clamps were fitted to her labia, then mercilessly tugged, stretching her slick nether lips. Constance winced in sympathy, unable to imagine the terrible torment the helpless captive must be suffering. While this was happening, the other master sucked the stiff brown nipples of her fortunate companion and fondled lovingly between her thighs.

Following sixty seconds of pussy torture that must have felt more like an hour to the slave on the receiving end, the clamps were removed and the second round of the game commenced. This involved a greased red rubber ball, the size of a golf ball, being inserted in the vagina of either woman. Their masters then began lashing between their thighs with a cat o' nine tails, hard enough to cause discomfort rather than real pain. The first slave to lose her slippery ball was deemed the loser, or winner, depending on the colour on the underside of the sticker peeled from her breasts. Once again, it was the blonde who first lost control, the ball popping from her pussy and rolling off the stage. This time she was not so fortunate. Her label had a white underside, which meant her companion received the pleasure, while she was subjected to the pain.

A master from the audience was invited to administer sixty seconds' worth of his best to the apprehensively trembling girl. He obliged by energetically flogging her thighs with a long thin whip, while the relieved brunette received another welcome treat from her master's vibrator.

As the game continued the punishments meted out to the slaves became ever more severe. Both, in turn, had their breasts roped tightly and several heavy objects suspended from their clamped nipples and pussies, the blonde receiving slightly more of the sadism than her companion. At the end of the hour their masters released them from their bondage and the appreciative audience applauded the show. Constance was as shocked as she was excited by what she had witnessed. As she watched the two naked slaves being led away by their masters she was uncertain whether she ought to pity or envy them.

Upon her return to the bar, G presented her with a hand-written note, which read:

Dear CB, your master awaits you in the darkroom.

'Who left this for me?' she demanded.

'An admirer,' G told her. She gestured to her right. 'The door's just over there.'

Constance decided she needed another drink before making up her mind whether or not to accept the mysterious invitation. She could control what happened in a fantasy; whatever lurked in the club darkroom was another matter.

'G, what exactly is it like in there?' she enquired when

she managed to catch the barmaid's attention again.

'I'd rather not spoil the surprise,' G replied. 'But you won't come to any harm, if that's what you're afraid of.'

Constance was not sure what she was afraid of. Almost from the moment she had stepped into the club she had felt her self-control slowly but surely slipping away. It was as though she was caught in a web that was drawing her ever deeper into a twilight world where the boundaries between fantasy and reality were no longer discernible. She could finish her drink and leave the club, a wiser and more enlightened woman, but she knew she would have to come back.

Reasoning that she ought to at least satisfy her curiosity, she summoned up her courage and strode towards the darkroom, hoping she did not look as nervous as she felt.

Once the door creaked shut behind her she was in almost complete darkness. All she could see were two rows of tiny red lights, inches above the level of her head. There were six on either side of her, at intervals of about three feet. She heard a moan from the darkness and what sounded like a whip striking flesh. She almost turned and ran, but forced herself instead to take a forward step, her high heeled footfall on the wooden floor sounding like a small explosion.

The darkroom was warm and claustrophobic. Her spine tingling, Constance felt like the damsel in distress in a horror film, waiting for some form of hideous monster to spring from the darkness at any instant.

She heard the moan again, unmistakably feminine, only a few feet away. She wanted to call out, but did not dare. Besides, she did not even know who she was looking for. She sensed a movement to her left and uttered a startled cry when a leather-gloved hand brushed the back of hers.

'No need to be frightened,' came a whispered male voice.

'Who are you?' she responded nervously, edging backwards from the source of the voice.

'Not knowing is part of the adventure,' came the reply. 'Take a couple of steps towards the red light directly in front of you. We both know you haven't come this far just to turn and run away.'

Constance had the uneasy feeling that this unseen man was reading her mind. She took one tentative step forward, then another, coaxed like a reluctant puppy by his whispers. Though she knew he could only be a few feet away, being unable to see the slightest thing had her nerves on edge.

'Now, hold out your right hand,' he whispered, after she had taken half a dozen steps.

Constance obeyed hesitantly, her every reaction taking place in slow motion. Her fingertips brushed cool rubber, beneath which bulged the firmness of a male torso. She instinctively withdrew her hand for a few seconds, then touched the rubber-sheathed body again. The only sound from the man standing at arm's length was his deep breathing. His second skin was tautly stretched and slippery smooth to the touch.

She formed a mental picture of the man as her hand glided slowly over his belly and chest. All she could tell for certain was that he was heavily built, though not fat. The rest she had to leave to her imagination. Her hand reached his chin, touching rubber rather than flesh. He was wearing what felt like a gas mask, plastic goggles covering his eyes. Constance found the sinister uniform perversely exciting. Even if the darkroom should suddenly be bathed in light, she would still be unable to see the person beneath.

The rhythmic breathing from the mask became more laboured as her hand began travelling in a downward direction. She touched what she first thought was some kind of latex object protruding from between the thighs of the masked man, then realised it was his erect penis. It bulged within a rubber sheath chained to the front of his suit. She traced a fingertip along the length of his shaft and was startled when rubber gave way to hot flesh, halfway to the crown. In that instant she would have given anything for a flash-light.

'Now it's my turn,' he whispered.

'To do what?' she pleaded softly.

'To get to know you more intimately. Follow me.'

He took her hand and she allowed herself to be led through a heavy velvet curtain, into what felt like a long, narrow cubicle. He walked with slow, carefully measured paces, as though instinctively aware of the layout of where he was leading her.

A few paces further on, he directed her to stop and raise her hands above her head. She obeyed with only the slightest hesitation, her heart pounding and perspiration dampening her brow. She heard him grunt. Something clinked, then cold steel touched her wrists. In the instant it took her to realise what was happening the manacles had snapped shut. Her cry of protest was cut short by a gloved finger pressed to her lips.

'Trust me,' the masked man whispered.

Chained to an iron bar, Constance had little choice. She held her breath as he unfastened her dress at the back and eased it down over her body. All she wore underneath was a black silk cache-sex and hold-up stockings. Gloved hands cupped her breasts, teasing her tingling nipples to full stiffness by squeezing them between thumb and forefinger. Though still quivering nervously, she permitted herself a gentle sigh of pleasure.

Several delicious minutes later his hands left her breasts and moved down over the slope of her waist. Hooking a thumb in the string of her sex-pouch, he stretched it out from her back, then snapped it against her skin. He did this three more times before the elastic finally snapped and the flimsy strip of silk fell to the floor. A fingertip nuzzled the soft down of her pubis. Constance instinctively parted her thighs as his hand slid in between. When he eased his finger between the soaking folds of her labia she was unable to contain a muffled cry of ecstasy. Her only regret was that he was not penetrating her with his cock, the damp crown of which was pressed lightly against her left thigh.

Whoever this man was, he knew how to use his finger to maximum effect. Constance could not have done it better herself if she were playing this erotic scene in her mind, rather than participating for real. The man thrust a second finger up inside her and began pushing into her aggressively with both digits. She responded by bucking her hips and moaning loudly, clenching her fists and straining against the manacles on her wrists. She did not care who might hear. Her pleasure was merely heightened by the near certainty that she and the man in rubber were not alone.

She could not remember a climax as intense as that which electrified every nerve of her body a few minutes later. Her sex juices flowed so copiously she thought she must be melting. When the man withdrew his hand from between her thighs, he presented his soaked and scented fingers to her lips. She had no hesitation in sucking the leather clean of her own juices.

He left her then. When she realised he was gone panic replaced the pleasant afterglow of her orgasm. She had expected him to take full advantage of her helplessness, not to abandon her in the darkness, chained up and naked.

'Where are you?' she whimpered. 'Unlock these handcuffs, now!'

Silence was the only response. Constance was about to shout when she heard somebody creeping up on her from behind. She turned her head, but was still unable to see a thing. A bare-chested figure embraced her around the waist from behind, his stiff cock nuzzling the cleft of her buttocks. The cold metal of a pair of nipple rings touched her back. A second man, wearing what felt like a studded leather jacket, pressed against the front of her body, rubbing the tip of his cock against her belly.

Keeping her sandwiched so tightly between them that she could scarcely breathe, the two men began masturbating. Neither spoke to her, restricting their sounds to heavy breathing and low grunts. The man with his cock gripped between her buttocks climaxed first, his semen spurting over both cheeks and up her back. When the last drop had been spilt he wiped up the creamy rivulets, then brought both hands around to her mouth. Constance would have preferred his semen to be delivered direct, but licking it off his sticky gloves was a tolerable substitute.

She remained standing in the darkroom for at least another hour, during which time she was masturbated upon by a further five men, all of whom cleaned her with their fingers afterwards and then presented them to Constance to be licked clean. Finally the rubber-clad master returned, unlocked her handcuffs, then departed again. She scrabbled around on the floor for several panic-stricken minutes before finding her dress. Her sex-pouch had obviously been taken as a souvenir.

The following evening she returned home from work to discover a mysterious message on her answering machine.

'Hello, Constance – or should I say CB? If you enjoyed last night, call me. The number is...'

There was no mistaking the voice of KT. Constance had been expecting to hear from him again. She was only slightly surprised that he had somehow managed to obtain both her full name and telephone number.

'Basic detective work,' he explained, when she called the number he had given her and demanded an explanation. 'I presumed you wouldn't mind.'

'You presume a lot about me,' she retorted.

'And I have yet to be proved wrong,' he said. 'I hope your visit to the darkroom lived up to expectations.'

'You were there?'

'That's for me to know and for you to perhaps never find out.'

'Why are you so damned secretive?' she demanded angrily. 'You could at least tell me your full name.'

'What do you stand to gain from knowing that?' KT responded. 'All you need to know about me, for the moment, is that I hold all the cards in this little game of ours.'

'And the object of this game is?' she snapped.

'Nothing less than the fulfilment of your every fantasy, my dear Constance. Of course it won't come cheaply. As you may already have guessed, I'm an extremely demanding master.'

'I may not be able to live up to your expectations,'

she said

'We'll soon see,' he replied.

Constance had a thousand questions for this exciting and somewhat menacing figure who was proposing to become her master, but was curtly informed that they would have to wait. Before KT revealed the slightest detail about himself, she would have to prove that she was sincere in her desire to submit to him. Once she had proved herself suitable there would be time for all questions to be answered.

Her duty, in this assessment period, was to reveal to him her innermost fantasies. He could call her at any time of the day or night, wherever she might be, and demand a pornographically detailed confession. There would be no such thing as a bad time, if she truly wanted to be his. He was so persuasive, it was frightening. Though far from certain what she was letting herself in for, she agreed to his conditions.

Rather foolishly she assumed he would call at reasonably convenient times. KT had other ideas. On one occasion she was in the middle of an important business lunch when the mobile telephone in her purse shrilled. When she heard the voice on the other end of the line she had to excuse herself, race to the toilet and breathe down the line a fantasy about being arrested for drink-driving, then taken to the police station and offered a choice of being formally charged or stripped, spanked and screwed by half a dozen officers. Naturally, she chose the latter. Five minutes later she returned to her table, florid-faced and breathless. What if somebody had overheard her waxing pornographic in the cubicle?

His next call, the following afternoon, was even more inconvenient. Constance was giving a female friend a lift home from the health club they both frequented, when their conversation was interrupted by the telephone.

'This really isn't a good time,' she pleaded. 'Can you call me back in twenty minutes?'

'You know the rules,' KT replied. 'No exceptions.'

Further protests about his bad timing met with no sympathy. Unless she started talking dirty within ninety seconds he would hang up. With a despairing look to her friend she murmured something about an important message she had forgotten, pulled over and parked awkwardly on a double yellow line. Leaving the engine running, she leapt out of the Porsche and ducked down a nearby alleyway. The conditions were far from ideal for erotic storytelling, but Constance was not one to shrink from a challenge. She started with a man in a long rubber mac chasing her down an alleyway and took her story from there, her panting lending authenticity to the tale.

She had reached the point in her narrative where the man in the rubber mac was ripping off her panties, when she noticed, in real life, two teenage boys standing nearby, obviously eavesdropping intently. She lowered her voice and slunk further down the alley, but they merely followed.

'Master, there are people listening,' she whispered in desperation.

'There were people listening to S/M-FM,' he replied. 'Carry on.'

'But—'

'I said carry on!' he snapped.

Constance finished her kinky story in a near-whisper,

motioning angrily for the greatly amused boys to go away and mind their own business. The instant her master permitted her to hang up she fled from the alley, as though she were being pursued for real. She found her friend pleading with a grim-faced traffic warden, who was slapping a parking ticket on the windscreen of her Porsche.

The telephone relationship with KT continued for over a fortnight. During that time he refused to answer any questions or engage in any manner of polite conversation with her. Whenever she answered the phone the sound of his voice was the signal for her to supply aural sex, on demand. She suspected it was not so much the content of her stories that excited KT, as the knowledge that he was using and controlling her like a mechanical toy and she was meekly playing along.

Just when she was growing impatient with the game, he decided she had at last earnt her reward. It was time for a face-to-face meeting.

Chapter Four

Constance felt her palms sweating on the steering wheel as she piloted the Porsche along a ribbon of dark tarmac, lined on both sides by trees. In a few more minutes she would be meeting the man who had succeeded in stripping her mind bare and probably already knew her better than she knew herself. It was not what he might do to her that made her nervous, but rather how she might react to him. What if he did not live up to the image his voice had painted in her mind? What if he were old, fat, ugly, or even somehow deformed? As she had never seen him, it was entirely possible she had allowed her mind to be seduced by a monster.

The house at the end of the long driveway was an imposing structure, with ivy covered walls and huge windows that seemed to glare balefully at the outside world. Constance parked her Porsche and lit a calming cigarette before getting out. Her heart pounded almost as loudly as her pink stiletto heels as she ascended the five stone steps to the front porch. She glanced at her wristwatch before ringing the doorbell. Fifteen minutes late. Not a good start.

Moments later the door was opened and she was greeted by a grey-haired figure in the uniform of a butler.

'I'm Constance Brooking,' she began. 'I've—'

'The master is waiting for you,' he interrupted tersely. 'Please follow me.'

The butler led her down a long, gloomy corridor, lined with surrealistic paintings. It reminded her of a charmless gallery she had once visited. He knocked on one of the stout oak doors at the far end and a voice bade them enter.

Constance followed him through the door and found herself in a library. Standing behind an ornate desk was a tall, slender man in his late thirties, with a flowing mane of jet black hair and a neatly groomed goatee beard. She was greatly relieved by his handsome features and high cheekbones, though unnerved by the intensity of the emerald green eyes that peered through his tinted spectacles.

'Sorry I'm late,' she blurted. 'This place wasn't as easy to find as I thought.'

'Address me as master,' he snapped, in the voice that had become familiar. 'And put out that filthy cigarette. Only whores and cheap sluts smoke in the presence of gentlemen, and I trust you are neither.'

'Sorry, master,' Constance said hastily. Blushing, she looked around for an ashtray, found none, walked across to the empty fireplace and discarded her cigarette. She was conscious of the two men watching her and glanced uncomfortably at the butler.

'You need not concern yourself with Matthews,' her master told her. 'He is fully aware of who and what you are.' He beckoned imperiously. 'Come, kneel before my desk.'

Quivering with a mixture of shame and excitement, she approached the desk. As she fell to her knees she noticed a closed circuit TV camera high on the wall to her left.

'Are we being watched, master?' she asked.

He planted both palms on the top of his desk and leant forward to study her. 'My, aren't you the curious one? What would you say if I were to tell you to mind your

40

own damned business?'

'I would say, please pardon my impudence, master,' she responded.

He smiled thinly. 'Your impudence is pardoned, slave. It is natural that you should be curious, of course, so let me explain a few things. Firstly, though you may have been under the impression that you have been sharing your most intimate fantasies only with me, that would not be strictly true.' He nodded to the butler. 'Sound please, Matthews.'

The manservant slid open a wall cabinet and pressed the play button on the hi-fi system inside. Seconds later, Constance was horrified to hear her own sultry tones wafting from a pair of speakers on the wall.

'Master, there is something I've been longing to tell you – something I thought I would never tell another person. It's one of my favourite fantasies. When I think about it, it's so exciting, but talking about it, even to you, is making me blush.'

'Unburden yourself, Constance,' urged the silken tones of KT. 'If you are to be my slave, you can have no secrets from me. Tell me your fantasy in every detail. Imagine you are an erotic artist. My mind is the canvas, your words the brushes and paints you will use to create a masterpiece that we shall both treasure.'

She cleared her throat, then began speaking, hesitantly at first. 'It's one of those freak tropical summer nights, hot and muggy, with rain bucketing down. I'm tired, but I can't sleep – and not just because of the heat. The sound of the rain beating against my window is making me horny. I don't know why such a commonplace sound should have such an effect on me, but it does.

'After a while I decide to go for a drive, wearing nothing but an ankle-length raincoat. I haven't

41

consciously planned what I'm going to do next. It just seems to happen naturally. I drive to this secluded spot I know, getting hotter and hornier with every mile. It's way past midnight, so there's nobody about. I park the car, throw off my raincoat and skip and dance around the field, giggling like a naked lunatic, illuminated by the headlights. I can't describe the feeling of the warm rain on my skin and the sense of utter freedom. It's just so sexy! When I'm thoroughly drenched, I roll around on the grass and masturbate, opening my legs like a bitch in heat. At that point I don't care if somebody comes along and thinks they've found someone that's escaped from an asylum. I *have* escaped from an asylum, in a manner of speaking and, God, am I enjoying it!

'I fuck myself with two fingers, thrusting deep into my slit, until I orgasm. Afterwards I just lie back on the grass and let the rain bathe me. It's only when I decide to go home that I discover I've locked myself out of my car.' Her breathing became heavier. 'Imagine: it's late at night, pouring with rain and I'm stranded in the middle of nowhere, naked and completely helpless. What can I do? I can hardly go looking for a phone in this state. What if some man comes along and finds me? I'd be completely at his mercy. He could do whatever he wanted with me, force me to do anything. There's no way I could resist.

'I'm still trying to decide what I should do when a car pulls up a short way down the road and a man gets out. He must have seen my lights. As he starts to walk towards me a second man emerges from the car, then another. There are four of them coming towards me, all big and mean-looking. I know they have no intention of helping me. These are the kind of men who think of only one thing when they see a woman.

42

'I try to run, but they're too fast for me. When they catch me I scream and kick, but they're much too strong. They overpower me easily, then the first one takes me while the others hold me down on the wet grass. He's rough. The others encourage him to screw me harder. I scream and beg for mercy at the top of my voice but they don't care. Nobody can hear me.

'The four of them take me, one after the other, but even then they're not finished with me. I'm forced to kneel and suck their big cocks while they laugh at me and call me the most obscene names. I've never been so humiliated or felt so dirty. After I've sucked the four of them off and swallowed their come, two of them drag me through the mud, while the other two beat me on the bottom and thighs with their studded leather belts. One of them wants to have me again, but the others tell him not to degrade himself, pointing out that I look like a pig, covered from head to foot in mud. They leave me lying there and drive off laughing. Can you picture it, master?'

'Oh, yessss,' KT breathed.

He signalled for Matthews to switch off the tape. Constance was not easily embarrassed, but right then she was blushing to the roots of her blonde hair. She had never dreamt that he might record her candid confessions.

'Is this the only one you taped?' she asked quietly, hastening to add the word 'master'.

'What do you think, my dear slave?' he replied. 'Now, prepare yourself for a further shock. I haven't just been recording your fantasies. I've been sharing them, too.'

'Sharing them?' she cried.

He nodded. 'With some trusted members of The Master's Masque, as well as my S/M-FM colleagues.

They have found your revelations most interesting. By speaking to me on air that night you took your first step on the path to enlightenment. By coming to the club and sharing more of your fantasies, you proved that you were not just a cheap voyeur.'

'But, master, I trusted you!' Constance wailed, instantly reviling herself for sounding like a spoilt little girl.

'Did I, at any stage, lead you to believe you were sharing your fantasies with me alone?' he demanded, stepping from behind his desk.

'No,' she blurted. 'But...'

'Enough of your pathetic play-acting,' he snapped. 'I can hardly be blamed for your jumping to conclusions. I thought you had the makings of a genuine slave, but perhaps I was mistaken. You seem unable to accept the first and most golden of rules – that of unquestioning obedience to the will of your master. Get out of my house and stop wasting my time.'

'No master, please don't reject me,' she wailed, gazing imploringly up at him. 'I didn't mean to offend you, I swear.'

'I am not a patient man,' he warned. 'However, I am prepared to give you one more chance.' He slid open a top drawer of his desk, produced a long, slender cane and whacked the desktop so hard that Constance jumped. 'Take off your jacket and blouse and hand them to Matthews!' he barked.

She reacted hurriedly, anxious not to further displease him. She handed the jacket of her pink silk two-piece suit to the butler, then hurriedly unbuttoned her blouse. He dutifully eased it off her shoulders and took it from her. Underneath, she was wearing a bra of shimmering ivory-coloured silk. The half-cups snugly embraced and

44

uplifted her firm round breasts.

Her master stroked the generous display of creamy cleavage with the tip of his cane, watching her nipples swelling against the fabric of her bra. He then ordered her to unzip her skirt. Feeling as though she were starring in one of her own erotic fantasies, she unhesitatingly obeyed. The pink silk pooled around her knees. Her knickers, cut high on her hips and only partially covering her firm buttocks, matched her bra, as did her silk stockings and suspenders.

Constance thrust out her chest and basked in the admiration of her master. She was justifiably proud of her long-limbed, perfectly formed body, and had delighted in making men's mouths water for as long as she could remember. She shuddered as the tip of the cane glided down her belly, over her silk-sheathed mound and in between her thighs. Her hands were poised, ready to unclasp her bra at the front, even before her master uttered the command.

Matthews slid the straps down over her arms and draped her bra over his right arm, along with the other items of her clothing. Her nipples were like bullets shooting from cocoa-shaded areolae. The butler could not resist licking his lips, even though the demeanour of the master remained impassive. The cane traced the outline of her slit and she felt a warm dampness in her knickers. Almost unconsciously, her hands cupped her breasts.

'Did I give you permission to play with yourself?'

Her master's shout was like a bucket of icy water. Constance's hands could not have leapt from her breasts any quicker if they were red hot.

'Lesson number two. You do not pleasure yourself without my permission,' he told her. 'As your master, I

45

must have complete control over your sexuality. Do you understand?'

'Of course, master,' she answered. 'Please forgive me.'

'Forgiveness must be earnt,' he said sternly. 'I'm tempted to cane you but, as you have not yet been accepted as my slave, that would be an inappropriate honour. You may lick my boots instead.'

Crouching down before him, her bottom raised for the delectation of Matthews, she eagerly ran her tongue over KT's calf-high black leather boots. Her knickers rode up into the cleft of her buttocks, leaving the splendid milky globes on full display. In her state of high arousal she would have welcomed either her master's cock or cane, but she was not yet worthy of either.

When she had licked every inch of his boots, he ordered her to sit on his desk and masturbate. She adopted the required position, hooking her high heels on the edge of the desk, with her knees drawn up and her thighs wide apart. She then slipped her right hand down the front of her knickers and penetrated her soaking slit with two fingers. The two men watched intently, their bulges at their groins swelling ever more prominently. It took less than a minute for her to finger herself to an orgasm that took her breath away. Afterwards, she sucked her sticky fingers clean, without any need to fake the pleasure of the task.

She considered begging her master to take her, in any way he pleased, but then realised that that would be disrespectful. Nevertheless, when he curtly instructed her to get dressed again there was no concealing her disappointment. The butler poured him a cognac from a crystal decanter and handed it to him. Constance was not offered a drink.

'Now, to business,' he announced, returning to his

chair. 'As I said already, I'm not the only person who has enjoyed listening to your fantasies. You have more to offer The Master's Masque than just your delectable body. I have a new show in mind for S/M-FM, something I know our listeners will love. *Slave in the Hot Seat*, every Saturday from one until three a.m. You'll be the perfect presenter.'

'Me?' Constance cried. 'But I know nothing about radio. I can't—'

'What you need to know can quickly be learnt,' he interrupted. 'Come with me. I'd like you to see the nerve-centre of the nation's most subversive radio station for yourself.'

The 'station' was located in a small room at the rear of the house and consisted of little more than the broadcasting essentials. Constance was somewhat disappointed. She had imagined the headquarters of S/M-FM as a well-equipped dungeon in the bowels of The Master's Masque club.

'We've been broadcasting for four months and haven't been raided yet... touch wood,' KT told her. 'The fewer people know about this place the better – so not a word to anyone.'

She nodded. 'Of course. But there's something about all this that puzzles me. You, the club, and all the others involved in it are surrounded by such secrecy – yet you risk it all by running a pirate radio station.'

'I like to live dangerously,' he answered. 'How about you?'

'What if I refuse to be your *Slave in the Hot Seat*?' she asked.

KT smiled. 'But you're not going to refuse, are you?'

The following Saturday, just after one a.m., Constance the respectable businesswoman became a bona-fide pirate broadcaster, identifying herself only by her initials. KT had done little to assuage her nervousness beforehand, reasoning that it made her sound all the more authentically submissive. He stood behind her, menacingly brandishing a cane. G had helped her to prepare a rough script, but she was otherwise on her own. If her show was a success, the master had promised her an unspecified reward. Should she disappoint him, she would be severely punished.

'Hi, my name is CB, and I'm your *Slave in the Hot Seat*,' she began, trying to forget that an audience was listening to her every word. 'I'd first like to thank my master for giving me this opportunity to become the first woman to have her own show on S/M-FM. I sincerely hope I shall not disappoint him, or indeed you. I know there are many masters listening right now, eager to hear my confessions and tell me their fantasies. Please call and permit me to submit to you, otherwise my master shall be severely displeased and I will be punished. Is there something you would like me to do for you, something you would like to do to me? Your wish is my command.'

A tap of KT's cane on her bare right shoulder reminded her to give out the number to call. She then began to describe herself in sensual detail, changing only the colour of her hair and eyes, in the hope of avoiding recognition. She added that she was wearing only high heels, black lace bra and panties. That was not a lie. To enhance her sense of vulnerability KT had ordered her to strip down to her underwear before going on air. She was sitting on a hard wooden stool with her legs spread wide apart. She would be required to remain thus until the end of the show.

She did not have to wait long for her first caller – a plummy-toned gentleman who demanded that she address him as 'sir'. He remembered her from her previous on-air call to KT and ordered her to tell him what had happened on her visit to The Master's Masque. She detailed the events that had taken place in the darkroom, and her own feelings throughout the erotic ordeal.

'I was one of those men you entertained while you were handcuffed,' the caller said when she had finished.

Constance was too surprised to reply. Whether or not he was telling the truth, she would never know.

Her next caller admitted a fantasy of his own, in which Constance was the helpless victim in his dungeon. She made what she thought were all the right noises as he detailed how she was chained to a rack, whipped, caned, and then shaven of her pubic hair. When KT judged her cries to be less than whole-hearted, he struck the exposed upper half of her buttocks with his cane. The greatest shock of all was how much she enjoyed it.

Within a short while she found herself entering into the spirit of the show and responding enthusiastically to the explicit fantasies of her callers, urging the more reserved of them to treat her as the submissive slut of their dreams, to be used for their total pleasure. One particular master, who identified himself as Ron, wished to take the game a step further.

'Are you available, or is this just make-believe?' he demanded.

Constance glanced at KT, who nodded.

'Yes, master, I'm available,' she replied.

'In that case, I want to meet you,' he said. 'If you are what you say you are, you should have no objections.'

'Er, I'd very much like to meet you,' KT's cane tapped her shoulder. 'But of course you'll have to make the necessary arrangements with my master,' she added hastily.

Such was the response to her broadcast that she remained on air until almost four a.m. After he had thanked the audience for listening and signed off for the night, KT announced his verdict on her performance.

'Constance, you are a natural,' he said. 'From now on you can consider yourself a regular on S/M-FM. You would like that, I presume?'

'I can't believe how much I enjoyed it,' she said, smiling. 'I'd love to do it again, master. Is that the reward you had in mind?'

He shook his head. 'I had no specific reward in mind – not until that chap called Ron said he would like to meet you. That, my dear, is your reward.'

Constance was aghast. 'You expect me to really meet him? But... but I thought we were just playing a game.'

'A game in which I set the limits,' KT replied. 'He's already spoken with G and arranged a time and place for your rendezvous. Nine o'clock tonight. He can't wait to get his hands on you.'

'But I only spoke to him for a few minutes,' she protested. 'He could be some kind of maniac, or anything. No, it's too dangerous. I'm not doing it.'

'You must learn to trust me,' he said patiently. 'In the unlikely event of this chap turning out to be a psychopathic pervert, I'll be standing by to rescue you. Don't say you're losing your appetite for danger, just as it's getting so exciting?'

'I'm not doing it, and you can't force me,' she declared firmly.

He shrugged. 'Please yourself. G will be glad to take

your place and I'm sure I'll have no trouble finding a replacement slave for the "Hot Seat". I thought you were made of sterner stuff, Constance.'

She had always prided herself on an iron-clad ability to resist emotional blackmail, especially where men were concerned. Unlike in the club, KT was now asking her to place herself in real physical danger. Yet, despite her grave reservations, there was a part of her that yearned to embrace the danger and experience the wild thrill of sex with a potentially lethal stranger. It was to this treacherous instinct that KT applied all his powers of persuasion. Knowing she might well live to regret it, Constance finally agreed, with great reluctance, to meet her admirer.

Chapter Five

KT picked her up from her home at seven-thirty that evening. In accordance with his instructions, she was dressed for the tryst in a loose-fitting denim shirt and blue jeans, with no underwear. When she pleaded with him to at least tell her where she was meeting the mystery man, he replied that she would find out soon enough.

In the course of the day she had managed to justify her madness by convincing herself that Ron would fail to show up. In all probability he was just a lonely and frustrated man who had used S/M-FM radio as a cheap alternative to a sex line. Such a man would never have the guts to keep an appointment with an unknown woman, even if he did believe she was serious about wanting to meet him.

Over an hour passed before KT's silver Rover reached its destination, at the end of a pot-holed country lane. Ahead lay a dense forest. The last house they had passed was several miles back.

'Right, out you get,' he told her.

'Here?' she exclaimed.

He nodded. 'This is the place. Hurry up. I want to get you ready and get myself out of sight before he arrives.'

Constance knew it would be pointless to plead with him. She had committed herself to whatever was about to happen and did not wish to humiliate herself and anger him by going back on her word. She consoled herself with a mental reminder that Ron was unlikely to show up. With any luck KT would then use the occasion to ravish her himself. She assumed he had been prevented from doing so at the mansion by the presence of G. He would not have that excuse this time. Constance had no idea of the nature of his relationship with the red-haired slave, nor did she care. KT epitomised her ideal of a real man – handsome, arrogant and masterful. She was his for the taking, wherever and whenever he pleased. If G had any objection that was just too bad.

He took a small black sack from the boot of his car, then led Constance down a narrow path through the forest. With every step her trepidation increased. She had expected her rendezvous with Ron to take place in an hotel, not some remote woodland where only a few wild animals would hear her screams, should the worst happen.

They walked for several minutes, finally emerging into a clearing among the trees. She refrained from commenting on the fact that KT obviously knew his way around the forest. Pointing to a large oak tree at the edge of the clearing, he ordered her to stand with her back to it. He then reached into his sack and produced a length of thick rope.

'You're not going to tie me up?' she cried.

'That's exactly what I'm going to do,' he replied. 'Now, stretch your arms out behind your back.'

'But I'll be completely at his mercy,' she protested.

He sighed. 'That, my slave, is the whole idea. So stop behaving like a silly little girl and do as you're told.'

Constance almost told him to go to hell, but instead she obediently stretched back her arms. He tied the rope around her left wrist, then pulled it tightly around the thick tree trunk and similarly secured her right. He forced a second rope between her teeth, pulled it tight and knotted it around the tree, binding and gagging her in one.

'Mmmmmfffff!' she whimpered, struggling futilely against the ropes.

'Don't waste your time trying to break free,' he told her. 'I'm a bondage expert. All you have to do now is wait for your date to arrive. I'll be... somewhere, should you need me. Have fun.'

With that, he picked up his sack, turned and left her. Constance continued to struggle for a few more minutes, but his expertise with the ropes had been no idle boast. She cursed her own foolishness and vowed that, if she survived this lesson in terror, she would forever more turn her back on KT and his bizarre games.

As the minutes ticked tortuously by and the forest remained eerily silent, she grew increasingly confident that Ron would fail to appear. The thought that KT might have simply brought her here in order to abandon her was too terrible to contemplate.

After what seemed an eternity she heard the crackle of twigs underfoot and the sound of somebody slowly approaching from behind. She could not move her head to look around, but prayed it was KT returning to free her. Her hopes were dashed, a moment later, when the figure of a balding and portly man, in his mid-fifties, stepped into view.

In his ankle-length tan raincoat and olive green wellington boots, he resembled a stereotypical dirty old man. He silently surveyed his helpless and terror-stricken captive through eyes that radiated bestial lust.

'You're better-looking than I'd ever dreamt possible,' he said, eventually. 'I was half expecting to have made a wasted journey, but how wrong can a man be? So considerate of your master to have prepared you so well for me. Let's have a better look at you, shall we?'

With trembling fingers he began unbuttoning Constance's shirt. Up close, he smelt of stale cigar smoke. Though she knew it was a forlorn hope, she silently pleaded for KT to save her from this man. As the creamy globes of her breasts came into view, his breathing became more frantic and his fingers worked with increased zeal on her buttons. When the last one was undone he pulled her shirt open and feasted his eyes on her naked upper body.

'I've surely died and gone to heaven,' he panted, caressing her breasts with damp palms. 'I'd normally pay a small fortune for such a perfect woman, but I can do as I please with you for free.'

Constance could have died with shame when she felt her nipples stiffen against his palms. She could not permit herself to take any pleasure from the attentions of this lecherous little man. It was bad enough that she should be at his mercy, without giving him the additional satisfaction of knowing she was enjoying it.

Having fondled her breasts for several minutes and sucked greedily on both nipples, he reached for the buckle of her belt. She was tempted to kick him at that point, but in her present position that might not be wise. Besides, the moist tingling between her thighs betrayed a reaction she could not bear to consciously admit to herself.

He undid her belt and buttons, then fell to his knees and tugged her tight jeans down over her slender hips. The sight of her bare sex caused him to grunt excitedly. He pulled off her shoes, completely removed her jeans, and then pushed her ankles apart. Gazing lovingly at the moist folds of her slit, puckering through her dark blonde thatch, he began licking his way slowly upwards from her ankles. When his tongue had covered every inch of the front of both legs, he parted her labia with both thumbs and commenced an intimate feast, slurping noisily and murmuring his appreciation of her nectar. Constance chomped on the rope between her teeth, whimpering in ecstasy rather than protest. She moved her legs further apart and gently thrust her crotch against his face, leaving him in no doubt about the delightful effect his eagerly burrowing tongue was having upon her.

A few minutes later he raised her legs onto his shoulders and she wrapped them tightly around his neck. This was a much better position for him to bury his face between her thighs and enjoy her juicy fruit more thoroughly. His hands squeezed her buttocks, right thumb gently caressing the bud of her anus. As her first orgasm, several minutes later, sent sensual shock-waves through her entire body, he pushed the tip of his thumb into her nether orifice. Even had she been able to speak, Constance would not have protested at this exceptional liberty.

He continued to lap and slurp on her sex and wriggle his thumb in her bottom until she was near the point of her second climax. Then he disengaged her legs from around his neck and stood up, appreciatively smacking his lips.

'Don't worry, my dear,' he grinned, unbuckling the belt of his raincoat. 'I'm far from finished with you.'

He flung open the raincoat, revealing himself to be completely naked underneath. His pot-bellied physique was far from appealing, but the thick cock that jutted from below it was a reasonable compensation. Not long ago Constance would not have looked twice at such a man. Now she ached for him as though he were a muscular blond Adonis.

He raised her legs and she wrapped them around his lower back, urging the bulbous crown of his cock towards the mouth of her sex. With a hoarse cry of pleasure he eased the full length of his thick shaft into her well-oiled tunnel.

As he proceeded to fuck her with short, aggressive stabs of his cock, he squeezed her breasts and pinched her throbbing nipples. The discomfort of her position and the rope biting into her wrists served only to heighten her pleasure. Wherever KT was watching from, she hoped he was enjoying the show.

Shortly after Constance had climaxed for the second time, he uttered a guttural cry and lowered his perspiration-sheened and crimson face to the soft cushions of her breasts. She shuddered as she felt his hot, thick semen flood her depths. Afterwards, instead of withdrawing, he kissed her breasts as he recovered his breath. She kept him wrapped between her legs, savouring the warmth of his semen and the sensation of his cock gradually losing its stiffness inside her.

'What a woman,' he gasped, finally raising his head. 'If I were your master, I wouldn't dream of sharing you with another man.'

The only response Constance could manage was a muffled whimper. The man resumed kissing and fondling her breasts. Sooner than she would have expected, she felt his cock stiffen again. He resumed his thrusts, gently at first, increasing the momentum as his tool returned to full erection. This second time was far less hurried and he was determined to enjoy it to the full. He managed to maintain the languidly thrusting tempo for at least twenty minutes, before his cock finally spewed its second creamy payload into Constance. In that time her breath was taken away by two further orgasms. She made a mental note to never again judge a book by the cover.

It was getting dark by the time the fat man finally withdrew his wet and flaccid cock from her and belted up his raincoat. A hurried goodbye and then he was gone, leaving the exhausted slave trussed to the tree. Another twenty minutes passed before KT returned to release her, by which time the chill air and deepening darkness had brought goose-bumps to her skin.

'Now that wasn't so bad, was it?' he asked as she hurriedly pulled her jeans back on.

'It was... different.'

'I'm glad you enjoyed it,' he said, folding his ropes. 'It won't be the last such encounter, that I can promise you.'

More than anything else that had happened to her since that first call to S/M-FM, the encounter in the woods marked the turning point in Constance's life. Though the sex in itself had been most enjoyable, the real thrill of the occasion had been her state of total helplessness. How that man in the raincoat and wellingtons must have savoured the sight of such a beautiful young slut tied to a tree, completely at his mercy! Her only regret was that he had not brought a Polaroid camera and presented her with a memento of the occasion.

During the following week, she found herself counting down the hours to her next broadcast on S/M-FM. KT further whetted her anticipation by calling her at work on Wednesday afternoon, to inform her that he had a very special game planned for the next edition of *Slave in the Hot Seat*. No more details would be forthcoming until Saturday night.

She arrived at his mansion several hours earlier than expected, dressed in a whorish ensemble of scarlet high heels, matching leather micro-skirt and see-through fishnet vest. If KT's butler was pleasantly surprised by the sight that greeted him when he answered the front door, he kept the fact well hidden.

'The master wasn't expecting you so early,' he curtly informed her.

'I couldn't wait,' she admitted with a coy smile. 'May I come in?'

'I suppose so,' he replied, stepping aside. 'But you'll have to wait in the study. He is—' he paused momentarily, clearly considering the appropriate terminology, '—busy, and left strict instructions that he wasn't to be disturbed.'

Constance was disappointed, but knew better than to insist on seeing him. Matthews escorted her to the study, poured her a drink and invited her to make herself at home. It would be at least an hour before KT was ready to join her.

Left alone, she suddenly realised that this was an ideal opportunity to perhaps learn a few of her master's closely guarded secrets. Discovering even his full name would be something of an achievement. She mitigated a pang of guilt by telling herself that he was probably 'busy' upstairs with G.

His desktop was bare, so her only option was to try the drawers. The first one she opened contained a cane, cat o'nine tails, thick leather strap and a set of handcuffs. She took out the cane and flexed it, the feel of the hard wood sending a sensual shudder through her body. If KT did catch her rifling through his possessions, she hoped this was what he would use to punish her.

The second drawer down revealed an even more

intriguing discovery – a single sheet of white paper, bearing a crest in the form of a set of handcuffs resting on a spike-heeled shoe. Printed in blood red gothic script underneath were the words, *Slave Contract*. Constance took a sip from her drink, glanced towards the door, then sat back in KT's chair and began reading.

I, the undersigned, being of legally consenting age, do hereby surrender myself completely to my master. I do so of my own free will, in a spirit of servitude and unselfish obedience. I will, at all times, obey without question the commands of my master and attend to his needs above all others. Should I fail in my duties, or in any way displease him, it is his right to punish me as he sees fit. I will accept such punishments without protest and strive continually to be nothing less than the perfect slave. In addition to submitting to my master's every sexual desire, I will attend to domestic and any other duties assigned by him. This document binds master and slave to their respective roles, until such time as either party expresses, in writing, their desire to change it.

The contract was signed by Mr Kenton Turley (master) and Miss Gina Lessways (slave).

Pleased, yet also slightly dismayed by what she had learnt, Constance replaced the contract in the drawer and continued her search. In the third drawer, on top of a small pile of documents, lay a video cassette. Written on the label was the name, *Constance*.

She stared at the cassette for several minutes, as if by doing so she could somehow decipher what was on it. Was it possible that KT had videotaped her at The Master's Masque, or with the man in the woods? There was only one way to find out.

She slid aside several wooden panels on the wall, before finding the one that concealed a video player and TV screen. She inserted the cassette, switched on the machine and stood back to watch. When the face of KT appeared she uttered a small gasp.

'Good evening, Constance,' he began. 'I had hoped you might arrive a little early and, once again, you have not disappointed me. If you are watching this, then you have been snooping where you had no right to snoop. I'm waiting for you upstairs, second door on the left. Come up and be punished, at once.'

As she made her way upstairs, Constance was more annoyed by her own stupidity than the fiendish machinations of KT. Whatever punishment awaited her, it would be no more than she deserved.

She knocked on the door and he called out for her to enter. She stepped into a large bedroom decorated in a lurid shade of pink, with mirrors on all four walls and on the ceiling above the purple satin-draped four-poster bed. Late evening sunlight spilled through the open French windows, gleaming on the thigh-high purple rubber boots and matching cat-suit Gina wore. Smiling, she beckoned Constance forward.

The bare-chested figure of KT stood by the head of the bed, a riding crop tucked into the studded belt of his skin-tight faded blue jeans. Lying on the black velvet cushion of the chair beside him was a set of handcuffs and steel clamps.

'Oh, Constance, you are so delightfully predictable,' he greeted her. 'Gina is none too pleased to see you, though. You see, we had a little bet. She thought you wouldn't turn up early and do a little detective work. I was certain you would. As she lost the bet, she gets punished. But you first. Get on your knees and crawl over here, on the double.'

Constance did as she was told, her face flushing with shame. When she reached KT, he ordered her to remove her vest. Her nipples stiffened when he touched them with the tip of his riding crop.

'I've been so looking forward to this moment,' he declared, caressing her breasts with the crop. 'Had I lost the bet, Gina would have had the privilege of punishing you.'

Constance frowned. 'But for what, master? If you had lost the bet, there would be no reason to punish me.'

He smiled. 'We would have found an excuse, never fear. Now, lift those breasts nice and high. I want to give them a taste of what your bottom will shortly be receiving. Come on! You're only making it worse for yourself by trying my patience.'

Trembling, Constance lifted her breasts with both hands and squeezed them together. Gina knelt behind her and gripped her wrists firmly, obviously intending not to let go until Constance had been fully punished. She shut her eyes and whimpered in terror as KT drew back the riding crop. She heard it whistle through the air, felt the breeze as it descended past her face, then the fiery agony of its cracking impact on her breasts. A shrill cry burst from her. Instinctively, she tried to retreat out of range, but Gina's iron grip on her wrists and her right knee pressed into the small of her back prevented her from going anywhere.

KT allowed a moment for the fire to spread through her breasts, before administering a second searing stroke of the crop.

'Owww... Master, have mercy!' she cried.

'If you're going to play big girl games, you must accept big girl punishments!' he snapped, raising the crop for the third time.

Half a dozen resounding whacks later, the first instalment of her punishment was complete. The throbbing of the six fiery lines branded on the upper half of her breasts brought tears to her eyes, yet she could not deny the equally strong sensations of pleasure.

At KT's command, Gina unzipped Constance's skirt and tugged it down to her knees. The tiny panties she wore underneath were transparent pink silk. As Gina pulled these down, KT instructed Constance to put her hands behind her back. He passed the handcuffs to his slave and she snapped them shut around Constance's wrists. She then picked one of the chrome clamps up off the chair. Constance's cry of protest became a shriek of pain as the steel jaws bit her right nipple. Gina affixed the other clamp to the opposite bud and gave the small steel balls that dangled by chains from both a small tug.

'You'll soon get used to the minor discomforts,' KT assured her as she continued to gasp in agony. 'Right, let's have a look at your bottom.'

Remaining on her knees, Constance bent over the chair, resting her chin on the velvet cushion. The steel balls dangling freely from her nipples exacerbated the agony in her breasts. To make sure that Constance did not move, Gina raised her right foot and planted her spike-heeled boot on the back of her neck.

'These white cheeks are begging for the crop,' KT mused, studying her submissively presented rear. 'Shall we say a dozen strokes?'

'No!' Constance shrieked.

'The slave seems to feel that's not enough, master,' said Gina.

'Very well – sixteen then,' he said.

'Master, no, I didn't—!'

'She's still not happy,' Gina said, pressing harder on Constance's neck with her boot.

'Then we shall have to make it an even two dozen,' said KT. He tapped Constance's buttocks with the crop. 'Any advances on twenty-four?'

Knowing full well what would happen if she responded again, she wisely remained silent. She clenched her buttocks and bit her lower lip in anticipation of the first burning crack of the crop. KT took careful aim, before delivering a savage lash that caused her buttocks to quiver and raised an angry furrow on the creamy flesh. Her responsive yelp was everything a master could have hoped for.

The thrashing seemed to last forever, each stroke of the crop burning more fiercely than the previous. Having administered the agreed two dozen, KT stepped back to admire his handiwork. The crimson stripes criss-crossed on Constance's buttocks were as pleasing to behold as they were painful to endure. Gina removed her boot from the other woman's neck. As Constance rose to her feet, blinking tears from her eyes, her skirt and panties slipped down to her ankles.

'That's you dealt with, for now,' he announced. 'You won't be needing your clothes for the rest of the evening. Now, go and kneel in the corner while I deal with Gina.'

Constance slunk away like a chastened schoolgirl, and took up her position in the corner, facing the wall. By peeking sideways at one of the mirrors, she would still be able to see the other woman receive whatever punishment she had earnt by losing the bet with her master. For the part Gina had so willingly played in her own punishment, Constance hoped it would be exceptionally severe.

Gina paid the price of her wager without protest,

peeling her cat-suit down to her hips, then kneeling at her master's feet. After he had punished her breasts with a dozen stiff strokes of the riding crop, she fell to all fours and began licking his boots. His manhood bulged impressively in his tight jeans and Constance was delighted to see that he was feasting his eyes on her, rather than his grovelling slave.

Constance was still naked and wearing her nipple clamps when she went on air, several hours later. KT's special game was a phone-in contest, in which his *Slave in the Hot Seat* was the prize. Any master who was seriously interested in having Constance as his slave for a whole night was invited to call in with a good reason why he should have her. KT would decide the winner. She had already agreed to accept his decision and give herself willingly to the winner of the contest.

During the next two hours, she took over twenty calls from men who were eager to get their hands on her. Their reasons for wanting her for a night ranged from the romantic to the depraved. Finally, KT went back on air and announced that she had been won by a man who called himself the Stablemaster, and who had claimed she should go to him because he could lick her into shape, in more ways than one.

Chapter Six

The following Thursday night Constance returned to The Master's Masque. She was dressed exactly as KT had specified, in a narrow-rimmed black hat, a white silk blouse, a black tie and virtually poured-on black rubber shorts. Gleaming ox-blood DM's laced almost to her knees added the finishing touch to her striking outfit. The approving looks were far more numerous than she could have attracted in the most expensive ensemble from her boutique. She hoped the Stablemaster would show due appreciation.

Constance knew absolutely nothing about the man who had won her for the night. Psychopath? Gentleman? Pervert? She would just have to wait to find out. In the event of something untoward occurring, KT would be on hand to rescue her.

She was glad to see that Gina had been given the night off. Old-fashioned jealousy was the principal reason behind her increasing dislike for KT's slave. After all, compared to Constance, the red-haired woman was almost plain. Why did KT keep her when such an attractive alternative was available?

Gina's replacement on bar duty was a heavily built blonde in a studded black leather basque and fishnet tights. Constance took a stool and asked for a Bloody Mary and 'reserved' collar. KT had insisted on the latter, as a symbol of respect for her master and a signal to all others that she was spoken for. She leant over the bar, her nose almost buried in the barmaid's cleavage as the other woman fastened a collar around her throat; the word 'reserved' was studded in gleaming chrome letters on the thick black leather.

KT had informed her that the Stablemaster would be meeting her 'after ten', refusing to be any more specific. If he kept her waiting into the early hours, which would not surprise her, he was liable to have a drunk slave on his hands. It was highly unlikely that he would fail to show up at all.

Constance was still sipping her first drink when a tall woman approached the bar. Her chestnut hair was tied back in a ponytail and her slender body sheathed in an ankle-length dress of shiny black rubber.

She carefully regarded Constance for a few seconds, then cleared her throat and spoke. 'You're waiting for the Stablemaster?'

Though the look was feminine, the voice was unmistakably male, reminding Constance that she had not yet lost her ability to be shocked.

'You're him?' she responded, trying to conceal her disappointment. It was impossible to reconcile the dual images of a transvestite and a dominant master.

'Shall we go?' He ignored her question.

'Where to, exactly?'

'Just follow me.'

He waited impatiently while she finished her drink. Telling him she had changed her mind momentarily seemed like a good idea but, she decided, what the hell? Going with a TV would be a new experience, if nothing else.

When she slid from her stool, he began walking towards the rear of the club. He held open a door and she found herself facing a narrow dimly lit staircase. 'The club have provided us with a fully equipped private room for the night,' he explained. 'More suitable than an hotel, I think you'll agree.'

'I didn't realise you could rent rooms here,' Constance replied.

The TV smiled. 'Here, you can do just about anything.'

She followed him up the steep flight of steps to a black painted door at the top of the landing. He pushed it open and she followed him inside, her uneasiness increasing with every step. The room was small and windowless, a jungle of dangling chains, racks of punishment tools, and bizarre items of black furniture. The multi-coloured bulbs in the high chandelier cast an eerie, pinkish green light over the claustrophobic space. Standing in one corner, his fists gripping a set of iron manacles dangling from heavy chains, was a broad-shouldered, shaven-headed man of forty-something. He was wearing an ankle-length robe of rich red satin.

'Good evening, sweet thing,' he greeted in an intoxicating Scottish brogue. 'So glad you didn't get cold feet.'

'I'm a woman of my word,' Constance replied. 'I, er, wasn't expecting there to be two of you.'

He frowned. 'Is that a problem? If it is, just say so. I wouldn't want you to be uncomfortable.'

'I'm just surprised,' she said, her glance darting from one to the other.

He smiled. 'This kinky world of ours is full of surprises. I'm the man who likes to be known as the Stablemaster. My friend's alias is Truelove. What shall we call you?'

She shrugged.

'How about "Prize"?' he suggested. 'That is what you are, after all.'

Truelove poured Constance a glass of vodka and the

Stablemaster invited her to sit. She moved towards the single chair, only noticing the pointed chrome studs on the wooden seat when she sat on them. Both men smiled when she yelped and leapt upright again.

'The fittings are rather functional,' said the Stablemaster, a half-note of apology in his voice. 'Perhaps it would have been better if we had met somewhere less intimidating.'

'This is fine,' she assured him, carefully studying each item of grimly functional furniture and mentally speculating on its possible uses. 'I'm just not very used to meeting strange men in dungeons.'

His eyes lit up. 'Aha, a relative newcomer! I never would have guessed from hearing you on S/M-FM. You sounded so uninhibited, if you don't mind my saying so. You're single?'

'By choice, I assure you.'

'Waiting for the master of your dreams to come along,' he said. 'I can well imagine you as a career woman – with your own business, perhaps?'

'I'd really rather not discuss personal details,' she replied. 'I'm sure you understand.'

He nodded. 'Absolutely. Safer to play by the rules of the game.'

'More fun too,' she added.

'Perhaps we should get on with establishing the statute of limitations for tonight's game,' he suggested.

'What does that mean?'

'I forget you're new to all this,' he said, somewhat patronisingly. 'As your master, it's important that I know the limits to which you are willing to go. Are there any particular acts you would absolutely refuse to have any part of?'

'I wouldn't be here if I wasn't open-minded,'

Constance replied. 'What is it about this game of yours that I might find so repugnant?'

'It's basically a game of chance, involving acts of S/M and bondage,' the Stablemaster explained. 'I am the master, Truelove my assistant, and you our submissive plaything. Okay, so far?'

She nodded.

'What will happen to you depends on the roll of a dice,' he continued. 'Let me show you.' He led her to the round iron table in the centre of the room and opened out a large snakes-and-ladders type board. There were four segments, each consisting of thirty-six numbered squares, with arrows pointing in various directions.

'The game begins here in the red section, which is the dungeon.' He held up a tiny plastic figure of a naked girl in chains. 'This is you, the slave. The objective of the game is for you to get from the dungeon to freedom, via the Master's Bedroom and the Slave Auction. The symbol in each numbered square represents a different form of punishment and you will be subjected to quite a few of these as you progress through each section. Should you land on one that throws up something you would rather not do, I can, at my discretion, offer you an alternative. I should warn you that this game is designed to test to the full the endurance limits of a slave. Once you begin, I shall expect you to see it through to the end.'

'Or else?'

He shrugged. 'As you said, you're a woman of your word. I don't see you chickening out. Any other questions?'

Constance put down her glass. 'Shall we begin?'

Before the first roll of the dice she was required to strip down to her high heels and stockings. Emboldened by the large vodka she had hurriedly consumed, she performed an erotic striptease for her two appreciative companions, casting off her inhibitions along with her clothes. It was becoming ever easier to slip into her carefree alter ego – the anonymous, sex-breathing slave tramp of S/M-FM, who was free to be whoever she wanted to be and whatever her masters desired. When she was all but naked the Stablemaster applauded, then ordered her to raise her hands above her head.

'You will enjoy this game,' he promised, slipping a set of rubber padded manacles around her wrists.

The feeling of delicious helplessness when the restraints were snapped shut caused her nipples to stiffen instantly. For better or worse, her fate was now in the hands of these two men. The fittings and tools in the room around her were suddenly infused with all manner of erotic possibility. Standing on the tips of her toes, Constance had a clear view of the game board on the table.

Truelove threw the dice and moved the slave figurine onto a square numbered eleven and decorated with the symbol of a coiled whip on a pair of breasts. With a satisfied grin the Stablemaster took a long thin whip from a rack on the wall, cracking it on the wooden floor as he took up his position a few feet in front of Constance. Knowing what was about to happen, she bit her lower lip, every muscle involuntarily tightening. She threw back her head as he recoiled the whip. The knotted tongue of black leather hissed through the air and licked fire across both breasts with a resounding *thwack*! She whimpered and jerked, the sharp after-burn bringing tears to her eyes.

The full eleven lashes left her globes throbbing and raggedly striped. After the Stablemaster had laid down his whip, his companion threw the dice again, yielding a one. Following the direction of the arrow, he moved the slave figure into an adjoining square, which was numbered six and decorated with a shark head symbol.

'Oh dear, we are off to a painful start,' the Stablemaster sighed.

'Wh-what does that mean?' Constance pleaded.

'It would be much more in keeping with the spirit of the game if you did not ask such questions,' he replied. 'Besides, you won't have to wait long to find out.'

Her eyes followed him as he took down a fearsome-looking chain from the wall. Instead of links, it was made up of small copper shark heads, with jagged teeth of white plastic. There were twenty such objects on the long chain, joined to one another by small metal hooks. He detached two sets of three and Constance realised the meaning of the number six on the board. She stifled a shriek of terror as he pulled open the jaws of one of the copper shark heads and placed it over her right nipple. The teeth looked sharp enough to bite it clean off.

Her shriek of agony filled the room as the jaws snapped tightly over her nipple. The pain was accentuated by the weight of the three metal objects left dangling from her teat. Another scream was breaking from her throat even before a second jaw was clamped to her left breast.

'You're doing fine, my Prize,' the Stablemaster reassured her, patting her bottom.

Constance would have laughed, had her breasts not felt like they were providing dinner for a real live Jaws.

The next roll of the dice resulted in her being fitted with a red rubber ball gag, strapped tightly around her head, denying her the relief of even being able to scream.

The plastic slave figure then progressed onto a square numbered twenty, with a picture of a cane. There was no need to wonder about the nature of that punishment.

Standing by the board, the transvestite master clicked his fingers in time to the beat of cane on quivering flesh as the Stablemaster administered twenty full-blooded strokes to her bare buttocks, each laying a livid red line on a fresh strip of pale skin. Constance would have been yelling for him to stop halfway through, had the gag not prevented her from uttering more than a hoarse whimper of protest.

It had not occurred to her that the sadistic board game might take much longer than a bout of Trivial Pursuit. The dice was rolled again and the slave figure moved to a numberless square decorated with an erect phallus. However, the result was not what Constance expected. The Stablemaster produced a long pink latex vibrator. He bound the two attached studded leather straps tightly around her thighs, then pushed the shaft of the object up into her sex. A pair of steel clips at the base of the phallus was attached to her labia, providing a painful counterbalance to the pleasure of the gentle palpitations when the vibrator was switched on.

Another roll of the dice earnt her two dozen stinging slaps of a wooden paddle, which toasted every inch of her already throbbing rear cheeks. She blinked tears from her eyes as she watched Truelove move the little plastic angel in bondage onto another square, depicting what looked horribly like a noose. The short length of thick rope the Stablemaster took from the wall had a hangman's knot fashioned at either end. He draped the rope around her shoulders, slipped a noose over both breasts and drew them so tightly that the harsh fabric of the rope bit into her soft flesh.

Constance did not know how much more of this she could bear. There was no denying the pleasurable aspects of what she was being subjected to – the vibrator and arse-reddenings were particularly stimulating – but the point was surely not far off when the pain and discomfort began to outweigh the pleasure. As she was gagged, she did not see how she could let her tormentor know she had had enough.

The next punishment consisted of several round ice cubes being placed in the cleft of her tightly roped breasts and two more inserted in her rectum. The Stablemaster did at least have the decency to use a squirt of KY jelly, before subjecting her to the latter indignity.

Following the next throw of the dice a steel spreader bar was placed between her feet and strapped to her ankles. He adjusted the breadth of the bar until her legs were as wide apart as was possible without causing severe discomfort. She shuddered as rivulets from the melting ice cubes between her breasts ran down over her belly. Far worse, however, was the shameful sensation of icy droplets trickling from her bottom and their soft patter on the floorboards, just audible above the hum of the vibrator that was sensually torturing her clitoris.

'At last, we leave the Dungeon!' the Stablemaster announced, following the next throw of the dice. 'I think we deserve a short break before the Slave Auction.' So saying, he and his companion left the room, leaving Constance trussed up and the door wide open. Minutes ticked interminably by as she anxiously awaited their return.

Eventually she heard footsteps on the stairs, the sound filling her with a mixture of relief and trepidation. A young man appeared in the doorway, wearing a low-peaked black leather cap decorated with studs and chains. His faded jeans looked like they had been attacked by a razor-wielding maniac and his leather waistcoat was heavy with military medals and heavy metal regalia. A smile crossed his stubbled face as he stepped into the room, delighted by Constance's look of wide-eyed consternation.

'Hope you don't mind me coming in for a minute,' he said in a Cockney accent. 'Bit careless of your master to leave the door open like that.' He scanned the room. 'Where is he anyway? S'all right, you don't have to answer.' He looked her up and down as if she were a mannequin in a shop window. 'You're a bit of a babe, ain't ya? Wouldn't mind 'avin' you to meself for a while. Dear, oh dear! What've you done to deserve all this?' He set her nipple attachments swinging and she winced in agony. 'They must be hell on your poor tits. I see he's given your arse a good seeing-to, as well.' He smacked her left buttock. 'Jesus, it's hot enough to fry bacon on! You don't look at all comfortable, darlin'.'

Constance kept her eyes on the doorway, willing the Stablemaster to return before this intruder was tempted to take any liberties with her. The coarse young man did not seem at all concerned by the prospect of being caught in the room. He stroked and prodded Constance, all the while crudely continuing to compliment her physical attributes. Eventually, much to her relief, his attention was diverted to the board game on the table.

'I wonder what this is all about,' he mused, leaning over to carefully study it. 'Better not touch anything, just to be on the safe side. Wouldn't want to get on the wrong side of your master.' He turned back to Constance. 'I wonder how long he'll be gone for. Long enough for me to have a little fun with you, eh?'

75

She whimpered and vigorously shook her head.

He grinned. 'If I didn't know better, I'd think you couldn't wait to get rid of me. Know what? I think I'll take a chance and live dangerously. If your master does come back before I'm finished with you, we'll just have to hope he understands. I'm sure you won't object to me taking out your gag, will you?'

She hesitated, then shook her head.

He reached for the strap at the back of her head. 'I didn't think so. You don't have to worry. I won't hurt you. Just a quick blow-job an' I'll be on my way. Okay?'

'Okay,' Constance gasped as the ball gag popped from between her lips.

The young man unzipped his jeans, then wrapped both fists around a set of manacles dangling overhead, took a deep breath and raised himself off the floor. His powerful biceps bulged as he hauled himself up, until his stiff cock was level with Constance's mouth.

'Better 'urry!' he grunted. 'I won't be able to stay up 'ere for long!'

Opening her mouth, she thrust her head forward. The purple crown and several inches of thick cock slipped past her red glossed lips and she went hungrily to work, temporarily forgetting the sadistic Stablemaster and his cross-dressing companion. The vein in the young man's temple throbbed as he watched her lips and tongue slide sensually over his cock.

Constance had always considered the taste and feel of a hard, hot cock between her lips to be one of life's supreme pleasures, but under the present bizarre circumstances, it was a particularly favourable treat. She just hoped the young master could hold on until she was finished.

From his groans and breathless exclamations, it was

76

impossible to tell whether the agony or ecstasy he was enduring was the greater. His nostrils flared, his face turned a deep shade of pink and his straining muscles were sheened with perspiration. Constance sucked him with all the urgency she could muster, almost as desperate for him to climax as he himself was.

'I can't... hold on much... longer!' he cried.

Her lips enveloped him in a silken clinch, her tongue slapping the crown of his cock. He uttered a long, loud groan that could surely be heard downstairs, then a hot burst of thick semen hit the back of her throat. She ravenously gulped down the powerful, creamy flood, so delicious she wished it would never end.

'Can't hold!' the young man cried desperately.

His cock slipped from Constance's mouth, the remainder of his semen splattering her chin and throat as he let go of the manacles and fell to the floor.

She was still licking her lips when he staggered back to his feet.

'That was... fuckin' amazing,' he gasped, tucking his wet tool back into his jeans. He wiped the semen from her with his fingers. After she had sucked them clean he kissed her for a few seconds, then whispered that it was time he was gone. Before leaving, never to be seen by her again, he replaced the ball gag in her mouth and secured the strap.

A few moments later the Stablemaster and Truelove returned. If they had any suspicions of her visitor, they kept them to themselves.

'We now find ourselves at the Slave Auction stage of our game,' the Stablemaster announced. 'Time to free the slave from the shackles of the Dungeon.'

As soon as Constance had been released from her manacles and all her accessories removed, the game resumed. Truelove cast the dice and moved the slave figure onto a number six square and the symbol of a horse. The Stablemaster directed Constance to a crude wooden horse positioned near the table. The object was fitted with a black leather saddle, bristling with conical silver studs. When she hesitated to climb aboard, he reached for a riding crop and informed her that she could have a dozen lashes of that across her backside instead. She wasn't certain which would be the lesser evil, but decided she might as well continue with the spirit of the game, at least for the time being.

The cold studs, though not sharp enough to puncture her skin, felt like nails gouging her tender nether cheeks. At the Stablemaster's command, she slipped her wrists into the leather cuffs on either side of the neck of the wooden horse and he buckled them tightly. Her ankles were secured to the stirrups in a similar fashion.

The game continued with the dice being rolled again and the Stablemaster reaching for a harness from his collection of restraint devices. Cups of wet-look red latex, with nipple peepholes, were fitted over Constance's breasts and secured in place by a strap at the back. Attached to this garment was a second strap of thick elastic. He ordered her to raise her bottom from the saddle, drew the strap down between her thighs and clipped the free end to the front of the rubber bra. The strap chafed unpleasantly in the cleft of her buttocks and between the folds of her labia.

'Aha, a choice move!' the Stablemaster exclaimed, following the next roll of the dice. From a box in one corner of the table he picked one from a small pile of black plastic chips, each the diameter of a two-penny coin. 'You have a decision to make, Prize,' he told Constance. 'There is a symbol on both sides of this coin, which stands for a different form of punishment. You can call heads or tails and accept whatever punishment results, or you can choose the less painful option of answering a single question.'

'What kind of question?' she demanded.

He smiled mysteriously. 'You won't know that unless you first decide to answer.'

'What if I don't know the answer?'

'You'll know it,' he assured her. 'Well, what's it to be, call or question?'

Constance suspected the latter would not be as straightforward as he made it sound. On the other hand, she was none too eager for another taste of whip or cane, especially with the game far from reaching its conclusion. She opted to gamble on answering the question.

'What is your full name?' the Stablemaster demanded.

'Constance Elizabeth Brooking,' she replied. The triumphant look that crossed his face made her instantly regret not having answered with a false name.

'That didn't hurt too much, did it?' he smiled. 'Throw the dice, Truelove. Constance is eager to get on with the game.'

The subsequent punishment brought yet another harness into play. Two bars of hard black plastic were bolted to the neck of the wooden horse. At the opposite end of these bars was a rubber padded iron collar, which the Stablemaster placed around Constance's neck, adjusted to fit snugly, then padlocked at the back. A fresh set of clamps was then fitted to her nipples. These were attached to short bungee straps, which were hooked to the far ends of the plastic bars. She was now perched in an acutely uncomfortable position, unable to alleviate the painful tug of the straps on her nipples by leaning forward.

A further roll of the dice instituted yet further discomfort. A latex hood that matched the wrapping on her breasts was pulled over her head and joined to her collar by four steel clips. The tight-fitting sheath completely covered her eyes and the back of her head, leaving the lower half of her face uncovered. A strap at the back of the hood was hooked to the rear end of the wooden horse, tugging her head back and forcing her face upwards. Being unable to see what her masters were doing filled her with a greater sense of alarm than her state of near-complete bondage. They were now free to cheat at the game and administer their pet punishments, rather than leaving her fate to a roll of the dice.

For the next instalment of the game a thick roll of sticky black rubber tape was wrapped around her upper thighs and the middle of the wooden horse, binding her tightly to the studded saddle. She heard the rattle of the dice on the table top again, then the voice of the Stablemaster announcing that she had moved to the third section of the game – the Master's Chamber.

'Don't leave me like this!' she cried, hearing their footsteps as they moved towards the door.

Neither of her tormentors replied. She did not hear the door shut, so she knew they were once again leaving her exposed to anybody who should happen to peer in.

A short while after their departure she heard two sets of footsteps on the stairs. There was a momentary pause when they reached the landing, then the pair proceeded into the room.

'Master, is that you?' she demanded, in a trembling voice.

When nobody answered, Constance instinctively realised that she was again at the mercy of uninvited guests. As they moved around, inspecting the room and the helpless captive, she struggled in vain to free her wrists, in order to rip off her hood and at least be able to see them. She squealed when a sharp fingernail touched her left shoulder, pressed against the pale flesh, then began raking slowly down along her back, leaving a burning microgroove in its wake. The second intruder managed to work a gloved hand between her thighs from the front, burrowing into her slit with a long finger. The scent of expensive perfume caressed her nostrils, confirming that these two people were not the Stablemaster and Truelove.

She could not help relishing the gloved finger vigorously frigging her, even as the razor-like fingernails continued to rake her back, those of the other hand setting to work with equal cruelty on her sensitive buttocks. Following several long minutes of such torture, the fingernails were replaced by a silken tongue that lapped slowly over the throbbing ridges. Constance shuddered from the unexpectedly sensual sensation, unconcerned for the time being by the certainty that the person licking and kissing her was a woman. The heavy breathing from in front of her left her in no doubt that the other half of the duo was a man.

She had no idea how long the erotic torture lasted. The man continued to finger her until she eventually cried out in the *frisson* of a wondrous climax. When his soaked finger was then presented to her lips she sucked it clean of her juices, without the slightest hesitation.

She thought the couple might leave then, but instead of departing footsteps she heard the rasp of a zipper, followed by a soft murmur of pleasure from one and an excited grunt from the other. From the ecstatic moans and soft wet smacking sounds that ensued over the next few minutes, she concluded that the master half of the pair was having his cock sucked. Her taste buds tingled enviously.

The master moaned loudly as he climaxed. Seconds later, Constance felt a soft pair of lips brush hers. Instinctively repulsed by the thought of kissing another woman, she resisted momentarily, before lust gained the upper hand. The woman crushed her lips against hers and a warm, sticky stream of semen oozed into her mouth. Constance gulped it down thirstily. The woman's semen-coated tongue followed and Constance sucked it as eagerly as if it were a cock. The lingering, feverish kiss was finally broken and the master and his slave slipped away.

Between the departure of the unseen couple and the return of her masters, Constance had a few moments in which to reflect on what was happening. It was too convenient that the Stablemaster and Truelove should remain absent on both occasions, while her unknown visitors amused themselves with her. She could only conclude that sharing her with other members of the club was a part of the game they had decided not to tell her about.

Upon their return, the two men set about releasing her from the wooden horse. A throw of the dice commenced the Master's Chamber section of the game. Truelove moved the plastic slave figure onto a square depicting a blackboard.

'Looks like I shall be playing headmaster,' the Stablemaster said. 'Which means you, Constance, are my pupil.' He reached for a cane on the wall. 'Throw the dice again, Truelove. Let's find out what our pretty pupil's first lesson is going to be.'

The dice rolled and the slave on the board was moved

to a square numbered thirty, with a symbol that Constance could not decipher.

'Physical education,' the Stablemaster announced. 'I hope you're as fit as you look, Constance.'

He placed a thick, curved black plastic phallus mounted on a rectangular steel plate on the floor and instructed her to squat over it, her arms raised high above her head and her legs wide apart. When she was in the required position, her labia brushing the head of the dildo, he informed her that she would now perform thirty squats, impaling herself fully on the dildo each time. Even before a crack of the cane on her buttocks signalled her to begin, her face was showing the strain.

'Keep those hands high!' he barked as she lowered herself onto the shaft for the first time. 'That's it, take it all in. Aaaand up!'

She almost lost her balance as she rose back up. The phallus slipped from between her thighs with a soft plop. She took a deep breath, then lowered herself onto it again, fervently wishing that it were a flesh and blood cock, instead of a cold length of hard plastic. A stinging whack from the Stablemaster's cane reminded her to keep her arms straight.

By the time she was halfway through her quota of thrusts and lunges, her shoulder and thigh muscles were beginning to ache unbearably. Her protestations to the man towering over her that she needed a rest were met with another whack of the cane. After she had finally managed to complete the exercise, he pushed her down onto the dildo once more and ordered her to remain there while the dice was cast again and her next torment decided.

The chosen subject was art. Gripping a felt-tipped marker with her clenched vaginal muscles, Constance was forced to stand spread-legged over a stool. On the plain sheet of paper tacked to the wooden seat, she was ordered to write her name. Her hands were cuffed behind her back. At her first four attempts, the marker slipped from her slick pussy. Before reinserting it each time, the Stablemaster punished her with two strokes of the cane.

'It's impossible!' she wailed.

'That's not the attitude of a good pupil,' he responded, in headmasterly tones. 'You'll keep on trying until you succeed. Just be grateful I haven't given you a hundred lines.'

Even getting the tip of the marker to the paper was extraordinarily difficult. With her teeth gritted in frustration, Constance clenched her internal muscles and tried desperately to guide the marker with the movements of her hips. Offered a choice, she would have almost preferred to suffer the torments of the wooden horse all over again. Eventually, when she was close to screaming point, her efforts resulted in a near illegible scrawl on the paper. Rather than make her try again, the Stablemaster punished her with six whacks of the cane to the backs of her thighs. The dice then rolled again.

'The headmaster's office,' the Stablemaster declared. 'Yet more punishment for you, my naughty girl.'

He sat on the stool and ordered Constance to bend over his knee. The square on the game board that the slave figure had been moved onto was numbered twenty-two. Eleven resounding whacks of his right palm were administered to each cheek, infusing her bottom with a fresh shade of crimson. The spanking left her convinced she would not be able to sit down comfortably for a week.

When the next throw of the dice dictated that she sit

in the studded chair and take a French lesson, she begged the Stablemaster to offer her an alternative.

'Bottom a bit sore?' he smirked. 'Very well, if you don't want to sit in the chair, you can have detention for fifteen minutes. How does that sound?'

She thought it had to be preferable to inflicting any further suffering on her raw rear. The Stablemaster slid aside a panel in one of the walls, revealing a small dark closet. Constance was handcuffed, then ordered to step inside. Before locking her in, he drew open another panel at the back of the closet. She uttered a horrified gasp when she found herself pressed against a sheet of transparent Perspex, staring into a brightly-lit booth beyond. There were air holes in the top of the screen and several larger openings at strategic points further down. The sliding of the panel must have activated some form of signal, because the closet door had barely slid shut behind her when an elderly grey-haired man in a loose-fitting black suit stepped into the lighted booth. Constance was wedged tightly into the closet, the tips of her breasts protruding through the Perspex cutouts.

The man slid a door shut behind him and they were alone together. He ogled her for a moment, lasciviously licking his lips, then reached with both hands for her breasts. He pinched and tweaked her nipples before proceeding to suck, first on the left, then the right. He then turned his attention to the hole further down the screen. It was large enough for him to fit one hand through. He wriggled a finger between Constance's tightly clenched thighs and worked it up into her sex. Never had she felt so cheapened and humiliated. It was almost enjoyable.

The confines of the closet did not permit her to part her thighs by more than an inch, but the old man still managed to penetrate her with the full length of his finger. He resumed his feasting on her nipples as he frigged her. By shutting her eyes she found it easier to abandon herself to the pleasure of what he was doing.

Throughout the brief, crudely erotic interlude, not a single word was spoken. Constance was near the point of climax when the old man abruptly withdrew his hand and stood up. He licked her honey from his finger, complimented her with a smile, then turned and left the booth.

'Selfish old git!' she muttered in frustration.

Before any more visitors had a chance to enter the booth, the closet door was opened again and the Stablemaster led her back into the room. One throw of the dice later, the plastic slave was in the Freedom section of the board.

'Just one more sacrifice for your master, and your duty is done,' said the Stablemaster.

'What do you mean by sacrifice?' she demanded warily.

Truelove handed him a pack of playing cards. He shuffled the deck, then invited Constance to pick one.

'Each card represents a different kind of sacrifice,' he explained. 'Depending on the one you pick, you might have to parade naked through the club, have your cunt shaved for an audience, or lie across the bar and fuck yourself with a beer bottle. The possibilities are numerous. On the other hand, if you pick one of the jokers in the pack, all you have to do is get dressed and go home a happy little slave.'

'What if I don't like the card I choose?'

He sighed. 'You've played the game with remarkable spirit and perseverance. It would be a shame if it were to finish on a sour note.'

Constance studied the pack, dreading the prospect of picking a card that resulted in any of the abject humiliations he had mentioned. Whatever the challenge, however, she knew she would not refuse to go through with it. In submission, as in business, her word was her bond.

'Here goes,' she sighed, before plucking a card from the middle of the deck. She could scarcely bear to look when the Stablemaster held it up for her inspection. The card was a ten of diamonds, with a picture of a camera in the centre.

'You have just consented to pose for some dirty pics,' he grinned. 'Ten, to be precise. Aren't you relieved?'

'Uh, yes, I suppose so,' she replied. 'Who gets to keep these pictures?'

'They'll be my souvenirs of an unforgettable night,' he answered. 'Don't worry. I won't be sending them off to any pervy magazines, or anything like that.'

Constance still had grave misgivings about 'dirty' photographs of herself in anybody's collection. But the Stablemaster persuaded her to trust him, swearing that if she cared to give him her address, he would send the snaps and negatives to her as soon as they were developed.

It was a decision she would very soon regret.

Chapter Seven

Late the following afternoon Constance's boutique received an unexpected visitor. Wearing sunglasses and a conservative grey trouser suit, with her red hair tied up in a bun, Gina was scarcely recognisable.

'What are you doing here?' Constance demanded in an alarmed whisper.

'Is that any way to greet a potential customer?' she replied. 'How are you feeling after last night's festivities?'

'Sore, if you must know,' Constance answered. 'Look, I'd really rather not discuss my nocturnal activities here.'

Gina smiled. 'The Stablemaster got his money's worth, I'll bet. KT and I were at the club, you know.'

'Really?'

She nodded. 'We even paid you a little visit, when you were on that wooden horse contraption.'

Constance blushed at the memory. 'That was you?'

'Uh-huh. Okay, I can see I'm embarrassing you, so I'll say no more on the subject for now. The real reason I dropped by is to exercise my credit card. KT and I are going to an important function on Saturday night and I want to look my best. I need something sexy, yet classy.'

'Saturday night?' Constance repeated. 'But that's...'

'S/M-FM night, I know. You won't be on your own, don't worry. You'll have a strong master by your side, to ensure everything runs smoothly.'

'Who?'

'A trusted friend of ours. You and he will get along

splendidly. Now, can you help me squander some money on a designer label, or do you just want to go somewhere quiet and talk bondage?'

Constance did not relish the prospect of going on air without the guiding presence of KT by her side, but she still arrived at his mansion that Saturday night. Her master for the night was a pleasant surprise – tall, handsome, in his early thirties and of Mediterranean appearance. He introduced himself as Marlo, which made a refreshing change from the initials and pseudonyms that seemed to go with the territory.

'You're becoming quite a radio star,' he said as they sipped glasses of wine in the studio. He handed her a glossy adult magazine. 'Take a look at this.'

The page he had opened contained adult entertainment related news and gossip. One column was devoted to the discovery of 'late night pirates of perversity and passion on the airwaves around Greater London'. S/M-FM was described as 'essential listening for subs, doms, fetishists and anyone interested in bizarre and kinky sex'. The 'sultry submissive who calls herself CB' was written of in particularly glowing terms. Constance had to read the article several times before she could believe it was her that was being referred to.

'They've even published the frequency to pick us up on,' smiled Marlo. 'I think we're going to have a lot more listeners from now on. KT is a very happy man.'

'I never dreamt it would come to this,' said Constance, lighting a cigarette. 'I thought we could only be heard by a few dozen people, at most.'

'S/M-FM has the potential to be *the* pirate radio station of sleaze,' said Marlo. 'It's a shame we don't stand a chance in hell of ever getting a licence to broadcast legally. Anyway, you're on air in less than an hour, so I hope you're hot. I thought you could start off with one of your fantasies – the filthier the better – while we wait for the calls to come in. You're doing the full four hours tonight: think you can keep the juices flowing that long?'

She smiled coyly. 'I'm relying on you to see that I do. Is it okay for me to call you master?'

'I think you and I are going to work very well together,' he replied with a smile.

From midnight to four a.m. Constance shared her fantasies and traded pornographic conversation with a continuous stream of callers. She revelled as never before in her every second on air, only regretting that she could not stay on longer. Afterwards, she and Marlo celebrated with a bottle of wine. She did not mind getting drunk, as she had no intention of driving home.

As befitted her submissive role, she waited for him to make the first move. He did not need any encouragement. He first kissed her breathless, then spread her on the thick red carpeted studio floor and peeled off her short figure-hugging black lycra dress. The black G-string panties she was wearing underneath offered even less of a challenge.

'Master, take me,' she breathed, fumbling with the zipper of his jeans.

'Wait,' he said, gently pushing her hands away. 'Let's put S/M-FM back on air and fuck for an audience.'

Once he had flicked the necessary switches, he flung off his clothes and joined the wet and wanton slave spread-eagled on the floor. Remembering the listeners, Constance gave full voice to her passion, screaming obscenities as her master's cock pistoned between her thighs. Being on air had a similar effect on him, and he left whoever might be listening in no doubt that the shrieking woman at the receiving end of his cock was a true-blue slut.

S/M-FM remained on air until almost seven a.m., by which time Constance and Marlo had finally exhausted their animal passions. They crawled to a spare upstairs bedroom, where they slept until noon, when KT returned and demanded a report on the night's events.

The afterglow of Marlo, broadcasting success and the compliments of KT lasted until the following Monday evening, when Constance found a sealed brown envelope slipped beneath the windscreen of her Porsche. Inside was a photograph from The Master's Masque, which showed her kneeling in the centre of the dungeon floor, thrusting the huge dildo in her right fist up between her widely parted thighs and performing fellatio on the matching phallus in her left hand.

She hurriedly thrust it back into the envelope before any passer-by managed to catch a glimpse. Why had the Stablemaster left the envelope on her windscreen, for anybody to pick up and open?

The question was answered half an hour later, when he called her on her mobile phone. 'The photographs came out well, didn't they?' he began.

'What the hell are you playing at?'

'Another of my little master and slave games,' he calmly replied. 'The last one was such a success that I find myself wanting to use you as my plaything again.'

'Well, I don't want to be your plaything,' Constance retorted. 'I thought it was understood that what happened at the club was a one-off.'

'Rules change,' came the response. 'These

photographs give me a huge advantage over you. If they were to fall into the wrong hands they could prove very embarrassing for a respectable businesswoman such as yourself. Are you getting the picture – if you'll pardon the expression?'

'What is it you want?' she asked, in as level a voice as she could manage.

'You,' he replied. 'Whenever, however, and wherever I want. I still have nine photographs of you. Each time you do something for me, I give you one back. When you have them all, then you're free.'

'And the alternative?'

'The alternative, my dear Constance, is these sexy photographs of you turning up in all manner of public places. It would be very easy to prove I'm not bluffing, if you don't believe me.'

'Why are you doing this?' she demanded. 'I played your game, did everything you asked. I trusted you!'

'What can I say? I'm a greedy and devious man,' he replied. 'I want to meet you tonight. I'll be expecting you no later than nine. Here's the address...'

The rendezvous point was a lock-up garage, in a neighbourhood where Constance was far from comfortable about parking her Porsche. The Stablemaster was waiting for her, as arranged, wearing a tan suit and multi-coloured tie. The sight of his smug features filled her with rage, but she thought it might be wiser to contain herself, for the moment.

'Where's your other half?' she demanded.

'This is a private arrangement between you and me,' he replied. 'Come, let me show you our little love-nest.'

He raised the garage door and she stepped cautiously inside. There was a large wooden chest in one corner and a black rubber-covered mattress on the floor. Ropes and chains hung from hooks on the back wall. A wide metal bar dangled from two chains bolted to the ceiling, a couple of feet behind the naked light bulb that illuminated the dingy cell. Constance suspected that she was not its first guest.

'It smells a bit,' she observed, wrinkling her nose at the faint scent of engine oil.

'Sorry, the cleaning lady's on holiday,' the Stablemaster smirked, slamming the door shut. 'You don't have to pretend to be impressed.'

'What *do* I have to do?' she snapped.

'Address me as master, for a start. I know you'd rather not be here – especially under these circumstances – but we don't always get what we want out of life, do we?'

'Unless we refuse to abide by rules of decent behaviour,' Constance responded icily. 'So, master, for having made the mistake of trusting you, I am now your sex slave, whether I like it or not. Correct?'

He smiled. 'I knew you'd understand. Cheer up. This isn't the beginning of a life sentence. You only have to earn nine photographs and your sentence is served. Anyway, after what happened when we last met, I think you may enjoy being my slave.'

'Don't you bet on it.'

'Now, Constance, is that any way to speak to your master?' he tutted. 'I can see you're in need of a few lessons in good manners.' He raised the lid of the chest and produced a long slender cane. 'Let's have you on your back, where you belong.'

Until she devised a way out of this blackmail situation, she decided it would be best to play along with the creep. She lay back on the mattress and spread her arms wide, looking and feeling as though she was selling herself up for her own sacrifice. Her master flexed his cane as he leant over her, a victorious smirk playing at the corners of his mouth. The fact that she was a far from willing plaything obviously greatly increased the pleasure of having her at his mercy.

He hooked the top of the cane in the hem of her knee-length sky-blue skirt and tugged it gradually up along her legs, savouring every further inch of smooth, pale flesh that was exposed. Not wishing to give him any excuse to punish her, Constance obligingly raised her bottom off the mattress to allow her skirt to be pulled up over her hips. She kept her hindquarters raised as he hooked the cane in the waistband of her white lace briefs and tugged them down, baring her severely manicured pubic mound.

He pulled off her panties, sniffed them, commented favourably on the scent, and then placed them across her face. 'You just stay as you are, my love,' he smiled. 'Your master will do all the necessary work.'

He tied a length of thick rope around her left ankle, slung the other end across the overhead bar and pulled downwards, until her leg was stretched at a sixty-degree angle to her body. He knotted the rope in position, then repeated the process on her right ankle. Standing between her thighs, he gazed at what Constance knew was a perfect vaginal vista.

Any hope that he would be content to tie her up and screw her was dispelled when he withdrew the cane from his belt and announced that he was about to punish her earlier impudence. She denied him the satisfaction of pleading for mercy and resolved to take her punishment without a whimper.

The Stablemaster seemed to know exactly what she

was thinking and was equally determined to make her squeal. She bit her lower lip, tossed her head from side to side and writhed on the mattress as the cane spread fire across her buttocks and the backs of her thighs, in a relentless broadside. Despite the severity of the punishment, she managed to keep her response to the cracking strokes muted to a few gasps and whimpers.

When his right arm eventually wearied, he threw down the cane and feverishly unzipped his trousers. Cupping Constance's cane-scorched buttocks in both hands, he sank his cock between the dewy folds of her sex. She vowed to keep just as silent while he was screwing her, regardless of how much she found herself enjoying it.

When he realised she was doing her utmost to appear frigid, he began slapping her buttocks with the palms of both hands, in time to the aggressive plunging of his shaft. Despite the stinging pain, Constance continued to defy him. Only when she eventually felt a burst of hot semen against her cervix did an involuntary cry of pleasure escape her lips.

The Stablemaster kept her tied up for almost two hours, during which time he reddened her breasts with his belt, punished her backside with a thin lath of timber and screwed her with a soft-centred chocolate bar, which she was then forced to eat. Afterwards he crouched over her, squeezed his cock between her breasts and thrust until he climaxed again, spurting a hot string of creamy pearls around her throat.

After she had been untied and was finished dressing, he produced a photograph from the inside pocket of his jacket and handed it to her. 'Your payment, as promised,' he smiled.

The picture showed Constance naked on all fours,

glancing over her left shoulder and pouting seductively for the camera. She studied the embarrassing exposure for a moment, then ripped the photograph into dozens of tiny pieces.

'I thought you'd want to keep it as a souvenir,' he said.

'It would only remind me of you,' she retorted. 'If you're quite finished with me I'd like to go home. I have work to do.'

'Of course,' he said. 'Thanks for another wonderful evening. I'll be in touch again, very soon. You have eight photographs left to earn, remember.'

Constance did not believe, for one moment, that he would surrender his hold over her once the full collection of photographs had been returned. He would still have the negatives and would certainly use them. Unless she wanted to be his slave for a very long time to come, she would have to find another way to break free of his clutches.

She was tempted to tell KT, but he was likely to be less than sympathetic to her plight. Instead she decided to enlist the services of a private detective who had served her well on a previous occasion, by unearthing the identity of a member of her staff who had been selling confidential business information to the owners of a rival boutique. The first step to getting the Stablemaster out of her life once and for all was to learn as much as possible about him.

For her next stint on SM/FM, the following Saturday night, KT had devised an on-air slave auction for the listeners. Constance would be sold to the highest bidder, with all proceeds being donated to the campaign of a dominatrix who was standing as a candidate in a local parliamentary by-election. Her resistance to the idea surprised KT.

'I've had my fill of sex with complete strangers, for now,' she complained. 'Besides, I've always voted for a conventional party.'

'What's brought on this change of heart?' he demanded. 'I thought you'd love the idea.'

'If I wanted to be a whore, I might just as well stand on a street corner,' she retorted.

KT sighed. 'Constance, it's a game. You sell yourself for one night and earn a few quid for a good cause in the process.'

'What good cause? This Mistress Amber hasn't a chance in hell of being elected.'

'True,' he agreed. 'But there's a lot of media interest in her campaign. She can enlighten the general public on S&M related issues – perhaps even initiate some intelligent debate on the subject. If nothing else, she at least adds a bit of colour to a dull campaign.'

Had it not been for the Stablemaster's baleful hold over her, Constance would have unhesitatingly agreed to the idea. But the last thing she needed right then was to fall into the clutches of another pervert who wanted to own her. However, against her better judgement, she allowed herself to be persuaded. The mess she was in was not of KT's doing, and she would hate to turn her back on S/M-FM and the myriad opportunities for sexual gratification it provided.

Two hours later she was pronounced 'sold' to an anonymous bidder, for the sum of sixteen hundred pounds.

'I didn't think you'd make even half that amount,'

KT said delightedly, as soon as they had finished broadcasting.

'Thanks for the vote of confidence,' she replied bitterly.

'What is wrong with you?' he demanded. 'Your heart just wasn't in this tonight.'

'Time of the month,' she lied.

He nodded sympathetically. 'In that case I shall spare you a caning. I do hope you won't let me down when the time comes for you to meet your buyer.'

Early the following Tuesday, a tall and slender blond man in his early thirties entered Constance's boutique. He told the assistant who approached him that he wished to deal with Miss Brooking personally. While he waited for her to finish dealing with another client, he browsed through the racks of designer wear with the eye of a connoisseur. As Constance finally approached him, he looked up and smiled.

'May I help you?' she enquired pleasantly.

'Constance – nice to see you again,' he greeted.

She frowned. 'I'm sorry, have we met before?'

'The Master's Masque,' he replied. 'Does the name Truelove ring any bells?'

'You?' she exclaimed, her face flushing. 'What do you want?'

'A little courteous service,' he answered. 'You do have some exquisite garments on sale here. A bit beyond my normal price range, but I feel like splashing out.'

'This is a respectable boutique,' she said quietly, scarcely able to contain her anger. 'You'll find plenty of alternative places more suited to your particular requirements.'

'But I like what I see here,' he insisted. 'This designer

gown, for example, is a tasty little number.' He whistled. 'Tasty little price tag too.'

'If you don't leave I shall call the police,' she whispered agitatedly.

'Be my guest,' he replied calmly. 'I'll be interested to hear what you tell them when they arrive. I'm not an expert on law, but I don't think it's illegal for a man to walk in here and express an interest in purchasing a criminally overpriced frock.'

Constance sighed. 'Okay, if you want to buy something, fine. But I'm perfectly within my rights in forbidding you to try it on.'

He laughed. 'You're becoming paranoid. Who said it was for me? As it happens, I'm looking for a birthday present for my girlfriend. This is her size and her favourite colour.' He removed the dress from the rack, held it up for scrutiny, then nodded. 'Yes, it's perfect. She'll love it.'

'Will there be anything else?' she asked.

'Now that you mention it, yes,' he answered. 'I think I might spoil her with a complete ensemble. Let's see what other goodies you can tempt me with.'

Constance did her best to treat Truelove, or whatever his real name was, as just another customer, though she had a horrible feeling there was something more to his visit than a mere shopping trip. Her suspicions were confirmed when he took his purchases to the counter.

'Oh, the Stablemaster sends his regards,' he said softly. 'He wants to meet you at ten o'clock tonight, in the usual place.'

'The bastard!' she hissed. 'He told me you knew nothing about this... other business.'

'The Stablemaster is a very devious man,' he replied. 'Not to be trusted. How much does this little lot come to?'

'Er, seven hundred and forty pounds,' she replied. 'How will you be paying?'

He produced his wallet from his jacket, withdrew a photograph and placed it face-down on the counter.

'My flexible friend,' he grinned.

Constance glanced nervously around, before picking up the photograph in trembling hands and taking a quick look. It was another from her blackmailer's pornographic collection, featuring her spread-eagled on the table in the clubroom, with her knees drawn up around her chin. One end of a huge double-ended pink latex dildo was buried between her thighs. Several inches of the other end were in her mouth.

'This is outrageous,' she said, her voice trembling.

'I'm sure your respectable customers couldn't agree more,' he replied. 'Bag this lot, if you don't mind. There's no need for a receipt.'

As soon as he left she had to retire to her office for a cigarette and a cup of coffee. She was trembling with rage. Being forced to acquiesce to the Stablemaster's perverse sexual demands was bad enough, but it did at least have its pleasurable compensations. Having to stand idly by while his sneering transvestite cohort raided her boutique was another matter. Nobody could be permitted to walk over Constance Brooking in that manner.

When she had somewhat calmed down again, she rang the number of the private detective she had hired. It was time to start fighting back.

When she left home, at eight-thirty that evening, the detective's car followed at a discreet distance. The plan was for him to get a good look at the Stablemaster, possibly even a photograph. He could then unearth his identity and as much information as possible about him. Constance's hope was that this would provide her with some means of retaliation.

The Stablemaster's blue Ford Sierra was parked inside the garage and he was waiting by the open door. Constance was more nervous than ever as she stepped out of her Porsche. Who knew how he might react if he spotted the private detective nearby? Luckily, there were a number of other vehicles in the vicinity and the Stablemaster's full attention was on his slave.

'You're late,' he rasped, glancing at his watch.

'I got delayed,' she replied.

'That's a dozen strokes of the cane earnt straight off,' he replied. 'Well, come on in. There's work to be done.'

As soon as the garage door had been slammed shut she rounded angrily on him.

'You told me that tranny friend of yours knew nothing about this. Yet he struts into my boutique this morning, picks up over seven hundred pounds worth of gear and pays with one of your photos.'

He sighed. 'That wasn't a very nice thing to do. But it could have been worse.'

'How do you mean?'

'He could have cleaned you out of several grands' worth.'

'You bastard!' she snarled. 'As if it's not enough to have me at your beck and call, you have to mess with my business as well. Do you think I'm just going to take this lying down?'

'You seem to have little choice at the moment,' he replied calmly. 'Okay, what my friend did was wrong and I'll see that it doesn't happen again. You have my word on that.'

'Oh well, that makes me feel so much better,' she

sneered.

'Now, now, let's not get uncivil,' he said, in a tone so patronising it made her flesh crawl. 'You know what I want from you and I have no interest in stealing from your precious boutique. It absolutely *will not* happen again. Okay?'

Constance did not believe him, but consoled herself with a reminder that she would soon be in a position to turn the tables on him. He directed her to take off everything but her high heeled shoes, then lie face down over the bonnet of the car with her arms and legs wide apart. She watched him take his cane from the chest and flex it menacingly. In spite of the intensity with which she despised him, the sight created a sensual tingle between her thighs. The greatest injustice was that the man she was submitting to should be such a creep.

He removed his tie and used it as a gag, knotting it tightly at the back of her head. He then took off his jacket and rolled up his shirt-sleeves, leaving her in no doubt that he intended to subject her bottom to a merciless flogging. She pressed her face to the cold metal of the bonnet, wincing in response to each stroke that slashed across her tender flanks. When the full dozen had been delivered, he put down the cane and produced a martinet from within his treasure chest.

'You didn't think I could let your impudence go unpunished, did you?' he demanded, when Constance began whimpering in protest. 'A couple of dozen lashes of this should make you think twice before talking back to your master again. Now, be a good girl and lie still, otherwise I shall have to tie you up.'

The martinet swished and the three tongues of hard leather bit cruelly into her buttocks and thighs. The features of the Stablemaster were set in grim concentration as he watched her flesh turn a serious shade of sunburn. When the thrashing finally ended, he unzipped his trousers and unceremoniously speared her from behind with the full length of his rock hard cock.

Having flogged and fucked her into submission, he handed her a tin of car wax and a cloth. Her neck-tie gag remained in place.

'Get waxing, slave,' he commanded. 'Unless you're in the mood for yet more of the cane, you'll have my motor gleaming like a mirror before you finish.'

Constance would have preferred to be tied up and ravished, but the choice was not hers to make. While she worked up a sweat, waxing and polishing the car, the Stablemaster stood right behind her, cane in hand. By the time she was finished her arms ached and she reeked of car wax. He carefully inspected every inch of the shiny blue bodywork, before grudgingly pronouncing himself satisfied.

Her final task of the evening was to kneel and suck his cock. A mouthful of semen was little enough reward for her labours. When she was dressed he handed her another photograph – a close-up of her face, with half the length of his cock between her lips. She barely glanced at it before tearing it up.

The following afternoon her private detective reported back to her with the results of his investigations. The Stablemaster's real name was Detective Inspector Charles Mountjoy, of the CID. He was stationed locally, divorced, lived alone and enjoyed a reputation as something of a hard man.

Now that she had the information, Constance realised there was little she could do with it. The fact that her blackmailer was a senior police officer meant it would be even harder to deal with him.

Discovering the identity of his partner in crime took a little longer. Constance gave the detective the video recording from her in-store security cameras, on which the face of the mystery man appeared. The results of his subsequent investigations were anything but reassuring. His name was Gareth Whiting, a former pimp and pornographer, who had served a number of prison sentences for his diverse criminal activities. He was now the proprietor of a semi-respectable Soho strip club, though he was reputed to be still involved in various illegal enterprises. All in all, the private detective surmised, not the kind of man it would be wise to become involved with.

Constance felt as if her world was falling around her ears. All she needed now was for the man who had 'bought' her in the radio auction to be a Mafia godfather.

Chapter Eight

By the end of the week, the cheque had arrived and KT had made all the necessary arrangements with her buyer, who was anxious to become acquainted with his slave. He telephoned Constance and told her to go to Suite 909 of the Saint Gabriel hotel, at eight o'clock on Saturday evening. S/M-FM would just have to manage without her for one night. Mr Ford was the name of the man who would be waiting for her.

'Not another sleaze-bag, I hope,' she sighed.

'What happened to your enthusiasm?' KT demanded. 'It's not that long ago you were leaping at any opportunity to further your career as a slave.'

'I'm under a lot of pressure at the moment,' she replied. 'Do you think perhaps this Mr Ford might wait a few weeks?'

'Absolutely not.' KT sounded appalled by the very idea. 'He paid for you on the understanding that you would be available at a time of his choosing. I just don't know what you're afraid of. You're meeting him in the Saint Gabriel, not some basement torture chamber. If you're not prepared to play by the rules of the game—'

'I shouldn't be playing at all,' she finished. 'I know. Okay, I'll meet this Mr Ford and give him the night of his life, for you and Mistress whatsername.'

'I knew I could count on you,' KT replied.

By the time she reached the chic Kensington hotel, at the appointed hour, Constance had managed to consign her woes to the back of her mind and slip fully into the role of upmarket call-girl. Her hair was in a ponytail and she was dressed in a figure-hugging suit of cream silk, the slit skirt of which ended several inches above her knees. In her matching silk stockings and stiletto heels she felt almost as sexy as she looked.

When her ring on the doorbell of suite 909 was answered, she was immediately glad that KT had not allowed her to change her mind. Her 'buyer' – a sandy-haired man of about forty-five – was tall and powerfully built, his boxer's nose and ruggedly hewn features rendering him attractive rather than strikingly handsome. Constance remembered the faint feeling of uneasiness she had felt the first time she met the Stablemaster. The instinct aroused by this man was the exact opposite and she decided to trust it.

'Well, well, this is a pleasant surprise,' he greeted her, in a warm mid-Atlantic accent. 'I didn't think you could possibly be as sexy in real life as you sounded on the radio, but you surpass my wildest expectations.'

Constance thanked him for the compliment as he ushered her into the luxurious suite. Room service had delivered a bottle of Dom Perignon, just before she arrived. As she settled into a leatherette-covered armchair he popped the cork and poured two glasses.

'I don't even know your name,' he said, seating himself in the chair opposite.

'Constance,' she replied. 'Do I call you Mr Ford, or master, or what?'

He smiled. 'Larry will do just fine. Cheers.' He took a sip from his glass. 'I have to tell you, I find this S/M-FM station of yours an intriguing concept. How do you get away with it?'

She shrugged. 'Just luck, I guess. It's not my station,

by the way. I just play the *Slave in the Hot Seat* for a couple of hours on Saturday night. It's a hobby.'

'A damned interesting hobby,' he added. 'I'd never have known such a station existed, but for a piece I read in a magazine. I'll make sure I tune in from now on, whenever I happen to be in town.'

'You don't live in London?'

'My business takes me to the four corners of the earth,' he replied. 'I'm lucky if I get to visit here more than twice in the same year. As a matter of fact, I fly to New York tomorrow afternoon – which is why I had to insist on meeting you tonight.'

She smiled and seductively crossed her legs. 'I'm glad you did, Larry. I just hope you will be too.'

The swelling in the crotch of his dark grey trousers told her he already was.

From her previous experiences, Constance had been expecting another hard night of bondage, punishment and domination. But Larry's mastery of her was much more subtle than whips and handcuffs. He stimulated her with effortless easy conversation, until the champagne bottle was empty, then politely enquired if she would object to performing a striptease for him. By that stage she would not have objected to performing anything for him.

He switched on MTV. She moved into the centre of the floor and began peeling off her clothes, grinding her hips to the rhythmic grunge of high-volume Soundgarden. Her master sat back and watched, entranced by the erotic exhibition. Constance performed like a professional, her excitement mounting with every garment she cast off. Midway through the second heavy rock track, she was down to her high heels and stockings.

Crouching with her legs spread wide, her luscious sex on full display, she beckoned Larry towards her. He sprang from his seat, the protuberance of his cock almost bursting through his trousers. Licking her lips in anticipation, she reached for his zipper and drew it slowly down. Her hand reached in and he gasped from the electrifying sensation of her soft fingers touching his cock. She withdrew the tumescent tool, stroked the length with her fingertips, then leant forward to enfold it with her lips.

For the next five minutes, though she crouched at her master's feet, it was she who was completely in control. Her mouth made passionate love to his cock, teasing him with deliberate leisure to the point of blissful release. She gulped down every drop of his thick, creamy nectar, then licked his cock clean with her tongue, purring with wholehearted pleasure.

He carried her to the bedroom afterwards, where she immediately resumed her loving oral ministrations. As soon as his cock was hard again she lay back on the cool sheets and drew her knees up to her chin, presenting herself to him like a whore in heat.

'Oh yes, master – take me,' she sighed as he guided his lance into the hot, drooling depths of her sex.

Much later, they shared a bottle of wine in bed together and listened to S/M-FM. KT was interviewing Mistress Amber, the by-election candidate whose cause he so passionately supported.

'You'll doubtless be glad to hear that you are the reason our *Slave in the Hot Seat* is not on duty tonight,' he told her. 'At this very moment she is entertaining the master who, last Saturday night, bid sixteen hundred pounds for her.'

'I hope she's giving him his money's worth,' the

gravel-toned dominatrix replied.

'Our slave knows how to please her master,' KT assured her. 'Any master.'

'I'll drink to that,' Larry grinned, his cock once more stirring to the lazy caress of Constance's fingertips.

After a late Sunday morning breakfast in bed, they showered together. The sight of her soap-lathered body beneath the steaming jets of water inflamed his passion all over again. After the number of times he had already taken her, it seemed impossible that he would be able to rise to the occasion yet again, but his stiff cock nuzzling the cleft of her buttocks proved otherwise. Pressing against the tiled wall, she thrust her lower body back to meet him. He wrapped her in his powerful arms and slid his cock into her already pleasantly aching slit.

It was with no little regret that she finally got dressed and prepared to leave. After she had kissed him goodbye he pressed several folded bank notes into her right fist.

'A small token of my appreciation,' he said with a smile. 'Thanks for a wonderful night, Constance.'

Only then did she realise that he thought she was a genuine call-girl. She resisted an impulse to set him straight. There was no need to complicate what had been a thoroughly enjoyable night for both of them.

KT telephoned her later that day, anxious for a report on what had happened. She was glad to inform him that the night had been a total success.

'He even gave me a two hundred quid tip,' she added. 'Perhaps I ought to consider a career change.'

'Perhaps indeed,' he replied, half seriously.

A few minutes later the telephone rang again. Constance's cheerful spirits nose-dived when she heard the voice on the other end of the line.

'I was looking for you last night,' the Stablemaster growled.

'I was otherwise engaged.'

'So I heard. Whoring on behalf of a fellow whore. How very charitable of you. I don't like you reneging on our deal, slave. You do remember the deal, don't you?'

'You don't own me,' she snapped.

'On the contrary,' he replied. 'I still have deeds of ownership – in the form of six very pornographic pictures of you. How would you like it if I sent one to a member of your staff tomorrow?'

'That would be a very nasty thing to do, Detective Inspector Mountjoy,' she retorted. She took a sadistic delight in the moment of stunned silence that followed.

'So, you've been doing a little detective work,' he said finally. 'What good can it do you? It doesn't change the fact that I still have the photographs. Should you be foolish enough to make a complaint, I can simply deny all knowledge of them. It would be the word of a nymphomaniac slut against that of a highly respected police officer. All you'd succeed in doing is making a complete fool of yourself.'

'What if I were to mention your friendship with a certain Mr Gareth Whiting?' she countered. 'He's hardly the sort of company a man in your position ought to be keeping.'

Another brief silence followed. When the Stablemaster spoke again there was a menacing edge to his voice. 'You would be well advised not to threaten me,' he said carefully. 'At the moment you and I are playing a harmless little game – nothing more. If you try to up the ante, a reddened backside will be the least of your worries, believe me.'

'Meaning?'

'Meaning you meet me in the usual place, at ten tonight.' Before Constance could say any more, he hung up.

She arrived at the garage deliberately early, having no wish to antagonise him further. No words were exchanged until the door was slammed shut.

'I'm actually surprised you showed up,' he said.

'I don't like unfinished business,' she replied, forcing far more confidence into her tone than she actually felt.

The Stablemaster smiled. 'Believe me, our business is far from unfinished. Any more threats you'd like to make, before I tie you up and thrash the arse off you?'

'No more games,' said Constance. 'I know enough about you and your friend to cause serious problems for you both, especially you. Give me the rest of the photographs and the negatives, and I'll forget we ever met.'

'Full marks for trying,' he said, when he had finished laughing. 'But you have nothing to incriminate me with. For your information, Gareth Whiting is working with me, helping CID nail down a villain we've been trying to get our hands on for some time. In return for his co-operation we turn a blind eye to some of his more... questionable activities. It's common police practice, and I have the full blessing of the top brass. As for the rest, where's your proof? Let's face it, Constance, I have you exactly where I want you, and there's not a thing you can do about it.'

'You bastard!' she spat. 'Why can't you just find yourself another slave and leave me alone?'

'Because I like you,' he replied. 'And because I enjoy

the power I have over you. However, just to show you I'm not completely unreasonable...' He reached inside his jacket and produced an envelope of photographs. 'Take a look. Be a good little slave for me tonight, and these are all yours. Payment in full.'

Constance opened the envelope and carefully inspected the contents. The remaining six photographs were there, along with the full set of negatives.

'Where's the catch?' she demanded suspiciously.

'There isn't one,' he replied, snatching back the envelope.

'How do I know you don't have copies hidden away somewhere?'

He smiled. 'You flatter yourself, Constance. The truth is, you don't mean that much to me. I've had my fun with you and, if you're honest, you've had a little fun of your own. This was never destined to be a long-term relationship.'

She wanted to believe him, but could not dispel the nagging suspicion that he was yet again cruelly toying with her. Finally, she decided she had little option but to take a chance.

The Stablemaster had obviously been looking forward to punishing her, both for being unavailable the previous night and for having the temerity to think she could play him at his own game. After she had stripped down to her high heels and peach lingerie, he manacled her wrists to the overhead bar and placed a strip of sticky black vinyl tape over her mouth.

Watching him rummage in his trunk of tools, she felt far greater trepidation than usual. Tied up and unable to even scream, she would be completely helpless if he had decided to punish her in a more permanent fashion. It was with a feeling of relief that she greeted the sight of a slimline black whip gripped in his right fist.

Her body jerked as the first lash cracked across the exposed half-moons of her buttocks, an angry red streak flaring across the lower portion of both buttocks. He paused for a few seconds, then let rip with the second stroke.

She felt the sharp bite of the firm leather a dozen times before he put the whip down again. The throbbing of her scorched buttocks was rendered all the more agonising by the certainty that her punishment was only just beginning.

The Stablemaster stepped in front of her, gripped the bodice of her silk body-stocking in both hands and ripped it open. He ogled and fondled her bare breasts for a few moments, then produced two yellow plastic clothes-pegs from a pocket of his jacket. She whimpered as he affixed them to her stiffened nipples.

A vigorous thrashing of her breasts with a cat o'nine tails followed, only ceasing when both soft globes were covered in livid claws of fire and tears were rolling down her cheeks. He ripped off the tattered remains of her lingerie, then crouched down before her and turned his sadistic attentions to her genitals. He had six more clothes-pegs in his pocket, three of which he clamped to each of her puffy nether lips. As he tugged repeatedly on them he looked up at her face, seeming pleased by her pained expression and the accompanying muffled whimpers. When he finally tired of this particular line of torture, he picked up the cat o'nine tails again, thrust the full length of the thick plastic handle up into her sex and proceeded to screw her with it.

He released her from the bar after that, peeled the tape from her mouth and ordered her to lie on the mattress, with her legs raised at a ninety-degree angle to her body.

He bound her left knee with one end of a long rope, which he then wrapped several times around her left wrist, twice around her chest, then her right wrist. The free end was then secured around her right ankle, leaving her bound in a highly uncomfortable and vulnerable position. She was still wearing the clothes pegs on her nipples and labia and the nine-tailed whip protruded obscenely from between her thighs.

'What a picture you make!' he leered. 'Speaking of pictures...' He produced the envelope again and selected a photograph of a smiling Constance standing with knees bent over an upended stool, the tip of one of the round wooden legs thrusting up into her vagina. 'This is my favourite of the bunch. What do you think?'

She shook her head to indicate her disagreement.

'You enjoyed it well enough at the time,' he reminded her. 'Look at your face, you dirty whore!'

He placed the photograph on her lower belly, then unzipped his trousers and knelt between her thighs. Watching him masturbate and listening to the stream of obscenities that poured from his lips, Constance had never felt more utterly humiliated. After he had climaxed over the photograph he carefully lifted it and brought it to her mouth. 'Tastier medicine than the whip,' he said, when she looked away in disgust.

Knowing that nothing would please him more than an excuse to punish her further, she opened her mouth. He tilted the photograph and the warm, thick semen drooled from the glossy surface onto her outstretched tongue. After she had swallowed the last creamy string, he ordered her to lick the photograph clean.

Shortly afterwards he untied her again and told her to get dressed. When she was ready to leave he handed her the envelope of photographs.

'All present and accounted for,' he smiled as she checked the contents.

'So, that's it then,' she said, unable to believe he was actually setting her free.

'Ah, not quite,' he replied. 'I don't have any more photographs to blackmail you with, but I've been having second thoughts about not seeing you again. I'd like if you could still be my part-time slave.'

'You're asking me?' she cried incredulously.

'As politely as I know how,' he answered. 'After all, it's not as though you don't enjoy submitting to a master.'

'To a master I trust and respect,' she corrected, vengefully tearing up the photographs. 'Not some sleazy, blackmailing, bent CID man.'

'I'll take that as a no, then.'

She flung the shredded photographs at his feet. 'Take it as a "fuck you", Mountjoy. Now open this door. I want to go home and take a long bath.'

He sighed. 'I had hoped you might be more reasonable, but now I see that I'm going to have to be a bit more persuasive. You realise you're a criminal, don't you?'

'What are you talking about?' she snapped.

'S/M-FM,' he replied. 'An illegal radio station, broadcasting highly illegal smut. I could have you and the rest of your Jolly Rogers put away for what you're doing. How do you think that would affect your respectable business?'

'I knew it was too good to be true,' Constance retorted angrily. 'You only gave me back the photographs because you'd thought of an even better way to keep me as your slave.'

'Clever girl,' he smiled. 'You don't have to give me your answer immediately. I'll be in touch in a few days. I'm sure you'll make the right decision.'

Chapter Nine

Constance did not sleep that night. Now that the Stablemaster's grip over her was more secure than ever, she realised she might never be free of him. It was within his power to destroy both her reputation and the business she had worked so hard to build. Given the slightest excuse, he would surely take a twisted pleasure in doing just that. The fact that she was indeed breaking the law by her association with S/M-FM left her with only one possible alternative to either a sentence to slavery or prison.

She tried to call KT at three a.m., but all she got was his answering machine. It was late the following evening before she finally managed to contact him.

'It's finished,' she told him bluntly. 'I want nothing more to do with you, the radio station, or anybody else associated with it. I'm sorry, but I have no choice. Please don't try to contact me again.'

'Constance, hold on,' he cried. 'What's wrong? What's brought all this on?'

'I have my reasons. It's nothing personal, believe me.'

'What is it, then?' he demanded. 'Don't you think you at least owe me an explanation?'

'I've just changed my mind about this whole submission business. It's not for me.'

'You expect me to believe that?'

'Believe what you like!' she snapped, before slamming down the receiver.

She should have known that would not be the end of

the matter – that KT would not rest until he received the explanation he was entitled to. She agonised over calling him back and apologising for her rudeness, but decided that might only make matters worse. With everything she held most precious at stake, guilt was not a luxury she could afford to indulge in. At least now her blackmailer had no further ammunition to threaten her with.

Two hours later the doorbell rang. Expecting it to be the Stablemaster, she lit a cigarette and braced herself to confront him. But when she opened the front door she found KT standing on the doorstep.

'May I come in?' he asked.

She hesitated, then stepped aside to allow him into the hallway.

'So are you going to tell me what's going on?' he demanded, taking a seat in the lounge.

He declined her offer of a drink. Constance poured herself one, then sat down. 'Okay,' she sighed. 'I suppose you deserve some kind of explanation.'

He listened in silence while she proceeded to relate the entire sordid tale of her relationship with the Stablemaster, omitting only the unimportant details.

'So you see, I have no choice but to break off all contact with you and everybody else associated with S/M-FM,' she finished. 'This bastard doesn't make idle threats.'

'Seemingly not,' KT agreed, pensively stroking his chin. 'But even if you do cut yourself off from us, there's no guarantee he'll leave you alone. He may have more photographs or bits of incriminating evidence. If you refuse to do as he says, S/M-FM will most definitely get busted and he'll probably have you arrested anyway, just out of sheer spite.'

'So you're saying I have no choice but to become his slave?'

'What I'm saying is, we have to find another way of dealing with him.'

'Can you think of one?'

'I will,' he assured her. 'Don't worry, Detective Inspector Mountjoy isn't going to put either of us out of business.'

Constance wished she could share his optimism, but just being able to unburden herself made her feel slightly better. At least she was no longer alone in her predicament. Some time later KT glanced at his watch and announced that he had better be going.

'Do you have to?' she pleaded, rising to her feet. 'I mean, couldn't you at least stay a little while longer?'

'Gina will be wondering what's happened to me.'

'You're her master; she'll understand,' Constance insisted. 'I... I really don't want to be alone tonight, thinking about that creep.'

'You sound like a frightened little girl,' he smiled. 'You wouldn't be trying to seduce me, now would you?'

She fell to her knees and gazed imploringly up into his dark eyes. 'And if I were, master?'

'Then I should be tempted to take advantage of you when you were at your most vulnerable,' he replied carefully, moving towards her.

He cradled her head in both hands and she pressed her face to the crotch of his tight blue jeans, feeling his cock stir within. Though sex had been the furthest thing from her mind when she had opened the door to him, her body now ached for him. This was the kind of comforting she required, and KT was not going to deny it to her.

She unzipped his jeans with her teeth and freed his cock with her fingers. If he thought her behaviour pathetic, so be it. Kneeling before a master she actually wanted was a refreshing antidote to the bitterness she felt towards the Stablemaster. The tip of her tongue lashed eagerly at the eye of KT's cock. He stroked her hair and thrust gently against her face, urging her to take him in her mouth. Constance was all too eager to oblige.

Several hours later, their mutual lust sated, he reluctantly disengaged himself from her perspiration-sheened body. She sat up and watched him get dressed, the taste of him still fresh in her mouth.

'I have a plan for dealing with our mutual friend,' he said as he buttoned up his shirt.

'What?' she cried excitedly, leaping naked from the bed.

'Come to my place tomorrow night and all will be revealed.'

A further eight days passed before the Stablemaster contacted her again, just when she was beginning to hope he had lost interest. She agreed, without hesitation, to meet him that night.

'You're looking well, slave,' he remarked, as soon as he had slammed the door of the lockup. 'I'm glad you came to the right decision regarding our... relationship.'

'You didn't give me much of a choice, Detective Inspector Mountjoy,' she retorted.

He glared. 'Master, is the correct form of address. You've just earnt yourself twelve strokes of the cane. Well, don't just stand there. Get that skirt off, and whatever you're wearing underneath it.'

'I had another visit from your friend, Gareth Whiting,' she said, ignoring the command. 'He helped himself to four hundred pounds worth of gear, warning me of what would happen if I tried to stop him. You promised I wouldn't have any more trouble from him.'

'You weren't supposed to.' He sounded genuinely surprised.

'It's bad enough that you should be blackmailing me,' she continued, her voice rising. 'I've almost got used to the idea of being your sex slave, but I don't like being threatened by a gangster.'

'I'll have another word with him,' he said impatiently. 'Now, I won't tell you again, get your arse bare for the cane. I didn't bring you here so that we could waste time arguing.'

Constance obediently stepped out of her skirt and pink G-string panties. The Stablemaster pushed her roughly up against the wall and ordered her to spread her arms and legs wide. The hem of her red sweater reached only to the slope of her buttocks, affording her no protection from the cane. He wielded it with a grim determination, each vicious stroke cracking like a pistol shot across her quivering buttocks. Though she tried not to cry out, it was impossible to prevent a few small shrieks from passing her lips.

By the time she left the garage, almost two hours later, her buttocks and thighs were smarting violently from a combination of cane, crop and open-handed spanking. Her breasts were sticky with semen and throbbing from being punished with the cat o'nine tails. She was safely inside her car before she permitted herself a satisfied smile.

The following evening she drove to KT's mansion, the shoes she had worn to her encounter with the Stablemaster tucked safely into a carrier bag. Planted inside the heel of the left shoe was a tiny transmitting device. The other contained a miniature sound recorder. She was not convinced the equipment could have worked, until KT plugged the recorder into a conventional tape machine and transferred its information to an ordinary cassette. Every word, every breath, every crack of leather on flesh that had taken place in the garage was clearly audible. KT and Gina insisted on listening to the entire tape, the latter seeming to derive particular pleasure from Constance's frequent squeals of pain.

'What now?' Constance asked afterwards.

'Now, I send a copy of this tape to Detective Inspector Mountjoy, along with a little warning note,' he replied. 'If he ever contacts you again, his superiors and any other parties who might be interested will receive their own copies. I think we can safely say we won't be having any more trouble from him.'

Constance breathed a sigh of relief. 'Thank God. And thank you, master. I'd still love to know how you're so familiar with this James Bond-type equipment.'

'I'm sure you would,' he answered. 'Let's just say that I have experience in security-related matters. There's something else I want to discuss with you, and now is as good a time as any. Would you fix us some drinks please, Gina?'

The red-haired slave, in the uniform of a maidservant, curtsied. 'Of course, master.'

'Unless I'm very much mistaken, you have become quite dedicated to our little broadcasting enterprise,' KT said, settling back into a sumptuous armchair.

'Very much so,' Constance replied. 'Going on air is almost as good as sex. I felt really sad when I thought I was going to have to give it up over that creep.'

'Well, you can forget about him now,' he said, taking a drink from Gina. 'However, this whole business got me thinking. As it stands, S/M-FM is in a very vulnerable position. We broadcast from the same place, at the same time each weekend, so the authorities would find it very easy to track us down. We've been lucky so far, but it's only a matter of time before this place is raided. We need alternative headquarters for the station, which is where you come in. Your house would be perfect.'

'My house?' she exclaimed, almost spilling her drink. 'You can't be serious.'

'Why not? From a broadcasting point of view it's ideally situated. And you live alone, with no nosy neighbours, nothing to interfere with the smooth running of a part-time pirate radio station.'

'In my own home?' Constance found the notion almost too preposterous for words.

'You've seen how little equipment is involved,' he said. 'The entire operation could be run from your attic. It would only be on Saturday nights. S/M-FM would broadcast from a room in The Master's Masque club on Fridays and from here on Sundays. By transmitting from three separate venues we make it harder for the powers-that-be to track us down.'

'You're beginning to sound like a gangster,' she half-joked.

'Captain of a pirate ship,' he corrected. 'I'll have all the equipment within a week, ready to set up. All I need from you is your permission. There will, of course, be a reward for your full co-operation.'

'What kind of reward?'

'Something very special,' he replied, with a mysterious smile.

Faced with KT's powers of persuasion, Constance was as malleable as a lump of putty. Ten days after she agreed to his request to broadcast from her attic, the equipment was installed and her favourite radio station was right under her own roof. Even though it was midweek she went on-air for an hour, reading extracts from the collected works of the Marquis de Sade, while KT checked that everything was working properly. At the end of the test broadcast he pronounced himself extremely pleased with the strength of the signal they had sent out.

'What about my signals, master?' Constance asked with a smile, rising from her seat behind the radio deck. 'Reading that stuff over the air always makes me so horny.'

'Wait here,' he replied.

He climbed down from the attic and she heard him go downstairs. He returned several minutes later and called her to come down. She lowered herself through the trapdoor and began descending the stepladder directly below. Halfway down, KT shouted for her to stop. She looked down and saw that he had paid a visit to the kitchen. He was holding a wooden spoon in his right hand and a wet dishcloth in his left. From where he was standing he could see all the way up her short black skirt.

'Lift your skirt,' he commanded, his stern voice sending a sensual shudder down her spine. 'Higher! Do I have to tell you what to do next?'

Constance hurriedly tugged her lacy white panties down over her thighs. She raised her left foot as they slipped to her ankles, then kicked them away with her right. KT ordered her to lean forward on the ladder, so that her bottom was perfectly presented for punishment. He warmed her up with the wooden spoon, dispensing a dozen hard whacks to each cheek. He then twisted the wet dishcloth into a highly effective whip and thrashed her bright pink, from the backs of her knees to the top of her buttocks.

'You can come down now,' he said, when he finally finished punishing her.

She scampered down the ladder, her skirt still rolled up around her waist. The instant her feet touched the floor he seized her roughly and pushed her back against the wall. She pretended to resist, knowing he would enjoy it all the more. He ripped her blouse open so that the buttons popped and flew like bullets. She continued to fight him as he fumbled with the clasp at the front of her bra.

'Must I tie you up before I can have my way with you?' he barked.

Constance responded with a whole-hearted effort to escape from his clutches. She made it to the door of her bedroom before he grabbed the strap at the back of her bra and yanked her to a halt.

'So you want to play rough, eh?' he rasped, locking an arm around her neck. 'Well, if that's what you want, that's what you'll get.'

He kicked the door fully open, dragged her choking and kicking into the room and flung her, face down, onto the bed. Before she had a chance to catch her breath her bra had been ripped open and her skirt was pulled down over her legs. As KT flung it aside she made a renewed effort to save herself, kicking blindly out at him, before attempting a dash towards the door. She knew she had not the slightest hope of getting away, even had she really wanted to. KT leapt upon her like a savage beast and wrestled her to the floor. He pinned her down with the full weight of his body on her legs, grabbed her ponytail in his right hand and jerked her head up.

'Ouch, master, you're hurting me,' she cried.

'Shut up, slut,' he retorted, his free hand reaching inside his brown leather jacket.

The snarled words of abuse were almost as exciting to Constance as a wily tongue on her clitoris. In the full-length closet mirror she saw herself – the helpless victim – overpowered by her brutal master. From inside his jacket he produced a thin black leather cord, with two chrome clamps on one end. She offered no further resistance, just a shriek of pain, as he fitted them to her labia. He knotted the other end of the cord tightly around her ponytail, then hauled her to her feet. She had to throw her head back in order to ease the agonising tug on her nether lips.

KT threw her onto the bed and ordered her not to move, if she knew what was good for her. Lying on her back, she watched him rummage like a burglar through the drawers of her dressing table. Having sifted through each one in turn he yanked out the top drawer, carried it over to the bed and emptied the contents over Constance.

He plucked a scarlet suspender belt from the underwear pile and used it to bind her wrists to one of the brass bars at the head of the bed. He then secured her ankles to the upper bedposts with a pair of pale silk stockings and stuffed a balled-up pair of black lace panties into her mouth.

'You look so much more attractive when you're helpless,' he said, stepping back to appraise his handiwork 'Now, I'm going to punish you like you've never been punished before.'

From the dressing table he picked up a round hairbrush, dealt several whacks of the wooden handle to her bottom, then began raking the hard plastic bristles over her tender buttocks and inner thighs. Her eyes bulging, she tossed her head from side to side and struggled in vain to break free of her bondage. KT dragged the hairbrush over the backs of her legs, all the way to her ankles and back, then once more over every inch of her violently throbbing rear cheeks. The bristles scraped up along her belly, leaving inflamed little furrows behind. Reaching her breasts, he paused momentarily, as though unable to make up his mind whether to proceed.

Constance was not fooled. She knew he was only teasing her.

Who needed a torture chamber when a sadist could find everything he needed in his victim's dressing table? After he had raked her breasts red with the hairbrush he placed it in the cleft between them, then dressed her in a half-cup bra of pink silk. When it was clasped at the front, the brush was squeezed tightly between her breasts, the bristles painfully pricking her soft flesh.

Using a set of eyebrow tweezers, he began plucking out single ribs of pubic hair, while Constance snorted through flaring nostrils and thrashed on the bed. She thought he would not stop until she had been plucked as bare as a Christmas turkey. After a few long and hideous minutes of this he put down the tweezers and picked up a card of hair clips. One by one he fitted them to her labia, nine to either side. He then took her sleek gold vibrator from the bottom drawer of the dressing table and flipped the switch at the base. Bliss superseded discomfort as the slender shaft was eased up inside her.

Only when he tired of teasing and tormenting her, seemingly hours later, did he finally make love to her. She remained trussed up, but he did take the panties out of her mouth so she could at least lend full voice to her passion.

Taking to the airwaves the following Saturday night, she felt exceptionally nervous. Broadcasting from the safety of KT's studio, she had given little thought to the dangers involved. With S/M-FM coming from her own attic it was not difficult to imagine the police beating a path to her door as she spoke. KT and Gina kept her company, the latter dealing with incoming calls. KT had set up the telephones so callers reached the station's usual number, not Constance's own private line.

She exchanged ideas and fantasies with the customary array of night creatures, including a few regular callers who were beginning to sound like old friends. One suggested that her master might like to tie her up and screw her on air. KT was only too glad to oblige. He described into the microphone each item of clothing he was removing from her and the method – two white silk scarves – used to bind her wrists to the rafters. She was on her knees, her rear end thrust back and thighs parted to receive him. Gina held the microphone close to the action, ensuring that the listeners heard every grunt, moan and cry of pleasure.

She was not untied again until after the four a.m. closedown.

What happened next had not been plotted in advance. It just seemed natural for KT and Gina to spend the remainder of the night as guests in her bed. However, the other slave insisted that there was a price to be paid if Constance wanted her master's cock again that night. Constance stood on a chair in the centre of the bedroom while Gina vengefully thrashed her buttocks with a thick leather strap. KT stood back and watched, ready to take Constance as soon as his slave finished flogging her.

'I did mention a reward, for your dedication to S/M-FM,' he said that afternoon. 'How would you like a very special holiday, Constance?'

'I haven't had a holiday in over two years,' she replied. 'But I can't just get up and go. My business needs me.'

'But what of your needs?' he responded. 'It wouldn't do to start neglecting them again, now would it?'

'My needs?' she repeated.

'Your needs as a submissive woman,' he explained. 'You've enjoyed everything that's happened to you in that area so far, am I right?'

'With the exception of that business with the Stablemaster, yes,' she replied.

'So it's only natural you would want to take your submission to the next stage,' he continued. 'Picture something, then tell me what you think. An adult holiday resort where all the men are masters, with all the women – staff and guests alike – totally submissive to them. A fantasy playground, free of the petty rules of political correctness that the real world forces us to observe.'

'A club, like The Master's Masque?'

'Something a bit more demanding. This is not the kind of place where you can just dress up in kinky clothes, play out a few fantasies, and then hurry on home again. This playground belongs to a select circle of masters. Membership involves more than having a broad mind and the ability to memorise a password. It demands the kind of commitment few slaves are willing to make.'

'But surely I have proved that I'm not just out for cheap thrills,' Constance protested.

'You've proved you have a fertile imagination and a taste for exotic games,' he answered. 'That doesn't make you in any way unique. I've been talking to my fellow Chargemasters – the shareholders in this resort and the men who lay down the law. Their verdict is that you are exceptionally attractive and a young woman of obvious refinement, the kind men take great pleasure in using and abusing. I assured them you are always glad to be on the receiving end of such treatment.'

Constance nodded vigorously.

'You won't find this resort of ours in any brochures or tourist guides,' he went on. 'It's exclusive, in the true sense of the word. I like to describe it as a university of servitude, where women such as you undergo the training that will weed out the thrill-seekers from the true submissives. Your next step along the path to slavery is to spend a weekend at the resort. During your stay you will be completely shut off from the outside world. No radio, no TV, no telephones, no newspapers. You will have to forget all about your business. You won't be kept prisoner, but if you leave before the time is up, for any reason whatsoever, you can never return.'

'That sounds rather harsh,' said Constance.

KT sighed heavily. 'I'm not trying to talk you into visiting a holiday camp. I suggest you spend a few days thinking it over. I'll call you before the weekend, when you can give me your answer.'

'How much does this resort cost?' she demanded.

'Female guests don't pay with money,' he replied. 'However, before you're allowed to visit, the Chargemasters require that you pass three tests. Fail any one, and this is as close as you'll ever get to the resort. I can only reveal the nature of the tests when you have given me a definite answer. But be warned, they won't be easy.'

Chapter Ten

Constance felt two hundred pairs of eyes on her as she stepped through the front door of the Black Dog. The smell of sweat, beer and illicit smoking materials hit her nostrils and the heavy metal thunder of the on-stage band almost blew her back out onto the pavement. If the motorcycles lined up outside the pub had stirred a vague discomfort inside her, the sight and sound of their owners was positively terrifying. The Black Dog was the kind of low-life booze palace she would only ever have visited in her nightmares, had she not been acting on the instructions of her master.

He had known she would accept the challenge, of course. The Playground was too intriguing a prospect to be turned down. It would not be easy to pass the three admission tests, let alone abandon her precious business for five days. But once she had made her mind up to do something, Constance would allow nothing to get in her way.

The visit to the Black Dog was her first test. She would have to pass this before the second was revealed. Her master's instructions had been explicit and somebody in the bar would be watching her, to ensure they were obeyed to the letter. She was dressed like a cheap blonde bimbo from a rock video, in high scarlet heels, with a matching rubber skirt that scarcely covered her hips and clearly advertised the fact that she was wearing no underwear. Her legs were bare and the only other item of clothing she wore was a tiny red rubber waistcoat that left her midriff exposed. Her bra-less breasts threatened to burst the two buttons that strained to hold the garment shut.

Constance realised that she was being forced to act out one of her fantasies, but the reality was somewhat less appealing. Tonight, in this sleazy bar, she was going to have to give herself to any man who wanted her, without question. There would be many. She could refuse none, no matter how unappealing and, even if she did not enjoy it as much as in her fantasy, she would have to give the performance of her life.

As she pushed her way to the bar she felt a rough hand on her bottom. She turned around to face the groper and smiled, successfully arresting her initial instinct to slap him across the face. He was thickset and bearded, with greasy black curls trailing halfway down his back. He wore the biker's uniform of scuffed black leather and ragged denim cut-offs and was the sort of crude creature Constance would not have allowed within a hundred yards of her, before tonight.

'Lookin' for someone?' he leered, taking a long swig from his bottle of beer.

'A man,' Constance replied, shouting to make herself heard above the music. 'Any man.'

Grinning, he grabbed her right hand and pushed it against his crotch. She felt his cock stiffening through his jeans. She moved closer and squeezed, feeling the first tingling of her own excitement. Perhaps, after all, she could take some pleasure from this experience. The biker turned to one of his Neanderthal companions.

'Oi, Ratcatcher, look at this,' he shouted.

The other biker, an even fatter and more repulsive example of the kind, looked away from his own woman and ran his eyes down Constance, coming to rest on her grasping right hand.

'Buy her a drink and you might get a blow-job,' he roared.

'You don't have to buy me a drink,' she responded, squeezing his erection even harder. She was prepared to take him on right there in the middle of the crowded floor, if that was what he wanted, but he pushed her roughly towards the nearby gent's toilet. She almost slipped on the wet floor as he herded her towards an empty cubicle. There were several men lined up at the urinals and all looked around when they heard her high heels on the tiles. But Constance no longer felt any shame. She would see her test through to the end, and do her best to enjoy it.

The biker did not bother to shut the cubicle door, before pushing her down onto the toilet bowl and unzipping his jeans. His cock was impressively large and faintly pungent. Constance lowered her head and slid the full fat length past her red-glossed lips. From behind him another man clapped his hands and roared encouragement.

Constance had a feeling she was going to be required to satisfy more than one man in this cubicle, and she was right. No sooner had the first biker spewed his creamy load to the back of her throat and withdrawn than another was taking his place. She did not even glance at his face as she hurriedly unzipped his jeans, hauled out his throbbing cock and fed it into her mouth.

The word spread like wildfire through the bar. There was a blonde cock-sucker in the toilet, taking on all comers, no questions asked. A queue of eager men formed. Most were drunk or stoned, all vulgar and scruffy. Even though loose women were as common as spilt beer in places like this, one who displayed such an animalistic lack of inhibition as Constance was still rare. She kept a mental count. In the fantasy scenario that so closely resembled this situation, she sucked off twelve men in a row. She actually had three more than that number before finally staggering to her feet. She needed a break.

'Not leaving us yet, babe?' growled a bearded and wild-eyed figure in an army surplus greatcoat.

'Of course not,' she replied. 'I'm having the time of my life, but it's a bit stuffy in here. Maybe we could go somewhere else.'

He grabbed her arm. 'Tell you what. I'll buy you a drink and take you to meet a friend of mine.'

A bottle of ice-cold lager was just the thing to wash down the lingering essence of the men. She half-drained the bottle in one swallow and followed the wild-eyed man through to the bar. Several pairs of hands groped her on the way and she smiled in response to every obscenity that was hurled. The man led her over to the pool table and introduced her to a handsome blond giant with a neatly trimmed beard and a fringed leather jacket festooned with metal badges.

'Slayer, this is the cock-sucker.'

The big man leant closer and inhaled. 'I can smell it on her. Put her up on the table and let's make sure she's the real thing. You can't always be sure, these days.'

Two men lifted Constance onto the pool table, laid her out on her back and spread her legs. Slayer thrust his right hand up under her skirt and grinned when he made contact with the hot wetness of her sex.

'She's all woman, all right.' He threw down his pool cue and reached for the zipper of his leather jeans. 'Your cunt thirsty too, eh?'

In response, Constance raised herself onto her elbows

and pushed herself towards him, her skirt riding up over her hips. The sight of the glistening petals of her sex was greeted with a cacophony of wolf whistles. Slayer cupped her bare buttocks in both huge hands and drew her onto the tumescent shaft of his cock. As he impaled her to the hilt another stiff cock sought her lips. She turned her head sideways and accepted it greedily. Another man popped open her waistcoat and proceeded to maul her aching breasts and slobber over her erect nipples. After a few minutes he had the inspiration to climb on top of her and squash his cock between her globes, grunting as he thrust towards her flushed face, her lips stretched tautly around the gnarled column that pumped back and forth between them.

Many more men took her on the pool table, sharing their cocks between her mouth and pussy. By the time they were finally finished with her she was stretched out on the beer-stained green baize, exhausted and completely naked. The emissions of the mob were coated over her satiated face and body.

It was well past closing time and the bikers began to disperse, but for Constance the night was not yet over. Slayer was a close friend of the lead singer in the band who had been playing in the pub and thought they might like to have a bit of fun with the nympho slut. He was not wrong. Constance spent a further two hours in the back of the band's van, eagerly giving herself to all five members of Roadkill. When they were finished with her, they discarded her in the car park of the Black Dog, naked and screwed half-senseless. At least they had the decency to toss out her clothes before speeding away. Constance was still in a state of shock early the following afternoon, when KT called to congratulate her on passing her first test with flying colours.

'I can't believe I did it!' she gasped. 'I was such a slut. And I enjoyed every minute of it.'

'You're a natural-born whore.'

'I suppose I must be.'

'Oh, you most certainly are,' he assured her. 'It's just taken you a long time to realise it. Now for your next test. Listen carefully.'

When he revealed what she was expected to do, Constance pleaded with him to reconsider. Degrading herself in a pub full of strangers was one thing, but what he was now demanding was simply unfair. He refused to entertain her pleas, reminding her that if she was serious about serving in the Playground, she would be expected to undergo far more arduous tasks.

'We can, of course, cancel the whole thing,' he added.

'No, master,' Constance conceded. 'I'll do it.'

Late the following afternoon, a well-dressed man in his fifties entered the boutique. She knew immediately that he was the customer she had been told to expect, and hurried to attend to him personally. He told her he was looking for an outfit for his wife. Something seductive for a special occasion. Before she even asked him what size the woman was, Constance knew what his answer would be. She was her size, down to the last centimetre.

Her heart pounding in her chest, she helped him to choose a number that he thought would be perfect for his wife. He agreed with her that the dress would probably be perfect, then asked her to select matching lingerie.

'I imagine she will look stunning in that outfit,' he said. 'But it is quite expensive and I have to be certain it's right. Perhaps you would be so kind as to model it for me.'

Constance smiled. 'Of course, sir. I'll be happy to model the dress.'

He returned her smile. 'Not just the dress, my dear. I want to see how the underwear looks too.'

She glanced nervously around, fearing that one of her assistants, or another customer, might have overheard. Then she quietly invited him to accompany her to her office at the back of the shop.

Before beginning her strip she suggested locking the door, so that they might not be disturbed. He insisted she leave it open. Somebody might come in. Then again, somebody might not. He sat back in her chair, planted his feet on her desk and watched her peel off her elegant black trouser suit, then unbutton her blouse. After what had happened in the Black Dog she had no inhibitions about stripping off for a complete stranger. She would even be happy to accommodate him sexually, as her master had hinted she might be required to do. But she was petrified at the thought of one of her employees walking in and catching her in the act.

'You have a lovely body,' the man commented as she slipped her bra straps down off her shoulders. 'I bet you like to keep yourself active – sexually, I mean.'

'I have been rather in demand, of late,' she admitted, stepping out of her pink panties and reaching for the new underwear on her desk.

'Let me have a good look at you first,' he said, snatching the garments out of reach. 'Stand up on the desk here and let me admire you.'

Constance came close to telling him what to do with himself, but to do so would put paid to her chance of visiting the Playground. So, casting an anxious glance towards the door, she climbed onto her desk, clad only in high heels and dark hold-up stockings, and permitted the man a thorough appraisal of her charms. Her office was on the first floor and a plate glass window overlooked the floor of the boutique. Anyone who glanced upwards would see the upper half of her naked body as she strutted upon her desk.

'What a lovely arse you have,' the man enthused, reaching up to fondle her buttocks with both hands.

She smiled and bent over slightly, affording him an even better view. 'It's nice of you to say so, sir.'

'I bet you really know how to please a man,' he continued. 'I can tell you're the type of girl who suffers from no inhibitions. You give yourself fully and freely, to any man who wants you.'

'You know me very well, sir,' Constance breathed, fully immersing herself in the role.

The touch of his hands was electrifying. She forgot about the open door and her boutique as she turned around and squatted before him, spreading her thighs wide. He leant over to inspect her sex, combing the dark curls and parting her fleshy folds with both thumbs. He sniffed her, briefly licked her, and then ordered her to get dressed for him. A few minutes earlier she would have jumped at the chance to cover herself up, but now she would have preferred to remain naked for as long as it took this man to pleasure himself with her.

However, she climbed down from the desk and obediently dressed in the peach silk bra and brief set he had chosen for her. The dress was an ankle-length creation of sky-blue silk, cut low at the front and high at the back, leaving a back view of her long legs, all the way to the tops of her thighs, as she walked. She was about to suggest it might look better without any underwear when the telephone rang. The man nodded for her to pick it up.

'All is going well, I trust,' said KT.

'Fine, master,' she responded. 'The... uh... customer seems quite pleased.'

'As a businesswoman, you don't need me to emphasise the importance of customer satisfaction,' he replied. 'Why don't you tell me a little story, Constance?'

'A story, master?'

'One of your exciting little fantasies. I'm sure our mutual friend would like to hear it too. He most certainly enjoyed listening to your other juicy tales.'

This had not been part of the plan and Constance was alarmed all over again. But she was not going to upset her master. It took her a moment to recall a fantasy she had not previously shared with him.

'I have a friend named Jill,' she began hesitantly, suspecting he would very much appreciate one of her lesbian fantasies. 'She's a few years older than me and married, but I think she's bisexual. I'm certain of it, in fact. Anyway, she comes to the boutique one evening, just as I am about to leave. She wants to buy some expensive lingerie.'

As she leant on the desk breathing her fantasy down the line to her master, the customer stood behind her, hiked her dress up over her waist and rolled her silk knickers down over her hips and legs. He had already unzipped his trousers and his cock was ready for her. She stepped out of her underwear and obligingly parted her thighs, without interrupting her explicit narrative.

'I've never before touched another woman in this way, but I can't help myself. I want Jill and she wants me. She kisses me and starts... ohhhh... master, it feels so good!'

Had anybody chanced to enter the office in the next few minutes, Constance would not have noticed him or her. The man whose name she did not even know was penetrating her from behind with long smooth strokes, while she titillated KT with an erotic tale that was unlikely ever to progress beyond fantasy. As soon as he had come the man withdrew, wiped his cock on her bottom and zipped up his trousers. She finished gasping her fantasy with evidence of the stranger's pleasure trickling down her thighs. By the time she was finished he had gone.

Constance was glad that particular test was finished. It was just sheer luck that nobody had walked into the office while the man guided her body back and forth to satisfy himself. Had a member of staff discovered her in such a position, she didn't know what she would have done.

KT called her again that night, to congratulate her on her success and reveal the details of her final test. She had twenty-four hours to prepare and was warned to adhere to every detail of his instructions. There would be no second chance.

At the appointed time, the following evening, she was leaning on a lamppost at the end of a street notorious as a red light area. Her stance and style of dress left no doubt as to the nature of her business. Beneath her ankle-length black rubber mac she was wearing a tight black string vest, with nothing underneath, a black leather mini-skirt and fishnet stockings. Her suspenders and several inches of thigh were clearly visible below the hem of her skirt. The mac served more than an aesthetic purpose. As it was raining heavily she would have been soaked to the skin without it. At least the rain was keeping the other girls off the street. Constance had a feeling they might not take kindly to her invading their turf and a fight was the last thing she needed. She hoped the rain kept the police away as well. The consequences of being arrested for soliciting did not bear thinking about.

Whenever a car approached she flung open her mac, giving the driver an eyeful of the shapely goods within. She would be required to service five tricks, before progressing to the final part of her test. To ensure she did not cheat, one of the five would be a master assigned to keeping an eye on her. As he would be reporting back to his fellow masters, and Constance had no idea which of the five clients he would be, she would have to service each with a boundless enthusiasm. She had not thought it would take very long, but a full twenty minutes passed before the first car cruised to a halt by the pavement. By then her hair was soaked and she did not feel in the least bit sexy or attractive. Nevertheless, as she approached the car, swaying on her high stiletto heels, she fixed a practised smile.

'Bad evening for it,' greeted the fat and balding driver.

'There's never a bad evening for it,' Constance replied, leaning close and offering him a flash of bare breasts beneath her vest.

'How much?' he demanded.

'Far less than you might think,' she responded. 'Why don't I get in and give you the best value for money you're ever likely to find?'

He insisted on knowing her exact terms before they went any further. When she told him he was incredulous.

'Are you taking the piss, lady?'

'I'm telling you the truth,' she replied. 'On my life. Any way you want: it's the same price. What do you say? It's bloody wet out here.'

Despite his reservations, the man found her offer

impossible to refuse. In the minute it took him to drive to a nearby side street, Constance had unzipped his trousers and was manipulating his cock to full hardness. As soon as he had parked, she lowered her head to his lap and treated him to what was probably the most exquisite blow-job he had ever received.

Afterwards he drove her back to her street corner and paid her the pound coin she had stated as her price. He tried to offer her a tip, probably out of guilt, but she pushed it away.

'A pound is more than I'm worth,' she told him, getting out of the car.

It was over two hours later that she emerged from the car of her fifth and final client, clasping another pound coin in her fist. Four of the clients had been easily pleased and conventional in tastes. The odd one out had tested Constance's claim to offer the best value for money he would ever find by ordering her to strip naked, kneel in a puddle outside the open door of his car and fuck herself with the handle of his flash-light, while she sucked him. She had shocked him by obeying his instructions without the slightest objection.

Thoroughly drenched, though elated at having passed the last of her three tests, Constance went in search of a taxi. She had earnt just about enough for her fare home. On the way there she peeled off her clothes in the back of the cab and tossed them out of the back window. Having handed her night's earnings to the astonished driver, she calmly walked naked across the street and up the driveway to her semi-detached house. She did not even consider what any of the neighbours might say, if they saw her.

Five minutes later the telephone rang. She knew who it was even before she picked up the receiver.

'Well done, Constance,' KT said. 'You have passed your preliminaries with flying colours. The Playground awaits you, unless you've changed your mind about wanting to be a slave.'

'I haven't changed my mind, master,' she hastily assured him. 'I want this more than ever, so please don't deny it to me now.'

'Nobody is denying you anything,' he replied. 'We just have to make certain you know what you're doing. The Playground is not for the faint-hearted.'

'Neither is what I've been through lately,' she responded.

'Quite,' he replied. 'At midday on Friday a car will arrive to take you to the resort. You must not tell a soul where you are going. Not that anybody would be likely to believe you anyway. Apart from a baggy T-shirt, which is the only thing you will be wearing, you will carry nothing. Not even a toothbrush. All necessities are provided with your accommodation. You will not hear from me again until your arrival. Any questions you may have will have to wait until then.'

Constance had plenty of questions, but he had already hung up.

Chapter Eleven

The white Rolls Royce cruised gracefully through the electronically controlled gates of the resort and wove a path along a long and winding stretch of tarmac, before finally halting in the shadow of a huge dazzlingly white house. Constance felt as if she had spent a lifetime in the luxury prison of the back of the car. The windows were blacked out and a smoked mirror panel separated her from the chauffeur. The Chargemasters either loved cloak-and-dagger games, or so prized their secrecy that they could not permit a willing captive even a glimpse of where she was being taken.

The chauffeur opened the rear door of the Rolls and Constance stepped out, revealing an expanse of flesh as her baggy lemon T-shirt rode up her hips. KT was waiting on the front porch, immaculately dressed in a pinstriped three-piece suit and gripping a thin riding crop in his fist. Kneeling beside him was a buxom blonde in her late thirties, wearing large round spectacles and crotchless fishnet tights, secured around her waist by a thin silver studded belt. A pair of large gold hoops dangled from the pierced nipples of her full round breasts and the sunlight glinted on a matching pair of hoops in her labia.

'So your courage did not desert you at the last moment,' said KT. 'It isn't unknown for a slave to pass her tests, only to then get cold feet.'

'I have no doubts, master,' said Constance. 'This is what I want.'

'Take off your T-shirt,' he commanded. 'You'll be spending much of your time here naked, so you might as well get used to it.'

Without hesitation she pulled the garment off over her head. Underneath, as instructed, she was completely naked.

'Barbara will escort you to your room and show you around,' he told her. 'At six p.m. sharp you will present yourself for inspection with the other girls.'

Constance walked past him, her eyes on the ample buttocks and swaying hips of the plump blonde as she followed her up the front steps. His riding crop sliced the air and cracked explosively across her buttocks. Constance yelped a loud shriek of pain and surprise, clutching at her crop-scorched cheeks.

'Just a little taste of what makes life at the resort so special,' smirked KT.

Constance's room was on the second floor of the guesthouse. Though clean and comfortable, it was far from the five-star luxury she was becoming accustomed to. She was about to ask Barbara where the bathroom was when she noticed the TV camera mounted over the door, scanning her room with an electronic eye.

'The masters watch us at all times,' the blonde woman explained. 'Slaves are allowed no privacy. It's creepy at first, but you'll get used to it.'

'How long have you been here?' asked Constance.

She smiled. 'This is my fourth visit. My master leaves me here for weeks at a time whenever he has to travel abroad on business. It's the best way of ensuring I don't get up to any mischief.'

'You don't mind?'

Barbara looked puzzled. 'Mind? Of course I don't

mind. I'm a slave. I'm serving as chambermaid for this week, but the masters have kindly given me the afternoon off, to show you around.'

'How many masters are there?' asked Constance.

'Oh, there must be about two hundred,' she replied. 'There's usually about thirty staying here at any one time. Come on, I'll take you on a tour of the Activities Area.'

In a conventional hotel she would have been referring to the gymnasium. But this place was anything but conventional. The huge and completely deserted leisure centre was like a cross between a torture chamber and a well-equipped gymnasium. Constance was both amazed and appalled by the range of equipment on display.

'This is one of my favourites,' said Barbara, showing her an exercise bicycle with a saddle-mounted vibrator and steel cuffs for her wrists and ankles. 'It has to be experienced to be believed.'

'I can well imagine,' mused Constance. 'Can I have a go?'

The blonde shook her head. 'We're not allowed to touch anything in here, unless there's a master present.'

'But there is a master present, my dear.'

Startled, both of them turned in the direction of the voice. Constance immediately recognised the silver-haired man as one of the clients she had served during her night of bargain-basement prostitution.

'I've been very much looking forward to seeing you again, Constance,' he continued, slowly approaching. 'You've given new meaning to the term "value for money". Help her aboard, Barbara. It's a lovely afternoon for a cycle ride.'

Constance started to have second thoughts as she mounted the exercise bicycle, but managed to keep a smile fixed. She shuddered as she lowered herself to the saddle and the vibrator slid smoothly into the moist depths of her sex. Barbara fitted the cuffs to her wrists and ankles, then the master got her underway with two sharp smacks of his right palm to her upthrust buttocks. As her feet bore down on the pedals the gold shaft of the vibrator began pistoning between her thighs.

'I think she is in need of a little encouragement,' said the master. 'Barbara, fetch me a cane.'

The slave scurried to one of the wall racks and brought back the kind of long thin cane a schoolmaster might once have used. The sight of it was enough to make Constance pedal faster, but her master did not intend it for decorative purposes. He drew it back and took careful aim. Constance shut her eyes, but she could hear it cutting through the air. She yelped as it exploded across her buttocks, burning a fiery mark across both cheeks.

'Poor Constance isn't yet fully familiar with the cane,' the master remarked, poised to deliver a second stroke. 'It may be some time before she appreciates its value. Move girl! Let's see how quickly you can cover four miles for me.'

'Ow!' she shrieked as he struck her again.

She did not realise how unfit she had allowed herself to become until, with the trip-meter on the handlebars registering barely two miles, she found herself gasping for breath. Her buttocks had already taken seven strokes of the cane and throbbed violently, in sweet contrast to the pleasurable sensations of the vibrator thrusting vigorously up into her. Her juices trickled down the gleaming shaft, just as the rivulets of sweat ran down her face and chest.

A further nine strokes of the cane and the equivalent of two gruelling miles of furious pedalling later, she was allowed to stop. Barbara freed her wrists and ankles, then helped her down off the bicycle. Had she not held onto her, Constance might well have collapsed.

'I shall be seeing you later this evening,' the master said, stroking her left breast with the tip of the cane. 'And this time, I shan't be paying.'

'What did he mean by that?' Barbara asked, once he was out of earshot.

When Constance told her she sighed. 'I'd love if my master forced me to do that. It must have been so humiliating!'

'It was,' Constance assured her. 'Did you not have to pass any tests to get in here?'

'Oh, yes – several,' she replied. 'I'll tell you about them, some time. But playing a cheap whore, in every sense of the word, must have been a really exciting experience.'

Constance nodded. 'There's no denying that. Oh, my poor bottom! I won't be able to sit down for days.'

'Mm, that's what I call a luscious colour,' Barbara said with a smile, admiring the handiwork of the master. 'Look in the mirror.'

Constance looked over her left shoulder and gasped at the reflection looking back at her from the full-length wall mirror. Her buttocks looked as though a crazed artist, using a tin of scarlet paint had painted them. Cane burns criss-crossed and blended into one another, leaving only patches of the milky undercoat of her buttocks visible.

'I bet it feels almost as good as it looks,' Barbara said with a smile.

Constance did not answer. For the moment she preferred to keep her feelings to herself.

From the gym, Barbara led her outside to the leisure

courts at the rear of the house. As it was a sunny afternoon, this was where most of the masters and slaves were to be found. Two attractive girls were playing a match on the tennis court. Both wore nothing but tennis shoes, white ankle socks and sunglasses. Their masters stood nearby within striking distance, with their long thin whips ready to punish the slightest mistake. To judge by the scarlet streaks on their buttocks and the backs of their thighs, the two slaves had been playing for some time.

Just as Constance was becoming intrigued in the performance on court she was startled by a hand squeezing her throbbing right buttock.

'New girl,' grinned a shaven-headed master in dark glasses. 'Sore bottom already?'

'Yes, master,' she gasped.

'Do you like to suck cock, new girl?'

'I... of course, master.'

He squeezed her cheek even harder in his big hand. 'That's what I like to hear. Come with me. You too, Barbara. There's enough for both of you.'

Meek as lambs, the two girls followed the mean-looking master back into the house. He ordered them to walk up the stairs in front of him and fondled their bottoms as they climbed the steps. Constance was trembling with excitement. She could still scarcely believe all of this was happening.

The master was staying on the third floor, in a suite known as the King's Chamber. This was as luxurious as anything offered by the best five-star hotel and a far cry from the small room Constance had been given.

'Turn on the TV,' he told Barbara. 'Let's see what's happening in the world. Constance, pour me a drink. Gin and tonic. No ice.'

Not very long ago any man who had dared speak to her as he did would have been sharply told where to stick his gin and tonic. But now it did not just feel like the most natural thing in the world to take orders from a man – it was a real pleasure.

He reclined in a luxurious leather armchair and stretched out his legs. Constance handed him his drink, Barbara the remote control, and then they stood to either side of the chair awaiting his next command.

'We have a few special channels here, Constance,' he said. 'They're called the house channels. There are fifteen: one for every slave room. You're on number eleven.'

Constance saw what looked like her own room on the screen. He flicked through the channels, bringing up a few more identical empty rooms, until he reached one that was occupied. A plump slave with long curly black hair was lying on the bed. Her thighs were parted and she was masturbating frenziedly, thrusting three fingers deep into her pouting sex. Scattered next to her on the bed was a vibrator, a candle, a hairbrush and a half-peeled banana.

'That's Maxie,' the master explained. 'She's been locked in her room, awaiting a disciplinary meeting this evening. She's been a bad girl. A master took her to his room last night. In the early hours he awoke to find her masturbating in the bathroom – without permission. A very serious offence. Her master ordered her to play with herself continuously until the disciplinary meeting, at six. Then her real punishment will be decided.'

'Perhaps he didn't—' Constance stopped herself, horrified by what she had almost said.

The master looked up at her. 'Perhaps he didn't what?'

She blushed. 'Nothing, master.'

'Out with it, girl!' he barked. 'You were about to say something. Perhaps he didn't satisfy her. Was that it?'

She remained silent, mentally cursing her own stupidity.

'So, you think the masters are here to satisfy the slaves?' he demanded.

'No, master, I didn't mean that,' she protested.

'I know what you meant,' he snapped. 'But as you've just arrived, I shall forgive your ignorance. I believe there should be something even more interesting happening on channel eight.'

He switched to the appropriate room where a girl was kneeling by her bed, a black hood pulled over her head. Otherwise, she was naked. A plump master stood behind her caning her buttocks. The only other action was in room fifteen, where a girl in a red rubber mask was crouched over on all fours, being taken in either end by a naked master.

'What did I bring you up here for, Constance?' the master in dark glasses demanded.

'To suck your cock, master,' she answered.

'Then do it.'

She fell instantly to her knees, reaching for the zipper of his slacks. He had not exaggerated when he said there was enough for her and Barbara. His cock was a good ten inches long and as thick as her wrist. The blonde maid joined her as she ran her tongue over the bulbous purple crown, mopping up a pearly tear that oozed from the slit. The master sipped his drink and sighed contentedly, dividing his attention between the two girls working oral magic on his throbbing member and the masked girl being fucked from head to hind in room fifteen.

Two pairs of soft hands and lips and two eager tongues

skilfully brought him to his explosive peak in not too many minutes. He climaxed with a low moan, both girls catching his creamy jets on their tongues with murmurs of genuine pleasure. They cleaned him with their tongues, licking up every last drop, but remained kneeling until he sat up and zipped up his trousers.

'You may go,' he told them. 'I'm sure the new girl is eager to continue her tour.'

Constance was far more eager to remain in his company, as she ached to accommodate his cock in her hot pussy. But she would just have to forego that pleasure, for the time being at least.

The afternoon continued its eventful course by the swimming pool, where Constance attracted the attention of a sunbathing master. In full view of at least a dozen others, he ordered her to pull down his swimming trunks and masturbate him. He seemed surprised by her lack of hesitation to comply – as Barbara explained to Constance, later, all but the most uninhibited of slaves needed a little time and encouragement to enter into the true spirit of the Playground.

She squatted between his thighs, smiling as she skilfully pumped his cock with her right fist. When he climaxed, she milked his thick cream over her breasts and cleaned him off with her tongue.

'You're going to love it here,' Barbara said afterwards. 'It's not every girl takes so easily to behaving like a complete slut.'

Constance accepted the compliment with a smile. 'If you'd called me a slut a month ago, I'd have slapped you across the face. Must be the ambience.'

'It's your true nature revealing itself,' the blonde woman replied. 'Outside, in so-called respectable society, that's where we're really slaves. We're forced to behave in a certain way and hide what we really are. I'd love to live like this all the time, naked and uninhibited, as nature intended, but I can't. I'm an upstanding member of society. A lady. It would hardly do for my master to bring me to dinner parties on a leash.'

Constance laughed. With the cold semen of one man drying on her breasts, the aftertaste of another in her mouth and the streaks of a caning on her backside, she was more content than she had felt in a very long time.

At precisely six that evening, eleven naked slaves were lined up for inspection in the courtyard of the hotel. As the new girl, Constance stood apart from the others. Barbara had earlier instructed her in the pose required for inspection. She had to stand with her legs wide apart, her hands behind back, her chest thrust out and her head bowed. She must not look a master in the eye, unless spoken to.

KT and three other men, each dressed in a three-piece pinstriped black suit and carrying a cane, moved along the line of girls, carefully scrutinising each. Once the ritual was completed the girls were commanded to bend over. Each then received three strokes of the cane across her bare buttocks. Then it was time for Constance to be inspected.

'What do you think?' KT asked the master in dark glasses, as they scrutinised her like a mannequin in a shop window.

'She's good with her mouth,' he replied. 'I took her to my room earlier.'

'Quite a horny bitch,' mused KT.

'She has a lovely arse,' observed one of the other men,

kneading her buttocks with a gloved hand. 'Good and firm. Able to take plenty of the cane.'

'Most of the men are going to want her tonight,' said the fourth man. 'I think the democratic thing would be to raffle her.'

'I have a better idea,' said KT. 'All those who want her can play for her in a snooker competition. The highest break wins.'

The other three men agreed that this was an excellent idea.

'What do you think, slave?' KT demanded.

Constance raised her head. 'I think it's a wonderful idea, master.'

He grinned. 'Of course you do. Right, there is one more item of business to be taken care of before dinner. The small matter of Miss Stickyfingers in room eight.'

As if on cue, the curly-haired slave was marched out into the garden by two masters. One gripped the chain attached to the iron collar around her throat. The other tugged a leash attached by steel clips to her outer labia.

'You look exhausted from playing with yourself all day,' KT sneered. 'Well, girl, what do you have to say for yourself?'

'I'm sorry, master,' she blurted miserably. 'I didn't mean—'

'Didn't mean to go to the bathroom in the middle of the night and play with yourself?' he exclaimed loudly. 'Could you not control your urges? Is that what you mean?'

She nodded. 'Yes, master.'

'Well, if you can't control yourself, you shall have to be controlled.'

He walked across to where a briefcase lay on the grass, opened it and produced a chastity belt made of thick leather. The inside of the belt bristled with conical studs of chrome and was fitted with a black phallus. Tears of shame welled in the eyes of the slave as the belt was placed between her thighs. The phallic plug was pushed up into her anus, then the belt was tightly strapped and padlocked around her waist. KT then produced a set of handcuffs from inside his jacket and manacled her wrists behind her back.

'You will be released at noon tomorrow,' he said. 'By which time I hope you will have learnt a valuable lesson. In the meantime, you won't be bored. You shall have a companion in your room for the night.'

He walked along the line of bent-over slaves and selected a slender middle-aged woman, with pierced nipples and peroxide blonde hair.

'You're quite partial to a nice young lady, aren't you, Mona?' he goaded.

'Yes, master.'

'Then take her to room eight. She's yours for the night. See to it her tongue is well exercised.'

While the masters enjoyed dinner in the dining room, waited upon by half a dozen slave girls, the slaves took their meal in the downstairs kitchen like servants from the Victorian era. Constance could not concentrate on the food, nor the conversation of her fellow slaves. She was too excited by thoughts of the night ahead. Though there was no shortage of available females in the resort, she knew she was the star attraction.

The snooker competition for her took place in the games room, a total of nine masters participating. Constance sat nearby, anxiously watching the proceedings. Eventually there was only one combatant remaining unbeaten.

'Well, well, this must be my lucky night!' smiled the master with dark glasses, stepping towards her. 'This is the first time I've won the privilege of breaking in a new slave.'

Constance felt as though the luck were all hers. The master led her to his suite and permitted her to enjoy a drink with him, before leading her to the bedroom.

'I have a little surprise for you,' he said as she draped herself provocatively across the bed, admiring herself in the huge round ceiling mirror. 'One of your fantasies is about to come true.'

A moment later her own husky tones wafted from the speakers of the stereo system. 'I lie across the bed, naked and wanton, aching for my master. I beg him to take me, any way he pleases. He teases me, slowly revealing himself, urging me to beg for it, like the tramp that I am. He is big, mean and handsome. His cock is the most magnificent creation I have ever seen. He touches it to my lips, my breasts, my thighs, but I am forbidden to touch it. I can't help myself. I reach for it. My lack of self-control angers him. He turns me over and spanks me hard, whacking me until my bottom is as red as sunburn. Then he handcuffs me to the head of the bed and blindfolds me, denying me the sight of his lovely big cock sliding past my lips and down to the back of my throat.

'He thrusts into my mouth in the same way as I long for my sex to be filled, his balls smacking against my chin. I want to suck him dry, drink down his come like wine, but he is a cruel and patient master. Instead of giving me what I want so badly, he takes his cock out of my mouth and begins beating my breasts with a leather strap. I scream from the pain and frustration.

'How he tortures me! He screws me half-crazy, then abandons me for what seems an age. When he returns he torments me further, rubbing his hard sticky cock over my body, smacking my face with it. I have never known a man with such ruthless self-discipline. How can he resist me, lying naked and begging for it?

'What seems like a lifetime later, he finally does take me, ramming deep into me like a wild animal, fondling my aching breasts and buttocks. He comes deep inside me, filling me to overflowing with a hot, creamy flood of his lovely spunk. Afterwards I lick his cock clean and keep on licking until he is hard again. Then it's the turn of my mouth to be taken once more.

'I have never known such pleasure. All night my masterful stud takes me, again and again. Even when my handcuffs and blindfold are removed I remain his helpless slave. He can do anything he pleases with me. Anything...'

Chapter Twelve

Constance was woken by a slant of sunlight through the blinds of the bedroom window. For a moment she thought she had been dreaming, but then she saw the sleeping figure of her master beside her. Her eyes travelled down along his hard-muscled dark-haired body to the tube of his cock, curled like a sleeping snake over his right thigh. Even at rest, it was the most magnificent specimen of manhood she had ever seen. Her aching pussy bore testament to its potency.

She realised that she knew next to nothing about the man with whom she had so delightfully enacted her fantasy. All he had told her was his name – Jonathan Covington. Constance had not pressed him for further information. After all, she was just a slave, a casual screw won in a snooker tournament. As soon as he woke up he would probably throw her out of his bed.

She could not take her eyes off the sleeping beauty of his cock. She hungered for it yet again. Almost instinctively, she slid down along the bed and kissed it lightly. Covington did not stir. She nuzzled his dark pubic curls with her tongue, then rolled it sensually up along the length of his flaccid shaft. One of her own dark pubic hairs was stuck to the purple crown. She removed it with her tongue, then gently lifted his cock from his thigh and wrapped her lips around the swollen head.

The master stirred and grunted softly as his member stiffened in her mouth. By the time he opened his eyes Constance was completely engrossed in the task, her golden hair cascading over his thighs and her head bobbing slowly up and down as she lovingly administered to his morning glory.

He lay back, sighing blissfully, hands behind his head, right up to the moment of climax. The flood of semen that gushed to the back of her throat surprised Constance, considering the copious amounts he had deposited throughout the course of the night.

Shortly afterwards she reluctantly returned to her room, where she showered and studied the trophies of her first day as a slave. Her buttocks glowed angrily from being thrashed and spanked, and her breasts, belly and thighs were streaked with several lesser shades of red.

Having dried herself off, she made her way downstairs. Another full day at the Playground lay ahead and she would doubtless be required to attend to the needs of several more masters.

'Your name is on the duty roster for tonight,' Barbara told her at breakfast. 'Four more masters are arriving and there's going to be a welcoming dinner. You'll be one of the serving girls.'

'Serving girls. Like a waitress, you mean?'

Barbara smiled. 'Something like that. How was last night?'

Constance sighed. 'Wonderful. I can honestly say I have never experienced anything like it.'

'Master Jon is a wonderful lover,' Barbara agreed.

Constance felt a momentary twinge of jealousy and hurriedly changed the subject. 'What exactly am I supposed to do now, after breakfast?'

'Go for a walk, a swim – whatever. Just make sure you're in the gym for midday. Slave training.'

Constance arrived ten minutes early, eager to discover exactly what slave training entailed. KT was already waiting, looking positively intimidating in knee-high boots, tight black leather trousers and a low-peaked leather cap. A wooden whip with a thick tongue of leather was gripped in his right fist.

'So gratifying to see an eager slave,' he greeted. 'Master John reports favourably on last night's performance.'

Constance blushed slightly. For some reason she had not expected him to share the details of their night together.

'Oh, yes, your fantasies have proved inspiring to many of the masters in the Playground,' he continued. 'Right, let's begin making you into the perfect slave I know you long to be. I was going to start you off on the exercise bike, but I'm told you're already familiar with that, so let's see how you fare on the rowing machine.'

With an encouraging flick of the whip to her tender buttocks, Constance mounted the exerciser. The hard wooden seat dug painfully into her nether cleft, but she suspected that would soon be the least of her discomforts. She stretched her legs straight out in front of her and KT secured them with leather straps. A pair of thin silver chains with steel clips on the end were attached to the oars. Constance winced as the clips were fastened to her nipples.

'Row, slave,' KT barked, flicking his whip across her breasts.

Constance gripped the oars tightly and began to row. Every outward thrust of the handles drew the chains taut and the steel clips tugged agonisingly on her nipples. The relief when she drew the oars back was incredible.

'Come on, put some effort into it,' KT snarled, striking

her buttocks with the whip. 'Imagine there's a big, juicy cock waiting to be sucked at the end of your journey. You don't want to keep your horny master waiting, do you?'

Constance whimpered, straining to redouble her efforts and telling herself that this was the price to be paid for the pleasure of the previous night. Her nipples throbbed mercilessly and the seat felt as if it were splitting her in two. She would have given anything to go back on the exercise bicycle.

Only when she was sweating and crying for mercy did KT finally free her from the machine. She was given a few minutes to recover, then ordered to lie back on a bench and pump iron, using the pulleys mounted on either side. As she strained with this fresh fitness sadism, KT took a long wooden lance from a rack on the wall. Mounted on one end of the lance was a long and thick pink dildo. As Constance pumped iron with every ounce of energy remaining, he thrust the dildo up between her thighs, in time with the up and down movements of her arms.

The press-ups that followed were marginally less strenuous. Crouching over a dildo sprouting like an obscene black flower from the floor, she managed twenty-six press-ups. At the end of each, several inches of the dildo penetrated her. KT added a lash of his whip each time she rose up, for good measure. At this stage several masters had gathered to watch the entertainment, even though it was available live on the TV screens in their rooms.

Once he had finished putting her through her paces in the gymnasium, KT patted her on the head, pronounced her a good slave, and decreed that she could have the rest of the afternoon to wander round at her leisure –

because she certainly wouldn't have any leisure later that evening.

The welcoming dinner for the new arrivals commenced at eight. Constance was one of four serving girls attending to the twenty-six men seated at the long dining table. All four maids wore an identical uniform, consisting of a small, lacy white cap and short black dress, with cutouts to leave their breasts and buttocks on full display.

As Constance leant over to serve soup to one master, the man seated next to him slipped a hand between her thighs. Startled, she overturned the soup bowl, spilling the contents over the other man's dinner jacket.

'Clumsy cow!' he roared, leaping to his feet. 'My jacket is ruined!'

'I'm so sorry, master,' she blurted.

'You will be,' he barked. 'Turn around.'

Before the rest of the men around the table, Constance had her bare bottom spanked vigorously. The man did not stop until his arm grew tired, by which time her cheeks were blazing red and felt like they had been scalded with boiling water. He then sat back down and she resumed her duties.

Throughout the evening the men continued to fondle and molest her freely and she received several more slaps to her throbbing cheeks. One man ordered her to suck his cock while he was eating dessert. While she was carrying out the command, another penetrated her with his finger, tickling her clitoris until she climaxed.

She was glad when the meal finally ended. She had hoped that Covington might choose to spend the night with her again, but he had not even spoken to her since she left his room. She knew she had no right to have expected anything more, but that did not stop her from nursing the forlorn hope that she had meant more to him than just a one-off night.

The after-dinner festivities took place on the floodlit front lawn of the Playground. They began with a nude wrestling match. The two volunteer combatants were covered in body oil and blindfolded, before being marched into the ring. They would wrestle until one submitted. The prize for the winner was the choice of which master she would spend the night with. The loser would be whipped and forced to lick the boots of three masters.

The wrestling was followed by a sack race. Four slaves crouched in bulky black canvas sacks that reached their throats and were bound by lengths of thick rope. They hopped from one end of the lawn to the other, the masters encouraging them with cheers and whiplashes. Once again, the winner was allowed to choose her master for the night.

None of the slaves were forced to take part in these events, but there was no shortage of earnest volunteers. Being allowed to choose one's master was a rare privilege, and one well worth striving for – which was why Constance held up her hand when KT called for three volunteers for the 'hen race'.

The three 'hens' were ordered to squat on the lawn. Their hands were then roped behind their backs and rubber chicken masks pulled over their heads. A box of eggs was brought from the kitchen and three empty cartons placed several yards in front of the slaves. A master carefully inserted an egg in the pussy of each hen, then KT commanded them to go to their boxes and 'lay'.

The three slaves began shuffling forward, delicately shuffling their feet, their haunches level with their ankles. Constance managed to progress only a few feet before the egg in her pussy burst and the slimy mess oozed down between her thighs. There was nothing to do but shuffle back and have a fresh egg inserted.

Three smashed eggs and what felt like an eternity of frustration later, she reached her designated carton, squatted over it and carefully laid her egg. The audience of masters cheered. One down, five to go. Her only consolation was the fact that the two other 'hens' were experiencing similar difficulties.

Practice made near perfect. Constance managed to complete the race, breaking only two more eggs. One girl was ahead of her and she would have certainly lost the race and been on the receiving end of a stiff caning, had her rival not carelessly dropped her sixth egg on top of another in the carton and broken both. Constance could not resist throwing a triumphant smile to the man she would choose as her master, as she neatly deposited her sixth glistening egg in the carton.

There was a sense of destiny about that second night with Covington, though he seemed far less delighted to be her chosen one than she would have liked. When he took her to his suite, still sticky with broken egg, he did not rush straight to the bedroom with her, as she had hoped. Instead, he reclined in his armchair, switched on the TV and ordered her to fix him a drink. He then stretched out his legs and told her to polish his calf-length black boots with her tongue.

While she was doing this, he scanned the rooms of the slaves. Most were unoccupied, the masters having taken their girls to their own rooms. The middle-aged woman in room four was lying bound, gagged and blindfolded on her bed, being vigorously screwed by a master in a black rubber mask. John watched for a while, then continued his surfing of the channels.

In seven, a blonde girl was down on all fours, thrusting a vibrator up between her thighs, while a master penetrated her anally. The girl in room twelve was entertaining two masters simultaneously and both in her mouth. The big-breasted occupant of room sixteen was kneeling before her master in an attitude of prayer, while he masturbated over her face. A master in room twenty-one was taking photographs of his dark-haired slave masturbating with a wine bottle.

By the time Covington tired of spying on the sexual activities in the slave rooms, every inch of his boots had been licked twice over and Constance was kneeling patiently at his feet, awaiting his next command. Hopefully, this would involve contact with the prominent bulge in his leather trousers.

If he had tormented her on the previous night before giving her what she craved, then tonight he was determined to torture her. He forced her to crawl to the bedroom with a cane gripped between her clenched buttocks. Each time she dropped it she received three strokes, then had to start again, from the front door. When she finally reached her goal he handcuffed her to the foot of the bed, then unzipped his trousers and presented his throbbing cock to her lips. But when she reached eagerly out to devour it, he grabbed a fistful of her hair in his fist.

'Patience, my horny slave,' he told her. 'I want to hear another of your stories. One you've never before shared with another soul.'

'Please, master, I can't think straight now,' she pleaded.

'I want you too much.'

'I'm not asking you to think straight,' he replied. 'In fact, I'd like to hear a lesbian story. So come on, tell me what you would like to do with another woman, if the two of you were alone together in this room with no masters to disturb you.'

The glistening crown of his throbbing cock was less than two inches from her lips. Close enough to smell, almost to taste. But she knew it would be cruelly denied to her until she gave him what he wanted.

He kept a grip on her hair, holding her greedy mouth at bay, while she made up a fantasy of herself and another girl. Whenever she faltered he gripped his cock in his free hand and brushed it tantalisingly against her lips, with the unspoken threat of denying it to her completely, unless she continued with her fantasy.

Half an hour later he was satisfied. Constance lunged forward the instant he let go of her hair, ravenously enveloping his erection between her lips. But the torture was far from over. After only a minute he sadistically withdrew from her mouth, freed her from the handcuffs and pushed her onto the bed. Using four silk scarves, he bound her wrists and ankles tightly to the posts, leaving her spread-eagled like a sacrificial offering. Then he left.

He returned over an hour later, completely naked, his cock gripped in his right fist. Constance was writhing on the bed in an agony of desire. Kneeling next to her, he began to masturbate, urging her to beg for his cock. She could not have pleaded for her life with greater fervour. When, several minutes later, he pumped his precious cream over her breasts, she almost screamed with joy.

For several more hours, as Constance lay tied to the bed, he used his cock to tease, humiliate and torment her in a way he could never have done with whips or nipple clamps. The more she begged for him, the more he resisted her. Even when her frustration reduced her to tears, she was permitted no more than a few precious moments of his shaft sliding into the oozing cleft between her thighs.

Chapter Thirteen

Constance had gone to the resort in the full expectation of having her life changed forever, but nothing could have prepared her for the emptiness she felt back in the real world. The boutique, once the love of her life, meant virtually nothing to her any more. Away from that place where fantasy and reality were indistinguishable, she remained in bondage, as surely as if she were still tied to her master's bedposts.

Jonathan Covington haunted her dreams and shadowed her every waking moment. She was still hurt and mystified by his treatment of her on that second night. The night had been one long drawn-out session of the most hideous torture imaginable. He had stroked her, teased her, penetrated her briefly, but never once rewarded her with the release she craved like a drug. Having finally tired of the cruel game he had released her and sent her crawling back to her room, whimpering like a rejected puppy. He had probably watched her lying on her bed, tossing and turning in a fever of frustration, not daring to relieve herself without permission. He had been nowhere in sight on Monday morning, when she had climbed miserably back into the limousine that would take her home, dressed only in the T-shirt she had arrived in.

She had to see him again, no matter what it cost. No man had ever managed to make such a dramatic impression on her, or so wholly commandeered her fantasies. If necessary, she was prepared to crawl to him on her hands and knees. However he forced her to grovel, whatever the price of her becoming his slave, she was prepared to pay.

In the meantime, there was KT. Constance had long since resigned herself to a role as his part-time plaything. He seemed to regard her as little more than a handy screw, available whenever he wished to make use of her. This was the arrangement she had willingly entered into the first time they met, so she knew she had no right to expect pride of place in his affections. Gina had the honour of being his slave and Constance would just have to live with that. However, she sensed a definite resentment smouldering below the carefree exterior of the other woman that made her suspect that Gina might not be as happy to share her master as she appeared. When she voiced her suspicions to KT, in the afterglow of a mid-afternoon soirée in a hotel bedroom, he merely laughed.

'Gina and I have an understanding. As her master I'm free to have anyone I please. As long as it's not kept secret from her, there's no jealousy.'

He studied Constance's buttocks, rosy from the spanking he had administered half an hour earlier, as she leant out of the bed to unearth her cigarette packet from the clothing strewn on the carpet. She lit one, then leant back against the headboard, thoughtfully focusing on the tendril of smoke that drifted upwards. KT's reassurance had sounded slightly less confident than he'd probably intended.

'But when we meet like this, that's secret,' she said quietly. 'You warned me never to mention it to her, remember?'

'She doesn't need to know every detail of every time you and I get together.'

Constance looked at him. 'She knows you and I are spending time alone together, and she's not happy about it. I can tell by the way she sometimes looks at me. She thinks I'm trying to take you away from her.'

'Rubbish,' he scoffed. 'Have you forgotten last Sunday morning, when we went off air? Gina didn't seem to mind you sucking my cock, or bending over for the cane. I don't recall any force being used when you and she shared that double-ended dildo while I was giving you both a good whipping.'

'It's different in a threesome,' Constance answered. 'With her there you and I don't have the same intimacy. She gets off on watching you punish me. It's what we do when we're alone that bothers her.'

'Even if she is jealous, why should you care?' KT demanded.

She smiled. 'I only care about having you, master.'

Stubbing out her half-smoked cigarette in the bedside ashtray, she slid down along the bed, gripped his stiffening cock in her fist and lowered her mouth to it. If he was having even the slightest doubts about his commitment to Gina, Constance resolved to use every means at her disposal to nurture them.

Constance had not had a birthday party since her twenty-first. For her twenty-ninth she received an unexpected present. A gift-wrapped package was delivered by courier to the boutique. The box inside contained a single red rose and a typewritten note, instructing her to go to The Master's Masque club at eleven o'clock that night and be prepared for a birthday surprise. Though the note was not signed, she assumed it was from KT.

She arrived at the club half an hour early, dressed to thrill in thigh-high black PVC boots and a matching low-cut dress, with two circular cutouts in the back which left her buttocks exposed. The pale moons peered through black fishnet tights. She turned more heads than usual as she strutted confidently towards the bar, the peak of her stud and chain-festooned black leather cap shading her eyes. She had expected KT to be waiting for her, but he was nowhere to be seen. Deciding he must be playing one of his games, she ordered a drink and waited for him to make his move.

Half an hour later, she was still waiting. The club was becoming crowded and several pairs of eyes were indiscreetly appraising her. Sitting on a stool, with her buttocks displayed and her breasts spilling out over the top of her dress, she looked like the most available woman on the planet. It was only a matter of time before a prospective master moved in.

'Playing, or just teasing?'

She looked round. The face of the man who had spoken was covered by a dark purple hood of glossy latex. He was heavy-set and hairy-chested, dressed in tight black jeans and a vest that matched his hood. In his right fist he held a riding crop. It took Constance only a moment to conclude that he was part of whatever fiendish birthday charade KT had devised.

'Playing.'

'How far are you prepared to go to please your master?'

She smiled. 'That's entirely up to my master.'

'Then step this way, my lovely slave,' he said, taking her arm.

He led her to a candle-lit room at the rear of the club, in which about two dozen people were seated around a circular wooden stage. Constance was hit by the glare of two spotlights as she stepped onto the platform. She scanned the shadowed faces of the men in the audience, but KT did not appear to be among them. He must have decided to let this masked man warm her up for him.

The stage was equipped with a set of stocks. At a nod from the master, Constance knelt and placed her throat and wrists in the grooves. The heavy wooden upper half descended with a loud thump, two steel clamps locking it into place. Cuffs of thick black leather, joined by a silver chain, were buckled tightly around her wrists. A heavy black hood was then placed over her head and the cord fastened beneath her chin. The only opening was a slit for her mouth.

After she had been secured in the stocks, nothing happened for a few moments. Then she felt the sharp bite of the riding crop on her backside. The hood muffled her shriek of pain and surprise. She had scarcely time to catch her breath before the crop struck her again, the crack resounding throughout the room, amplified by two microphones fitted unobtrusively on the stocks.

By the end of the twenty-four stroke thrashing, the fiery lines on Constance's buttocks were practically burning through the mesh of her tights. Somebody tugged at her hood and a stiff cock probed the mouth slit. As she welcomed it with open lips, the hands of another man tugged her dress up over her hips. She realised, with no small delight, that she was about to be taken by several men at once.

The man who was so eager to take her did not waste time taking off her tights. Instead, he ripped them apart at the crotch, then plunged his throbbing cock into the hot oiled depths of her eager sex. Another pair of hands peeled her dress down at the front, allowing her breasts to spill fully free. The bite of cold steel as both stiff nipples were simultaneously clamped sent an electrifying jolt through her body, the pain the perfect accompaniment to the intense pleasure of being taken by two men at once.

Constance was almost certain that neither of the men was KT. Not that it mattered. As long as their cocks were hard and they knew how to use them, she had no intention of complaining.

After a while she lost count of the number of men who screwed her. As soon as one was finished another was waiting to take his place. Whips licked her breasts at infrequent intervals, and fingers tugged on her nipple clamps to ensure a reasonable level of discomfort was maintained. Two masters began smacking her sore bottom with wooden paddles, keeping time with the man kneeling behind her, who was thrusting into her hard. At the point of climax, he withdrew his cock and milked it over her buttocks, his semen scalding the rose-red cheeks like molten wax.

She had no idea how long she remained on the platform, or how many men she was taken by. When she was eventually released from the stocks two men helped her to her feet. As her hood was yanked off, the audience around the stage broke into a thunderous round of applause. When her eyes readjusted to the light she realised she was standing with her breasts bare and her dress rolled up around her waist, before at least double the number of men that had been originally present. She had fully expected to find KT standing triumphantly next to her, but she recognised none of the men in the room.

Her near-perfect birthday in bondage was ruined upon her arrival home, at almost four a.m. While she was being screwed to heaven and back in the club, intruders had been busy in her home. Obscenities were scrawled in lipstick and dark eye-shadow on the walls of the hall and lounge. Furniture had been overturned, vases and mirrors smashed, and the video recorder had been hurled through the front of the TV set. In the kitchen, the contents of the refrigerator lay in a mess on the floor and the microwave was submerged in the overflowing sink.

Upstairs, the devastation was confined to her bedroom. The ragged remains of underwear and several expensive dresses were strewn on the floor. The walls were covered in more crude graffiti, and the bed littered with the smashed remains of a mirror. It was obvious the intruders had been intent on ransacking the place, rather than stealing anything. Sobbing softly, Constance slumped to her knees among the wreckage.

Several cigarettes and mugs of strong black coffee later, she had reached the only conclusion that made sense. The invasion of her home had been a crude act of revenge. The culprit could only be Detective Inspector Charles Mountjoy – the Stablemaster. He had probably been watching the house, waiting for the right opportunity to strike.

This was one of the reasons she did not report the matter to the police. The presence of a radio transmitter in her attic was another. Instead, she took a day off from the boutique and set about cleaning up the mess. Throughout the day she made several unsuccessful attempts to contact KT, needing the reassurance of a friendly voice. It was early evening before she finally located him on his mobile number. Like a knight in shining armour, he promised to be by her side within the hour.

Constance was somewhat uncomfortable with the sense of relief she felt upon seeing him. Needing a man to lean on had always struck her as a sign of weakness and she had resolved, from an early age, that she would never compromise her independence in such a way. Nevertheless, the urge to throw her arms around KT and cry on his strong shoulder was almost irresistible.

She was not sure whether to be more relieved or concerned when he informed her that the intruder could not possibly have been Charles Mountjoy. The Detective Inspector had been in hospital for the past four days, recovering from injuries sustained in the line of duty.

'Then it must have been his gangster friend,' Constance suggested.

'Unlikely,' KT replied. 'Whiting couldn't afford to take the risk. Besides, why would he bother? You can't have been that important to him. Maybe it was just common vandals, after all.'

She shook her head adamantly. 'No way. They knew the house was empty, so they must have been watching me. They switched off the alarm system, let themselves in, wrecked the place, but took nothing. It had to be somebody trying to get back at me.'

'It does look that way,' KT agreed. 'Where did you go last night?'

Constance smiled. 'As if you didn't know. With all the fuss over the burglary, I forgot to thank you.'

'For what?'

'For last night, of course. My birthday surprise at The Master's Masque. I really enjoyed myself.'

'I really don't know what you're talking about,' he said, appearing genuinely puzzled. 'I was in Manchester last night. I didn't get home until early this evening.'

'So you didn't send me the rose and the message?'

she demanded.

'Constance, I didn't even know it was your birthday,' he replied. 'You never mentioned it. Tell me all about this surprise I'm supposed to have given you.'

He listened attentively as she related the events of the previous night. She made no effort to deny how much she had enjoyed it.

'It's obvious you were set up,' he said afterwards. 'The invitation to the club was a ploy to get you out of the way, so that the intruders could be certain of having the house to themselves.'

'But who would want to do that, apart from Mountjoy?' she cried.

'Whoever it is, they did their homework,' KT replied. 'They knew your date of birth, and that you were a member of The Master's Masque – they even knew the code for your alarm system, so they didn't have to go to the trouble of breaking in. Christ knows what else they know about you.'

'Thanks, that makes me feel much better. What am I going to do?'

'I'll do a little detective work,' he said. 'It's probably just some crank with a grudge. My guess is they've made their point, so they won't bother you again.'

'All the same, I'd feel much better if you could stay with me tonight.' Constance almost cringed when she realised how pathetic her plea for protection sounded.

'I have a better idea,' he replied. 'Why don't you stay at my place for a few days, just until I see if I can get to the bottom of this?'

'I'd like that,' she said eagerly. 'But what about Gina?'

'Don't you worry about Gina,' he assured her. 'She won't have any objections.'

The idea of living in a *ménage à trois* held a certain appeal for Constance, though she would have preferred to have her master all to herself. Even though she was given a guest bedroom across the hall, she expected to spend most of her nights in KT's bed. Gina was even more enthusiastic about the arrangement, mainly because it afforded her ample opportunity to indulge in sapphic pleasures. Constance soon realised she had presented the couple with an ideal opportunity to keep her as a plaything. As long as most of the playing was done with KT, she did not mind.

The following Sunday morning, S/M-FM broadcast a two-hour live S/M session from the mansion. In addition to KT, Marlo and another middle-aged master she had not previously met were present. Constance, as always, was the *Slave in the Hot Seat*. Masters were invited to call in and decide what punishments she should suffer at the hands of the three men in the room.

'I'm hot, naked and kneeling at the feet of my masters,' she breathed into the microphone at the beginning of the show. 'What we are doing tonight on S/M-FM is making a *Slave in the Hot Seat video*, with you – the listeners – directing proceedings. My masters will carry out your instructions and I will, of course, willingly submit to all. The master who calls in with the most creative humiliation for me to submit to will receive a copy of the video, so please, show me no mercy.'

She had only agreed to this latest innovation when KT explained that the faces of all participants in the sado-session would be concealed. He and the middle-aged master wore reflective shades and garish silver face-paint. Constance wore a red latex mask, with apertures for her eyes and mouth. Marlo would be spending his time behind the camcorder.

As expected, the listeners to S/M-FM responded eagerly to the challenge. Within twenty minutes Constance was in full bondage. She was doubled over, wearing nothing but her hood and matching high heels. Her wrists were manacled to the chrome spreader bar between her ankles, which kept her legs wide apart. Two thick ropes suspended from the rafter directly overhead were bound tightly around her breasts. Another pair was knotted round her thighs, ensuring she was in no danger of losing her balance.

KT had set a few simple rules to ensure the challenge ran smoothly. No master was allowed more than ten minutes on-air. All directions would have to follow a reasonable logic, so one caller could not demand that Constance be tied up, only for the next to order her untied again. Within these constraints, virtually anything was possible.

She had asked for no mercy, and none was offered. Her nipples and labia were clamped, then KT's riding crop was called into action. The caller decreed that she receive two dozen strokes on her backside. While she was being thrashed, she would lick the boots of her other master.

This punishment, which left her buttocks streaked crimson, was but a preliminary for the next caller. He instructed both masters to give her a good spanking, stopping only when her rear cheeks were almost hot enough to burn toast on. As they carried out the request, Constance was required to keep her listeners entertained with an explicit confession. She obligingly related what had happened to her in the biker bar as part of her initiation tests. Her narrative was interspersed with squeals of pain and the sound of two palms slapping her fleshy buttocks.

'Why don't you start by screwing her?' the next caller demanded.

Without hesitation, the middle-aged master unzipped his trousers and smacked his cock against Constance's inflamed bottom. As soon as it had swollen to full stiffness, he penetrated her from behind.

'Is he fucking you, slave?' the caller demanded excitedly.

'Yes, master,' she gasped.

'Tell me how it feels.'

'It feels... good, master... Ohhh, so good!'

'Do you have any candles close to hand, gentlemen?' the caller enquired.

KT confirmed that they had. When Constance heard what the man on the other end of the line wanted done to her next, she protested at the top of her voice.

'What's the matter, slave?' the harsh voice sneered. 'Did I not hear you say you wanted no mercy?'

Ignoring her continuing pleas, KT lit a fat white candle and tilted it over her. As the wax melted, it dripped down onto her buttocks, each scalding droplet eliciting a sadistically gratifying yelp of agony. Encouraged by the sound, the master behind her increased the ferocity of his thrusts into her hot sex.

'Oh yes, that's what I like to hear!' From the tone of the caller's voice, it was obvious that he was masturbating. He urged her masters to fuck her even harder. It was almost as if he could see the action unfolding in the room.

KT and the other man were only too happy to carry out his wishes. By the time the caller reached his breathless climax, Constance's buttocks were practically covered in blobs of solidified candle wax. For the benefit of the video recording, the master inside her withdrew as he reached his peak. He came enthusiastically over her back and buttocks, providing a spectacular finish to part one of the video.

'CB has now been untied and is crawling around naked on all fours,' KT informed the listeners shortly afterwards. 'What shall we subject her to next? Masters, the camera is still rolling and you are in the director's seat. Your slave is at your mercy, so don't keep her waiting.'

As she crawled in a circle the second master flicked the white waxen lumps from her buttocks with the tip of the riding crop. Within minutes another caller was suggesting it might be a good idea to tie her up again.

Constance stood on a chair, a rope wound tightly around her waist, securing her hands by her sides. Her ankles were roped to the arms of the chair and her breasts bound together by yet another rope. At the caller's request, KT took up a slimline whip and began energetically flailing her squashed breasts with the hard leather tongue.

Before the entertainment finally ended, a further five callers had contributed their sadistic suggestions. Her bottom received ten strokes of the cane, weights were added to the clamps on her nipples and labia and her breasts were subjected to the hot wax treatment. For the final indignity, KT masturbated over her left shoe, then removed it and held it up for her to lick clean. The eye of the camcorder lingered on the sight of her tongue poking through the slit of her mask, lapping up the cream from the shiny black leather.

All the guests remained at the mansion for the rest of the night. Constance was too tired and sore to muster up much enthusiasm for an orgy, but a few glasses of wine and a soothing cold cream lovingly applied to her bottom by Marlo soon changed her mind. In his bedroom, KT played back the video of her earlier torments. The light from the television screen flickered over the five naked bodies on the king-sized bed. With two cocks stuffed into her mouth, a third in her pussy, and Gina's mouth on her breasts, the star was far too busy to cast more than an occasional glance at her blue movie début.

Chapter Fourteen

Constance returned home on Sunday evening, even though KT was no closer to discovering the identity of her malicious intruder. Whoever it was, she resolved they would not be allowed to drive her from her own home.

Among the messages on her answering machine was a call from a Mistress Amber. She left a contact number and requested Constance to give her a call. She had to think for a few minutes, before remembering that this was the woman whose recent foray into politics she had sold herself to assist. Even with all the media attention, the dominatrix had garnered less than five hundred votes.

She waited until late that night before returning the call. She was as curious to discover how the woman had obtained her home telephone number as she was to learn the reason for the call.

'KT was good enough to give me your number,' the husky-voiced mistress explained. 'Don't worry, I haven't written it down anywhere, so the police won't chance across it if I'm raided again.'

'What is it you want?' Constance demanded.

'To thank you for what you did for my campaign,' she replied.

'It was my pleasure.'

'I'm sure. Now, it would be my pleasure to repay you. I have an idea you might just find exciting.'

Constance knew she might well be setting herself up for yet more trouble, but Mistress Amber's idea appealed strongly to the foolhardy nature that was coming ever-increasingly to the fore. Nevertheless, it still took several days to make up her mind to accept the dubious reward for campaign services rendered.

She took a taxi to the Bayswater address and looked around nervously as she descended the steps to the basement apartment. Her recent unpleasant experiences made a certain degree of paranoia seem almost prudent.

A tall and slender woman answered the door. Constance was surprised to see that she was in her mid-twenties and exceptionally attractive, not at all the hard-faced, middle-aged madam she had been expecting. However, she was dressed for the role, in vertigo-inducing spike-heeled shoes, shiny black PVC stockings and a tiny matching dress that scarcely covered her hips and left an abundance of lightly tanned cleavage on display. She smiled at Constance's disguise of raincoat and headscarf.

'I'm glad you didn't change your mind about coming,' she breathed, escorting her into a small room.

'I almost did,' Constance replied, surveying the small pile of pornographic magazines spread out on the coffee table. 'Is this the waiting room?'

Amber laughed. 'Something like that. The client isn't due for at least half an hour, so you have time for a drink before you get changed.'

'Changed?'

'Into your working clothes,' she explained. 'This gentleman has a fondness for uniforms. He's one of my regulars – almost an old friend, at this stage. I wouldn't have invited you along otherwise.'

'Do you always have a partner when you're with him?' asked Constance.

'To tell you the truth, you're a special surprise,' Amber replied, handing her a glass of red wine. 'Like you, this man stuck his neck out to help me with my election campaign. I thought it would be a nice idea to reward you both at the same time. If you're having second thoughts about going through with this though, I won't be offended.'

'Actually, now I'm here, I'm rather looking forward to it,' Constance replied. 'Tell me more about this client of yours. Is he kinky?'

By the time the doorbell rang, half an hour later, both women had changed into uniform. Amber's crisp white nurse's outfit scarcely covered her hips, leaving several inches of lightly tanned thigh visible above the tops of her pale silk stockings. Constance's uniform consisted of her high heeled shoes and a similarly skimpy white dress.

Amber hurried to answer the door, leaving her alone in the playroom at the rear of the apartment. The furniture and fittings, the centrepiece of which was a double bed draped with a black rubber sheet, would have done the dungeons of The Master's Masque proud. Stroking the handle of one of the whips on the rack by the bed, Constance shuddered with anticipation. Amber had told her little about Mr W, but enough to make her confident she was going to enjoy making his acquaintance.

She was growing impatient by the time the door of the playroom finally opened again. Amber entered, followed by a heavily built man in his mid-fifties, wearing large gold-rimmed spectacles and a painfully obvious dark brown toupée. At the sight of Constance perched seductively on the black leather chair by the bed, he stopped as though he had run into a wall.

'I did tell you to expect something special,' Amber said, smiling at his gawking expression.

'Hello, master,' Constance greeted, her smile as inviting as her pose.

'Hello indeed,' he breathed, unable to believe his eyes.

'This is my friend, Connie,' Amber said, helping him out of his jacket. 'I hope you don't mind my inviting her to join us.'

'Oh, I think I shall be just about able to tolerate her presence,' he replied.

While Amber unhurriedly removed the client's clothes, arousing him with hints of the pleasures he was soon to experience, Constance remained in the chair, her legs seductively crossed. The man did not take his eyes off her for even an instant, and she in turn kept her gaze and smile unwaveringly fixed on him.

'Mm, now that's what I like to see,' Amber purred as she tugged his shorts down over his hips to reveal his swollen cock rearing against his hairy belly.

Constance licked her lips and murmured her agreement.

The man approached the bed and lay back like a king in repose, his eyes still feasting on Constance. Amber knelt beside him, gently stroking his belly with one hand and his cock with the other.

'Your friend doesn't say much,' he grunted.

'Connie is somewhat new to all this,' she answered. 'She's just a little shy.'

'Little prick-teaser, more like,' he retorted. 'She looks the kind of girl who prefers to give orders, rather than take them.'

'Oh no, master,' Constance protested. 'I know my place, I assure you.'

'In that case, you should know not to speak out of

185

turn,' he snapped. 'I think you need to be reminded in no uncertain terms of who's the boss here. Bring me a whip, at once.'

Amber had already warned her that her client would be eager to break in the 'new girl' and Constance was delighted that she was being proved correct. She already knew which one the master would want, but purposely lingered over the selection until he barked at her to hurry up.

Returning to the bed, she handed him the whip that Amber had previously advised her was his favourite. The handle, crafted from sterling silver and intricately embossed, resembled that of a ceremonial dagger. Instead of a lethal blade sprouting from the hilt, there were a dozen strands of hard black leather, woven into a single long devil tongue. Just touching it caused Constance to shudder with anticipation.

'You won't be the first young lady to be put in her place by this beauty,' the master told her, touching the cold steel of the handle to her lips. 'Handcuffs and ropes, if you please, Amber.'

Like a perfect servant, the other woman fetched the required items. Constance could not conceal her surprise when the master then commanded her to handcuff him to the head of the bed. In any previous bondage games it was always she who had been tied up. However, it was not her place to tell the customer what was best for him.

After he had been fitted with the handcuffs, he ordered Constance to crouch above him, as if about to lower herself onto his cock. Obeying his instructions, Amber unzipped her companion's dress halfway to her navel. Constance's breasts spilled forth, her rock-hard nipples brushing the master's hairy chest. It was clear that, though he was handcuffed, he had no intention of taking the submissive role. Instead, he was going to use Amber as a surrogate mistress.

Amber fitted Constance with a spiked black leather collar. Dangling from the back of this was a red elastic rope, with a set of steel clamps on the end. She produced another pair of stretchable ropes with clamps on either end. The ropes were first attached to Constance's nipples, then those of the master, who grunted excitedly.

'Get her arse bare for the whip,' he panted.

Quarter-moons of pale flesh were already visible below the hem of Constance's rubber dress. Amber tugged it up further, leaving her cheeks completely bare. She then drew the elastic rope dangling from Constance's collar into the cleft of her buttocks and fitted the clamps to her pussy. The tug on Constance's labia was more painful than she cared for, but she did not wish to spoil the fun by being a cry-baby.

In the large oval-shaped ceiling mirror directly above the bed, the master had a perfect view of her rear end. For starters, he decreed that she should receive twenty lashes. Amber applied the punishment zealously, having been warned that she would receive twice the amount herself, if the master thought that she was sparing her friend. Each crack of the whip on her buttocks was accompanied by a loud yelp from Constance.

'That's brought a pretty glow to her cheeks,' the master grinned afterwards. 'How was it for you, Connie?'

'Delightful, thank you, master,' she gasped.

'Delightful,' he repeated. 'Amber, this slave is obviously made of sterner stuff than I thought. Let's see how delightful she finds three dozen strokes of the cane.'

'Master, show some mercy!' Constance shrieked.

'You don't mean that,' he smiled, raising his hips and

thrusting upwards.

His cock-tip brushed her slick labia and she adjusted her position as much as her bondage permitted, to facilitate his entry. Her eyes were on Amber, who was thoughtfully inspecting the arsenal on the whip rack. With a loud grunt, the man buried almost the full length of his shaft between her thighs.

'Oh yes, master,' she moaned, the ropes gouging her thighs as she attempted to push downwards.

The weapon Amber took from the rack was a traditional cane only in shape. It was a quarter of an inch thick and made of hard black rubber. As Amber took up position behind her, Constance bit her lower lip. The master withdrew his cock until only the crown remained between her pursed pussy lips. At the end of his next thrust, the cane cracked, the rubber bending like the tongue of a whip across her buttocks. A lusty cry burst from Constance's throat.

'Not so quiet now, is she, Amber?' He grinned. 'And I've changed my mind. I want her silent while I enjoy her. She needs to know her place. Every time she cries out she'll get another stroke added to the total. Starting now. So that's thirty-seven. I want you to count every stroke and thank me on the slave's behalf.'

Amber nodded at his direction, and Constance felt another hard stroke of the rubber cane across her buttocks.

'That's one, thank you, master,' Amber said softly.

Constance bit her lip to stop herself crying out. Mr W looked at her, apparently satisfied, and resumed his thrusting. He took it slowly, pulling almost out of her each time. Constance tightened her internal muscles in anticipation of Amber's next strike, increasing both his pleasure and her own by the way she gripped his thick erection.

'That's two, thank you, master,' Amber said as he withdrew.

Each time he pushed back in, sliding slowly against the oiled flesh of her sex, Amber struck Constance's buttocks with the rubber cane. She placed the cuts neatly, laddering them all the way up the exposed moons and then criss-crossing downwards. It hurt more than Constance could possibly have dreamt – but the pleasure was there, too, heating her sex as her backside was warmed. Each cut of the cane made her jump slightly, which in turn tugged on the red elastic ropes, sending tingling sensations through her nipples. Sensations that Mr W obviously felt in his own nipples, tethered to hers, judging from the look of satisfaction on his face. Or maybe it was the sight in the oval mirror, she thought, that pleased him so much – the sight of her striped behind.

The punishment went on and on, until Constance was sure that no part of her buttocks had escaped the cane. It had taken a great effort on her part to keep back her gasps of pain – and her cries of pleasure as his cock continued to thrust in that slow, measured pace – but finally she heard Amber intone, 'That's thirty-seven, thank you, master.'

At that precise instant she felt his cock throbbing deep inside her, sending jet after jet of creamy semen into her sex. Constance was amazed and impressed by his self-control – many men would have come long before then, but he'd obviously held himself back, extracting every ounce of pleasure before allowing himself to climax. She'd already come twice, her sex quivering helplessly round his cock, almost in time to his measured thrusts and the sharp crack of the cane on her flesh.

Before he departed, over an hour later, the client thanked both women for giving him the time of his life. Even though her bottom was throbbing and there were rope burns on her arms, legs and breasts, Constance could truthfully reply that it had been her pleasure.

'Nothing pleases me more than a satisfied customer,' Amber said as they relaxed together. 'You and I make a great team. Have you ever thought of going into business full-time?'

Constance laughed. 'When I whore, it's strictly for pleasure.'

Chapter Fifteen

'The *Slave in the Hot Seat* video is selling as fast as I can make copies,' KT said happily.

'I thought that was only going to be for our own pleasure,' Constance grumbled. 'If I'd known you were going to be selling copies by the cartload I'd never have agreed to be in it.'

'What's the problem?' he retorted. 'There's no way anybody could ever identify you from it. You should be proud of yourself. Want to hear some more good news?'

'You've found out who broke into my house?'

'I've found a distributor who wants to market the video nationwide, as well as overseas. This could turn out to be a seriously profitable enterprise.'

'I only did it for fun,' she protested. 'I have no wish to be a pornographic movie star.'

He cocked an eyebrow. 'It's not that long ago you were telling me you didn't want to be a porno-pirate radio star either.'

Constance sighed heavily. 'I think I'm taking quite enough risks as it is, don't you?'

'The video is risk-free,' KT reminded her. 'As are the audio tapes.'

'Audio tapes?'

'Extracts from hot nights on S/M-FM,' he explained. 'It's taken me until now to realise the goldmine potential of this little radio station of ours.'

'My voice will be on those tapes,' she pointed out. 'I could be recognised.'

'Not getting tired of living dangerously, are you?' he teased. 'Speaking of which, I hope you haven't forgotten next Friday night.'

'The S/M-FM party,' she said. 'I wouldn't miss it for the world. But I still think it's odd having a birthday party for a station that's only been six months on air.'

'Pirate radio is a precarious business,' he replied. 'We might not be around in another six months, so we should celebrate when we can. Anyway, it's as good an excuse as any for an orgy.'

'And what role have you found for your loyal slave?' asked Constance.

'One she will enjoy immensely,' he answered.

Visitors gained entry to The Master's Masque by uttering the password that had been broadcast on S/M-FM the previous weekend. Once inside the club they found a circle of scantily clad slaves at their service. Constance was dressed in stiletto-heeled knee-high black boots and a toga of transparent white silk, underneath which she was naked. Along with nine other similarly attired slaves she stood in the centre of the floor, with her legs wide apart and her hands on her head. Each of the women wore a studded collar and a gold medallion stamped with her identity number. They were tethered on long chains to a vertical wooden pole.

Barbara and Gina stood to either side of Constance, the latter looking rather less excited than the occasion demanded. Six chargehands – masters in low-peaked leather caps and black leather uniforms – were perched on nearby stools, whips gripped in their gloved fists. KT was in charge of Constance and Gina.

Each visitor was presented with a leaflet explaining the party rules for the evening. Any man who wished to take one of the slaves was required to approach her chargehand first. They could inspect the group freely, but touching or even speaking to the slaves during inspection was forbidden. To ensure that as many masters as possible could take their pleasure, each would be allowed a maximum of forty-five minutes with the slave of his choice.

Constance felt deliciously degraded as a stream of strange men stepped up to inspect her. Though her companions in bondage were far from unattractive, it was she who proved the most alluring. A bearded man in dark glasses and military uniform, wearing a riding crop instead of a sword in the scabbard on his right hip, looked her over as though she were a particularly enticing bargain in a shop window. Her nipples stiffened against the fabric of her toga and she smiled encouragingly. The man looked from her to Barbara, unable to decide which of the pair was the most tempting. While he continued to procrastinate, a shaven-headed Asian with the physique of a heavyweight boxer spoke to KT, indicating her as he did.

'Could I take number six?' It had taken him the length of a glance to decide that Constance was the one he wanted.

'Certainly,' KT replied, rising from his stool.

As KT unhooked her chain from the pole, the bearded man turned to him. 'Unchain number seven for me, if you don't mind.'

The Asian master took Constance's chain and led her to one of the private playrooms at the rear of the club. Her heart was pounding and her loins were already liquid with desire.

'Introductions first,' he smiled, unclipping the chain

from her collar. 'I am Assad. And you are...?'

'Just number six, master,' she replied.

'As you wish,' he said, dropping the chain and stepping back to admire her in the soft light. 'It's a shame we can't have more than forty-five minutes together, but we shall just have to make the most of it.' He traced a fingertip over her lips. 'My God, you are a beautiful woman.'

Constance smiled coyly. 'Thank you, master.'

'And so submissive, too.'

He pushed his finger gently into her mouth. As she sucked it as though it were a cock, he slipped the straps of her toga off her shoulders. The feather-light garment slid to the floor and she thrust her naked body urgently against him. His free hand glided down over her waist and around to the firm slope of her buttocks.

'Take me, master,' she breathed, the instant his finger was withdrawn from her mouth.

In response, he crushed his lips to hers. Welcoming his tongue, Constance wrapped one arm tightly around his neck, her other hand reaching for the bulge between his thighs. She unzipped his trousers and reached inside, her fingers finding a rock-hard and delightfully thick erection.

No sooner had their mouths parted than she was falling to her knees, hungry to taste this new master and impress him with her oral artistry. Whatever he might have planned for her beforehand, it was the slave who was now in control. Her fingers and tongue caressed the dusky-brown staff that reared majestically from his trousers, then she wrapped it in her mouth, moaning softly when the bulbous crown touched the back of her throat.

Lost to her magic, the master leant back against the

wall, savouring the sight and sensations of her mouth sliding up and down his pulsing length. As she greedily sucked him, like a woman who had not tasted her favourite delicacy in months, she unbuckled his belt and tugged his trousers down to his knees. She needed both hands to fully cup the swollen eggs in his smoothly shaven sac. When his cock was trembling on the brink of climax she reluctantly freed it from the warmth of her mouth and looked up at him, a lewd smile dancing on her full wet lips.

'Don't stop,' he panted.

She kissed his dark-haired thighs and licked his balls, before taking each in turn in her mouth, tickling it with the tip of her tongue and bathing it in warm saliva. She licked her way back up along his shaft, then once more swallowed the full length. A few moments later she was rewarded with a torrent of hot cream that gushed down her throat with such force she almost choked.

Her master still had over half an hour remaining with her, and not a minute was wasted. The narrow bed, like all those in the clubrooms, was fully equipped for bondage. Constance was slightly disappointed that Assad did not appear inclined to tie her up or use a whip on her, but the night was still young, and she was certain her bottom would be well reddened before it ended.

After she had helped him out of his clothes, they lay down on the purple rubber sheets and she went back to work on his cock with her tongue and fingers. As the thickly veined snake began to swell once more against her lips, she felt a hand between her thighs, two fingers probing the soaking furrow of her sex. He guided her gently into the sixty-nine position, tasted her nectar on his fingers, then plunged his tongue into the pink flesh directly over his face.

One minute of his tongue teasing her swollen clitoris was enough to bring Constance to orgasm. She squealed at the top of her voice, ecstatic shudders rocking her entire body. The master continued to feast, bathing his face in her abundant juices. A louder cry burst from her lungs as he inserted a lubricated finger in her tight rear orifice.

A second breathtaking orgasm later, he obviously decided to give his tongue a rest and his cock a hot treat. Constance slithered down his body, her sex leaving a dewy trail on his dark skin. With her back turned to him she gripped his saliva-sheened cock in her fists and lowered herself onto it, with a long gasp of genuine pleasure. He thrust upwards, burying himself to the hilt in her tight wet tunnel.

She rode him aggressively, wildly tossing her head and kneading her breasts with both hands, her every fibre aflame with lust. In the mirror on the opposite wall the full whorish spectacle was reflected. The sight of the thick brown cock pistoning between her thighs and coated with her juices stoked her excitement to fever pitch.

'Ohhh... yes!' she squealed, seeing her master reach for a slender cane on the wall above the bed.

She paused, tensing with delicious anticipation. The cane sliced the air and scored a line of fire across the centre of both buttocks.

'Faster, slave!' he barked as she yelped.

Constance began riding him with renewed vigour, every deep thrust sending ripples of pleasure through her body. The cane struck her buttocks at regular intervals, the acid sting of each stroke almost too erotic to bear.

'Work, slave!' the master barked. 'Make me come!

Faster! Faster!'

By the time his semen erupted into her, Constance was breathless and glistening with perspiration. She cried out hoarsely in the throes of another wonderful orgasm. She slumped in an ecstatic stupor against the foot of the bed. The cane fell from Assad's grasp, and he too slumped in the afterglow. Constance only raised her head again when she felt his flaccid cock slip from her satiated sex.

Shortly afterwards, smelling of sex and still somewhat breathless, she was returned to the club and once again chained to the pole. The scarlet scorch-marks of the cane were clearly visible through the thin fabric of her toga, making her all the more irresistible to the men who gathered round to inspect her. In her absence, their number seemed to have doubled. Even if there had been forty slaves to choose from, all would have been kept fully occupied.

It was not long before she was being unchained again and led back to the playroom. Her second master – a bespectacled and slightly sinister-looking silver-haired figure in a skin of glossy black rubber – took full advantage of the facilities on offer, chaining her to the bed, face down, as soon as he had stripped her. After she had assured him he was free to use her as he pleased, there were no further questions. He unzipped the front of his one-piece suit and his stiff cock sprang free. Though it was nothing spectacular, Constance still eyed it with the relish of a nymphomaniac.

The master fitted her with a black leather face harness, secured at the back of her head with three thick straps. The device was equipped with a red rubber ball gag and enormous blindfold goggles. He then pinched a set of steel clamps to her nipples. Using the attached leather thongs as reins, he climbed between her legs and penetrated her roughly from behind. With each thrust of his cock he tugged on the thongs. All Constance could do in response was bite down on her gag and pray she would not have to endure this particular form of sadism for the full forty-five minutes.

Unfortunately for her tortured teats, the master was in no hurry to bring his pleasure to an end. The first time he was near the point of climax he withdrew and selected a broad leather tawse from the selection of punishment tools.

'Best keep your arse good and hot, eh, slave?' he mused.

Constance could only shake her head in reply, though she was not at all as terrified as she appeared at the prospect of a whacking. Leather smacked quivering flesh, and all the helpless slave could do was whimper. When every inch of her buttocks had been toasted, the master climbed onto the bed again and took the reins of her nipple clamps as he thrust his cock back into her.

Before the party ended in the early hours of the morning, a further seven masters had taken their pleasure with Constance. Her backside was raw from repeated punishments and the rest of her body throbbed pleasantly. All ten exhausted slaves agreed with their masters that the party had been an unqualified success.

Chapter Sixteen

Constance lit a cigarette as she waited for the traffic lights to turn green. She was not in a good mood. During the afternoon somebody had vandalised her precious Porsche by drawing a sharp object over the paintwork on both sides. It was not just the expense of a respray that was making her fume, but the certainty that the culprit was the same person who had broken into her home several weeks previously. Try as she might, she could think of nobody who hated her enough to carry out such a vindictive campaign.

A horn tooted to her left and she looked around. When she saw the driver behind the wheel of the maroon Jaguar, her look of annoyance turned to one of shock. Jonathan Covington was the last person she had expected to see.

He raised his right hand in a small wave. Constance was too shocked to return the greeting. The lights flashed amber and the Jaguar was gone, leaving her smiling inanely at his after-image. An angry honk from the car behind brought her to her senses.

Her anger forgotten, she set off in pursuit of the Jaguar. No speed limits were broken as Covington led her through the late rush-hour streets, taking an occasional glance in his rear-view mirror to confirm that she was still behind. To her dismay, she lost him at another set of traffic lights. She had almost given up hope of finding him again when, some minutes later, she spotted the Jaguar parked in front of the Royal Arch hotel.

She parked her Porsche nearby and walked back to the opulent hotel. What better place to renew their relationship? Her heart hammered excitedly.

Covington was not waiting for her in the lobby, nor did she find him in either the bar or the restaurant. When she politely enquired at reception, she was informed that he was not a guest in the hotel. She loitered for a while, then, beginning to feel foolish, decided she was wasting her time. If he had wanted her to find him he would not have made it so difficult.

Re-emerging from the hotel she was startled to see him sitting in his car, as though waiting for her. In her hurry to reach him she almost lost her footing on the steps. He threw her a glance, the ghost of a smile, then the Jaguar rocketed away from the kerb, leaving her standing in open-mouthed bewilderment.

The following afternoon a courier delivered a gift to her. A note attached to the gold-wrapped package, hand-inked in red, invited her to 'plug in, enjoy, and wait'. Constance was glad she was alone in her office when she unwrapped it.

Stamped on the box was the brand name *Lady Driver*. The device contained within resembled a stubby pink latex dildo, with a small ball sprouting on a stalk from the crown. A cable and small black plug attachment ran from the other end. Constance had to read the accompanying instruction leaflet carefully before she knew exactly what the thing was.

When she left the boutique, late that evening, she was not surprised to see the maroon Jaguar parked across the street. Covington looked at her until he was certain she recognised him, then turned his head away. She was about to run across to him when the mobile telephone in her purse shrilled. As she reached for it she saw him raise his own mobile to his ear.

'Ready to take a driving test, slave?' he asked.

Constance glanced around before replying in a near whisper. 'I shall be happy to do whatever you want, master.'

'That's what I had hoped you'd say. Are you ready to do absolutely anything I tell you, without question?'

'Yes.' Her body was already coming alive with familiar sensations.

'Get into your car and rig up your toy,' he told her. 'Let me know when you're done.'

Installing the *Lady Driver* simply involved plugging it into the cigarette lighter of the Porsche. As soon as she was finished she informed Covington.

'I don't think so,' he replied enigmatically. 'It's not much good just plugging in one end, now is it?'

'Master?'

'You know what to do.'

'But not here,' she pleaded. 'Somebody will see me.'

'Nobody need see a thing, as long as you're discreet,' he answered. 'Now come on, be a good slave and do as your master says. Otherwise...'

He left the threat unspoken. Constance took a deep breath, looked furtively around, then raised her hips off the car seat and slipped her right hand under her short blue skirt. The minute it took to pull her black lace panties down over her dark-stockinged legs felt more like an hour. Slipping the miniature dildo between her thighs and easing it between the wet lips of her hungry sex was far easier.

'You're now ready for your driving test,' the master informed her. 'Follow me.'

The instant Constance switched on the engine of her

Porsche the plugged-in sex device came to life, with a barely audible hum. She squealed as she felt the shaft undulate within her, the latex ball attachment quivering like the tongue of a devoted lover.

'If you think that feels good, wait till we start driving,' said Covington.

Constance only had to press her foot to the accelerator pedal to discover exactly what he meant. As the speed of the car's powerful engine increased, so too did the simultaneous tickle of the *Lady Driver*.

'I can't... can't drive... like... this...!' Constance gasped as the love-ball played a nerve-tingling rhythm on her clitoris.

'Of course you can,' he goaded. 'There's nothing a good slave can't do for her master. Or am I wrong about you?'

No reply was necessary. He continued to talk, becoming ever more explicit, as the Jaguar led the Porsche through the late evening traffic, making it almost impossible for her to concentrate on her driving. On several occasions she almost collided with his rear bumper. Failing even to notice a zebra crossing, she came within inches of knocking down an elderly lady. All the while Covington's blue tones caressed her ears, while the apparatus between her thighs became increasingly frenzied. Though the cable was not too noticeable and the activity beneath her skirt would not be apparent to a passer-by, the flushed look on Constance's face would certainly have given cause for wonder.

For ten minutes of slow, exquisitely tortuous driving, she willed herself to tread carefully on the accelerator pedal in order to retain a degree of control over the *Lady Driver*. Finally they reached a set of traffic lights. She was glad, for once, that they were red. She drew up behind him, bumper to bumper.

'Master, I... I can't go on... like this,' she panted into the mouthpiece of her mobile. 'I'll have an... accident!'

She saw his face reflected in his wing mirror, a wicked smile upon his lips.

'Come before the lights change,' he told her. 'You must be close.' He licked his lips. 'That's my tongue inside you, slave, and I want you to come now. I demand it.'

Her hands were white-knuckled and damp with perspiration, one gripping the steering wheel, the other her phone. The lights could change at any instant. Her master was right. She was tantalisingly close to the point of no return. She slammed her foot down on the accelerator. The device inside her responded with a ferocity that took her breath away. Just as the lights turned amber she climaxed. The pleasure was so intense she slumped against the steering wheel with a strangled cry of pleasure. For all the world she appeared to be in the throes of a cardiac arrest.

The insistent honking of several car horns to her rear brought her briskly back from her state of climactic rapture. She reached for the gearstick and the Porsche shot forward. Covington's Jaguar had already vanished.

'Congratulations, slave, you've passed part one of your driving test,' his disembodied voice teased just before the phone crackled and went dead.

Constance dropped her mobile onto the passenger seat, fumbled for the cable of the lewd toy, and with trembling fingers pulled it from between her thighs. She had had quite enough humiliation and danger for one evening.

Four days passed before he contacted her again. At five a.m. on Monday she was rudely woken by the bedside telephone.

'Sorry for waking you up at such an unearthly hour,' he began, in a tone that could not have contained less remorse.

'That's okay,' she whispered, slowly gathering her wits.

'I knew you'd understand. Are you alone?'

'Yes. But I suspect you already know that.'

'You might be right. Now get down to the garage and into your car, on the double. There's no need to get dressed.'

'But—'

'Obey, don't argue!' he snapped. 'Otherwise, I may have to slam the brakes on this relationship.'

A few minutes later, wearing only a pair of fluffy pink slippers, Constance entered the garage through the connecting door with the kitchen and switched on the light. Her master's voice on the cordless phone ordered her to open the main door. She pressed a button on the remote control box. As the automatic door was raised light flooded the garage, bathing her naked form and causing her to shade her sleepy eyes against the harsh brightness.

'Get into the car and get ready to play,' the instructions continued.

Obediently she relaxed on the driving seat, removed the *Lady Driver* from its hiding place beneath it, and fed it into her eagerly moist pussy. She turned the ignition key and the powerful engine throbbed into life. The slamming of a car door was followed by the thump of heavy boots on concrete. The shape of her master appeared in the garage doorway, the bright headlights from beyond throwing his silhouette into ominous black shadow. He had a whip slung over one shoulder, and the mobile phone in his free hand.

'Oh, master, I want you!' Constance panted into her receiver.

The whip whistled through the air and cracked like a gunshot on the garage floor.

'Spread yourself across the seats,' he commanded her. 'Face down, hands behind your neck. Good girl. Now pull in your knees and lift that sexy arse up nice and high. Come on, you can do better than that. I know you're not shy. That's perfect. Stay in that exact position. Move a muscle and you'll feel my whip. Don't look round. You'll know soon enough what I intend doing with you.'

Constance heard the clink of handcuffs as he leant into the car. The cold steel bands snapped shut around her wrists. He used his belt to bind her ankles together, then ordered her to open her mouth. When the phallic black handle of the whip was pushed between her lips she sucked it as keenly as if it were the genuine article. Meanwhile, an insistent finger probed her anus, massaging her sphincter into a suitably relaxed state. She was convinced he intended to bugger her and braced herself accordingly. Instead, he took the lubricated whip handle from her mouth and pushed it slowly into her tight rear hole. When her bottom was completely plugged and she was groaning in protest, he wound the tongue of the whip around her face, drawing it like a bit between her teeth. He knotted it at the back of her head, then stepped back to admire his handiwork.

'As you're in no position to drive, I shall just have to do it for you,' he said, moving his right foot towards the accelerator pedal. 'Is that okay with you, slave?'

A tortured groan and an uncertain nod were the only responses she could make.

Covington bore down on the pedal and the *Lady Driver*

leapt straight into sixth gear. Constance almost bit through the unyielding leather of the whip. A slap stung her buttocks and left behind a pink blotch. The roar of the sports car's tortured engine reverberated off the garage walls, while the rude rubber ball went berserk on her clitoris. While her master pumped the accelerator hard enough to drive her almost out of her mind with delight, he slapped her buttocks with equal intensity.

By the time he finally raised his foot again, Constance was coated in perspiration and breathless from the force of rapid-fire orgasms. The garage was filled with an acrid cloud of exhaust fumes.

'Shall I continue?' he demanded.

She shook her head. If the *Lady Driver* didn't take the last of her breath away, the carbon monoxide surely would.

'Perhaps you'd like a turn in my car,' he said, switching off the engine.

He untied her ankles, and then withdrew the glistening sex toy from her pussy. After he had helped her out of the car he ordered her to follow him. With one end of the whip between her teeth and the other between her buttocks, she staggered towards the Jaguar, tears streaming down her cheeks. The early morning air was more refreshing than any cold shower.

A few moments later she was face down over the bonnet of the Jaguar with her breasts squashed against the chilled metal. Without ceremony Covington pushed her legs apart and penetrated her from behind, the deep thrust of his cock rapidly reviving her erotic spirits.

He screwed her as aggressively as he had revved the engine of her car, his strong hands kneading her sore buttocks. As soon as he had taken his pleasure he zipped his trousers up and then unlocked her handcuffs. Without a parting word he climbed into his Jaguar. A moment later he was gone, leaving Constance standing naked in the driveway with the whip still wrapped around her and plugging her bottom. She felt outraged by the manner in which he had so casually used and abused her, and then taken his leave. Constance was starting to think she might just have found her ideal man.

Chapter Seventeen

Dear Constance,

You are a slut of the highest order, as you have so admirably proved on numerous occasions. Tomorrow afternoon you will do so again. What I'm about to suggest may seem outrageous, but I'm sure you won't let me down.

The remainder of the typewritten page contained detailed instructions for what seemed either a foolhardy dare or a particularly perverse test. There was no signature, or any clue to the identity of the sender, but Constance presumed it was Jonathan Covington. She had not heard from him for over a week and such a letter would have been totally in character. Obeying his instructions would take all the nerve she could muster and would mean being away from the boutique for the afternoon. Nevertheless, like the perfect slave that she was, she would not misplace his trust in her wanton ways.

The following afternoon the red Porsche purred to a halt in the parking lot of the motorway café named in the letter. Even though the sky was grey Constance donned her sunglasses as she stepped from the car, her faded black denim mini-skirt leaving plenty of fishnet-stockinged thigh visible. Lighting a cigarette, she pulled her clinging white cotton vest tighter over her bare breasts. Never had she felt more totally the whore. She looked around, but there was no sign of Covington. If he was watching from a safe distance, she hoped he was impressed.

The letter from her master had mentioned that this particular café was a favourite with long distance lorry drivers, and there were several dozen huge vehicles in the car park. Constance leant against her car, feeling as vulnerable as if she were wearing nothing. The honk of a horn to her left was followed by a wolf-whistle from another direction. She responded with a smile that made her appear completely at ease.

She had to wait longer than she had expected before somebody finally dared to approach her. The trucker that descended from his cab and waddled towards her was almost a caricature of the breed – bearded, bald and pot-bellied. Constance smiled at him as though he were a Hollywood idol, just to make sure he did not change his mind.

'Hiya love,' he greeted her in a coarse accent.

'Hi,' she beamed back, roaming over him with her eyes as she would a bronzed Adonis.

'Er... nice weather for it,' he grunted.

Her smile remained in place. 'For what, exactly?'

'For, uh, going about without much on,' he answered. 'Fancy a coffee?'

'I didn't come all this way for coffee,' Constance replied, taking a step towards him. 'That's a nice truck you have there. I wouldn't mind having a look inside.'

The trucker frowned. 'Listen, you're a fine looking lass an' all, but I don't pay for it.'

'Who's asking you to pay for it?' she responded sweetly.

With an alluring pucker of her scarlet lips, she began strutting in the direction of his truck. He watched her uncertainly for a few seconds, but there was never any question of him being able to resist her brazen invitation.

As she climbed up into the cab she made sure he had a good look up her skirt. With the scent of sex in her nostrils and her juices flowing freely, she was already forgetting that she had not come here entirely of her own free will. The whore had taken over and she was ready to savour her latest escapade.

The trucker bundled her into the rear of the cab, where they would be hidden from prying eyes by a thin curtain. Seconds later one calloused hand was rummaging roughly beneath her skirt while the fingers of the other fumbled with the zipper of his jeans. Constance lay back on the mat, her head resting on a rolled up sleeping bag, and surrendered to his coarse frenzy. He slobbered against her sweetly perfumed throat, and his breath and beard smelled of fried food. Her panties were dragged off in the same instant as his throbbing cock appeared in his fist.

'Christ, who are you?' he grunted as he lowered his bulk onto her, tugging her skirt up over her hips.

'Never mind – just make the most of me while you can,' she whispered, and squirmed under his crude treatment. She rolled her top up and her luscious breasts sprang free beneath his bulging eyes.

'Oh, I'll make the most of you all right!' he grunted, fumbling his fat tool into position. 'I'll fuck your lovely arse clean off you.'

'Oh *yesss*,' she sighed as he bucked and penetrated her with one aggressive thrust.

She spent over an hour in the back of the truck – much longer than she had intended. During that time she and the rampant trucker exchanged little in the way of conversation. He enacted many of his pent-up fantasies on her – fantasies accumulated over years of being on the road alone – correctly assuming that by practically throwing herself at him she had given him licence to use her as he pleased. He did not tell her his name, and neither did she ask.

When finally sated he pulled up his jeans and gruffly announced that it was time to get back on the road. Constance used her panties to wipe a trickle of semen from her chin before slipping them back on. She smoothed her skirt over her legs, straightened her straining vest, then left him with a satisfied smile and a sincere, 'Thank you.'

She adjourned to her Porsche and smoked a cigarette as she watched the other trucks in the car park. Round one had been an unqualified success, but her mission would not be accomplished until her master called her on her mobile phone. How would he know if she was complying with his wishes, unless he was watching her? She was about to take a walk around the car park to see if she could spot him, when her attention was grabbed by a young blond bearded man emerging from the café. He was wearing faded jeans, and a white T-shirt hugged his muscular torso.

This was too good an opportunity to pass up on, she thought. Constance stubbed out her cigarette, waited until he got closer, then stepped out of the car. One flash of her irresistibly seductive smile was all that was needed to stop him in mid-stride.

'Hi,' she purred. 'Lovely day, isn't it?'

'Lovely indeed,' he agreed, wandering over her with his eyes.

'I hope you're not in too much of a hurry.'

'Oh – why's that?'

She stepped closer, pulling her vest tighter over her bullet-hard nipples. 'I know this might sound a bit strange, but I'd really love to take a look at your truck I have a thing for artics, you might say.'

'I drive a van,' he replied. 'That white one over there. Here, are you selling something?'

'I'm giving it away for free.' Her eyes fell to the telltale bulge in his jeans. 'I can tell you're interested already.'

'This is some kind of wind-up, right?' He looked round. 'Where are the cameras?'

Constance laughed. 'Talk about looking a gift-horse in the mouth. Look, if you must know, I'm a bored housewife who gets a thrill out of getting off with strange men at service stations. But if you have better things to do I won't take up any more of your time.'

The stranger shook his head. 'Jesus, this is the kind of thing you read about in magazines.'

'But you never thought it happened in real life,' she added. 'I don't really want to stand out here chatting all day. Are we going to your van, or do I have to find myself a big, horny trucker?'

There was scarcely enough room for them both among the crates of industrial detergent in the back of the van. Any activity of a horizontal nature was definitely out of the question. Undeterred, Constance dropped to her knees and hurriedly unbuckled the delivery driver's belt.

'Mm, I just knew this was going to be a beauty!' she purred as his tumescent tool bucked against her lips.

Two hours and a further three men later, she was beginning to wonder whether her master would ever call. She was becoming uncomfortable with loitering in the car park and offering herself to complete strangers, with no more compunction than if she were asking them for the time of day. Her chief worry was that she might eventually get arrested.

She returned to her car with her panties balled up in her fist, leaving yet another trucker to hit the motorway with a smile on his face. While she had been busy with him a brown envelope had been placed on the windscreen of her Porsche. Inside was another typewritten and unsigned note.

Well done, Constance. Once again you have shown yourself to be a complete and utter slut. I'm waiting for you in the café.

Before going in she smoked another cigarette. When she was finished she repainted her lips, and then went forth to meet her master.

Instead of Jonathan Covington waiting for her, she found Gina. The red-haired woman was sitting alone at a table, sipping a cup of coffee. She looked up and smiled as Constance approached.

'What are you doing here?' Constance demanded quietly, taking the seat opposite her.

'Who were you expecting?'

'Jonathan Covington, I suppose.'

'Or KT, perhaps?'

She shrugged. 'Maybe. Certainly not you. Have you been here long?'

Gina smiled. 'All afternoon. I bet you had a great time servicing all those big, sweaty truckers. There's nothing you won't do for your master, is there?'

'I don't understand,' said Constance with a frown.

Gina leant closer. 'Then I'd better explain. It wasn't any master that sent you here to make a slut of yourself today. It was me. It was also me who vandalised your house and scratched your precious car.'

213

Constance's face drained of all colour. For a few moments she stared, speechless, while the woman across from her smirked.

'Why?' she finally demanded.

'Jealousy, I'm afraid,' Gina replied casually. 'You were trying to take something that was mine – KT. I didn't mind sharing, but you, the perfect boot-licking, cock-sucking slave, wanted him all for yourself. I demeaned myself as best I could to compete with you. I even begged him to stop seeing you, but he's used to getting whatever he wants and using women as he sees fit. Well, I've just torn up my slave contract and packed my bags, so you're welcome to crawl to his mansion and grovel to your heart's content. I hope you'll be very happy together – until he falls for a new plaything.'

'You two-faced bitch!' Constance was struggling to keep her voice down. 'You'll pay for what you did to me!'

'I think not,' Gina said. 'You see, I have enough evidence of S/M-FM and it's associated schemes to drop you and KT in deep shit. If I have to use it, I won't hesitate, believe me. He's already seen sense and agreed to a suitable pay-off. I've had my fun with you, so now we're just about quits. Aren't we?'

Chapter Eighteen

Much as she loathed having to capitulate to blackmail once again, Constance took consolation from the fact that her vengeful enemy was at least out of the way. KT assured her there was no danger of his ex-slave exacting future retribution. Within a week of their parting company, Gina had taken her money and left to start a new life in New Zealand, where her sister lived.

Not too long before, Constance would have unhesitatingly thrown herself at KT's feet and begged him to take her as his new slave. Now she was relieved that he did not present her with a slave contract. If she was going to enter into a full-time relationship, the only man she could envisage as her master was Jonathan Covington.

Another week passed before he contacted her again. Upon hearing his voice on the telephone, she could not have been happier had she won the lottery.

'And how are you, slave?' he enquired pleasantly. 'Still having fun with your *Lady Driver*?'

'To be honest, master, I haven't used it since,' Constance replied truthfully. 'I've been waiting to hear from you. I was beginning to think you'd forgotten about me.'

'I'm a very busy man,' he answered. 'Anyway, I'm sure you haven't been living the life of a nun in my absence.'

'I can't stop thinking about you. I have to see you

again.'

'You beg so beautifully,' he said. 'Continue.'

Constance took a deep breath. 'Master, I can hardly find the words to tell you how much I need you. More than anything in the world, I want to be your slave. I'll do absolutely anything you command. Give me a chance to prove myself worthy of you. Please!'

'Playing kinky games is one thing,' he said. 'But I'm not convinced you're ready to surrender yourself completely to the will of a master.'

'I'm old enough to decide for myself what I'm ready for.'

'Watch your mouth,' he snapped. 'I won't stand for impertinence from a slut like you. Do you understand?'

'Yes, master,' she replied quietly. 'I'm sorry.'

'Save your apologies,' he said icily. 'I shall have the cane waiting for you this very evening.'

'This evening?'

'That's right. I want you to meet me in the King Charles hotel at nine. Suite twelve-twenty. Wear something elegant, with no underwear. Don't be late.'

Constance was about to protest that she had already arranged to have dinner with a business associate this evening, but Covington had already hung up. She could not call him back – not that he would be likely to sympathise with her situation anyway. He already acted as though he owned her, which in a sense, he did. She would just have to cancel her prior arrangements.

At five to nine she swanned through the doors of the upmarket hotel, looking suitably elegant in an ankle-length dress of rich purple velvet, cut low at the back and accompanied by high heels and a pearl necklace. Her hair was tied up in an elaborate bun. She was conscious of heads turning as she made her way to the lift. She examined her make-up in the lift mirror as she rode up to the twelfth floor, and decided she looked stunning. Even Covington could not fail to be impressed.

He answered her knock almost immediately, looking as suave as ever in a black evening suit and bow-tie. His eyes ravished her as he ushered her into the room. He was not alone. Seated on the couch, sipping a glass of white wine, was a middle-aged man with swept-back silver hair and a neatly groomed moustache. He was dressed in the same formal wear as Covington.

'My word, Jonathan, you did not exaggerate the attractions of this one,' he smiled, rising to greet Constance.

Covington's hand caressed her bottom, confirming that she had obeyed his wishes regarding underwear.

'Meet Sir Terence DeMille,' he said. 'Owner of, among many other enterprises, the Playground resort.'

'Uh... I'm pleased to meet you, Sir Terence,' Constance blurted, shaking the proffered hand.

As she glanced around the room she noticed, laid out on the coffee table, a cane, a leather strap, a tawse, and a cat o'nine tails. While she exchanged pleasantries with Sir Terence, Covington casually unzipped her dress at the back and slid it down off her milky shoulders. It gathered around her ankles and she stood blushing before the man she had just met, wearing nothing but high heels and white silk hold-up stockings.

'A splendid young woman indeed,' Sir Terence marvelled, absorbing every detail of her nakedness. 'Sit down, my dear, make yourself comfortable. There are some matters of a business nature we would like to discuss with you.'

Constance sat opposite the two men and crossed her

legs, never more uncomfortable with her nudity. The strange formality of the occasion was not at all what she had been expecting. Covington poured her a drink. Sir Terence waited until they were all seated before speaking again.

'This meeting was my idea, Constance. I have a proposition to put to you that will be of benefit to us both. How would you feel about coming to work for me?'

She almost spilt her drink. 'Work for you, Sir Terence?'

He nodded. 'I have done a great deal of background research on you. After you left college you spent three successful years with a prestigious London fashion house. From there you went on to single-handedly build your own business. At the age of twenty-nine, you've achieved more than many people do in a lifetime. Now, you're ready for a fresh challenge. Am I right so far?'

'Well… yes.'

'How would you feel about working full time at the Playground?'

Constance was speechless. She looked at the two men in turn, unable to believe her ears.

'Well?' Covington prompted.

'I don't know what to say,' she blurted. 'I mean, this was the last thing I was expecting.'

'Allow me to explain,' said Sir Terence. 'I started the Playground five years ago, as an exclusive retreat where men could live out their sexual fantasies with attractive women who enjoyed being dominated. It was originally little more than a club for myself and a few friends and trusted acquaintances. I never dreamt it would take off the way it has. Our membership now comprises over two hundred and fifty masters from all over the world and at least three hundred slaves. It has become a business in its own right. Your friend, Kenton, is one of the people who has been doing a splendid job of running the Playground on my behalf for these past five years, and I listen closely to his advice. Unfortunately, his other commitments mean he no longer has as much time as the job requires, so I have to find somebody else to take over his share of the responsibilities. Somebody I can trust.'

'Me, running the Playground?' Constance exclaimed. 'But the women are the slaves there, Sir Terence. Surely your guests would resent a woman in a position of authority.'

He smiled. 'Tell me, Constance. Do you feel that men, in general, find you intimidating?'

'I suppose so,' she admitted carefully. 'I'm very confident. That seems to turn a lot of men off.'

'That's where you're wrong,' he said. 'They may think you cold and unapproachable, but that doesn't mean you turn them off. Quite the opposite, in fact. Now imagine if those same men were to meet you in a different situation. Still the same confident and gorgeous Constance, but with one vital difference. You were available to them...' He clicked his fingers. 'Just like that. You couldn't say no because, beneath that self-assured exterior, there was a slave willing to submit to whatever demands her master made upon her. No formalities. No complicated seduction routines. The man only has to say the word and you're his.'

Constance began to understand what he was proposing. She would bring her complete self to the Playground, the woman who had walked into the lobby of the hotel and the shameless whore who now sat naked before the two men. She would not be separating herself any more. It was another huge step along the path to total submission.

'You would be handsomely rewarded, of course,' Sir Terence continued. 'And not just in the sexual sense. Do you think you could disappear for a whole month, without your own business suffering?'

'I suppose so,' she replied, after a slight hesitation. 'I can think of nothing I would enjoy more than working at the Playground. But there's the other business.'

He nodded. 'S/M-FM. A noble cause and I fully appreciate your devotion to it, but I'm sure a temporary replacement can be found to keep your seat hot. If you do agree to accept this offer your initial training will involve a full month of total commitment. That's twenty-four hours a day, seven days a week. There won't be any time for outside concerns. I don't need your answer now. You might like a few days to think it over.'

Constance took a deep breath. 'I don't need any time to think it over, Sir Terence,' she said firmly. 'If you have the confidence in me to offer me the position, I would be honoured to accept.'

He smiled. 'Excellent. I'm so glad my faith in you hasn't been misplaced. We shall work out the details later, but now I believe Jonathan wishes to punish you.'

Covington stood up. 'On your feet, slave. I haven't forgotten your impudence on the telephone earlier today.' He pointed to the instruments on the coffee table. 'Choose one and hand it to me.'

Constance had already decided. She handed him the cane, then turned around and leant over her armchair, parting her legs slightly and thrusting her bottom out. Sir Terence rose and caressed her soft unblemished cheeks.

'What a divine bottom you have, my dear,' he crooned.

'Thank you, master,' she breathed in anticipation.

'God created you for the cane,' he continued. 'Once Jonathan has finished with you I shall take great pleasure in disciplining you myself.'

The instant he removed his hand from her bottom the cane swished and a lightning bolt of the sweetest pain scorched across her quivering rear cheeks. Jonathan waited, watching the scarlet welt blossom, before striking her again. With each resounding whack Constance uttered a small cry, though the last thing she wanted was for him to stop. Two dozen stinging strokes later, her shuddering buttocks were zigzagged with streaks of crimson. The sensual tingling between her thighs was a perfect accompaniment to the throbbing afterglow of the cane.

'Now it's my turn,' Sir Terence announced, gripping the leather strap tightly in his fist. 'Brace yourself, my dear. This is going to hurt.'

That was not an idle threat. The hard, thick strap was like petrol on the fire already infusing her buttocks. She gripped the arms of the chair tightly and hissed through clenched teeth as a relentless fusillade of full-blooded whacks turned her ruby, from the tops of her stockings to the small of her back. She came close to begging for mercy, before the punishment finally ended.

'What a beautiful shade that is,' Sir Terence panted, laying down the strap. 'Are you hot, my dear?'

'Yes, master,' Constance gasped, remaining in her punishment position.

He picked up his wine glass and slowly poured the chilled contents over her scorched globes. The instant relief was nigh on orgasmic. She shivered as the wine trickled into the shadowy valley between her buttocks and down her thighs, soaking her stockings.

Covington departed shortly afterwards, leaving her

alone with Sir Terence. She knew, without needing to be told, that she was expected to spend the night with him. His pleasure was her duty, as would be the pleasure of many men, once she took up her position at the Playground. From now on she would enjoy thinking of herself as a high-class whore.

She already liked Sir Terence and grew to like him more as they chatted. He had the same supercilious manner as Covington, but lacked the clichéd masterly coldness of the younger man. Even though she sat naked before him, basking in his continued admiration of her body, Constance felt more like a lady than a sexual object.

Several glasses of wine and a pleasant conversation later, he told her to go to the bathroom and fix him a hot bath. When it was ready, he joined her, having left his clothes in the bedroom. For a man of his age he was in extraordinarily good shape, with few wrinkles and only a small tyre of fat on his waist. His semi-erect penis was also a pleasant surprise and Constance eyed it with the purest desire as he stepped into the bath.

Like an authentic Geisha girl she lovingly bathed him, then towelled him dry and massaged him with talcum powder. He was a man obviously accustomed to being pampered and she did not intend to disappoint him.

Taking her hand, he led her to the bedroom and slid open the mirrored door of the closet. On a hanger next to his suit was a uniform of shiny black rubber, with matching thigh boots directly underneath.

'Put it on,' he told her, sitting back on the bed. 'It's in your size.'

Constance kicked off her shoes and peeled off her wet stockings, then took the outfit from the closet. She caressed the shiny material, finding even the feel of it in her fingers incredibly exciting. Sir Terence watched intently as she stepped into the split-crotch knickers. She winced as the rubber hugged the swell of her burning buttocks, like a second skin. The inside of the dress needed to be dusted with talc before she could slither into it. It fitted like a sheath, clinging lovingly to her every delectable curve. Two circular cutouts at the front allowed her breasts to remain on full display. She eased the elbow-length gloves up her arms, then pulled on the perfectly fitting thigh boots and zipped them up at the back. Admiring the finished result in the mirror, she noted with pleasure that Sir Terence's cock was now fully erect.

'You do look truly mouthwatering, my dear,' he enthused. 'Turn around. Oh yes, almost perfect.'

'Almost, master?'

He nodded. 'Your breasts would look so much more spectacular if we were to give them a little colour, don't you think?'

'Whatever you say, master,' she replied. 'Do you wish to punish me again?'

'Indeed I do,' he said. 'You'll find just the thing on the coffee table. Bring it to me.'

Tottering on the high heels of her thigh boots, Constance hurried out to the lounge and returned with the black leather tawse. She handed it to her master, then dropped to her knees before him. Arching her back, she thrust out her breasts in readiness to be punished. Her nipples were already swollen with anticipation.

'I do like to get every little detail just right,' said Sir Terence. 'You appreciate that, don't you, my dear?'

'Of course, Sir Terence. I'm your slave. You must do as you see fit with me.'

His cock swelled to even greater tumescence as he

treated her breasts to an energetic flogging with the tawse. Constance threw back her head and responded with a throaty sound that was somewhere between a cry of pain and a moan of pleasure.

Swish, thwack! Swish, thwack!

The rhythmic sound of harsh leather striking soft flesh filled the bedroom. The punishment did not cease until Constance's breasts were completely reddened and throbbing almost as violently as her bottom.

Sir Terence threw aside the tawse and thrust his thickly veined staff towards her moist and pouting lips. They peeled apart and his erection slipped eagerly within. She swallowed until her nose was buried in the dark bush of his pubic hair, then drew her head slowly back, coating his tool with her saliva. He shuddered in ecstasy as her silken tongue travelled sensually over his glistening purple crown. She stroked his cock with her rubber-gloved right hand, while she licked his crinkled scrotum and took both his swollen eggs in turn in her mouth, soaking and warming them. She licked her way back up his cock, covered it in silky kisses, then once more welcomed it into her hungry mouth.

The heavy breathing and soft moans of the old man were sweet music to her ears. With her mouth and tongue she made passionate love to his cock and balls, coaxing him to the brink of climax, but skilfully denying him the ultimate release. For now he was the slave, straining in the satin bondage of her cock-sucking craft. When finally she felt the tremor swelling from the base of his cock, she gripped it in her fist, threw back her head and milked his hot cream over her face and outstretched tongue, gasping as she was splattered in burst after burst of the powerful thick shower. As the last droplet spat onto her chin she flicked the seeping remains from his cock slit with the tip of her tongue. Not a drop was allowed to go to waste. She licked every sticky trace from her lips and gloves as Sir Terence slumped back onto the bed, breathless and blissfully drained.

'Everything I've heard about you is indeed true,' he panted, drawing her rubber-sheathed form tightly against him.

'And what have you heard, master?'

'That you really know how to satisfy a man. That you are uninhibited in the truest sense of the word. You showed your talent for obedience during your weekend at the Playground. Don't look so surprised. I had several people keeping a close eye on you. I had to be sure you were the right person before I took the risk of offering you the job.'

'You seem to know everything about me, Sir Terence,' she replied.

He smiled. 'Including your fantasies, my dear. I have been taking a keen interest in you, ever since Kenton first mentioned you. It would be a crime to allow a talent such as yours to go to waste.'

While he was speaking he guided her hands to his cock. As she stroked and manipulated him gradually back to full stiffness, he slipped a hand between her thighs and eased two fingers into her soaking sex. She spread her thighs wider, breathing urgently, aching to feel him inside her. In a few moments his cock had regained its full splendour and he ordered her to mount him.

'Oh master. Oh *yessss*,' she gasped, lowering herself onto his shaft, her rubber dress rolled up around her waist.

She began riding slowly up and down on him, her vagina gripping like a snug-fitting glove. He cupped her throbbing pink breasts and squeezed tightly, pinching her stiff nipples between thumb and forefinger. She was sweating in her skin of rubber, but the humid discomfort only added an additional edge to her pleasure. Gradually she increased the tempo, urging him towards his peak, eager for the prize of his hot seed in her torrid depths. She tossed her head from side to side, crying out in the throes of her first climax. Suddenly his hands left her breasts, gripped her hips and raised her from him. Her beautiful face twisted in the agony of being denied her release.

'Turn over,' he panted.

Constance eagerly fell onto all fours, enticingly presenting her bottom. He patted her rubber-covered buttocks, then slipped a skilful finger into the humid valley between them. She tensed as he stroked the crinkled bud of her rear entrance, then pushed his finger up inside.

'I presume you're not a virgin,' he said huskily, easing his finger deeper into her snug tunnel.

'A virgin, master?' she exclaimed, mystified.

'You've had anal sex before, I take it?'

'No... no master,' she stammered uncertainly. 'I... I haven't.'

'Then this is indeed my lucky night,' he smiled. 'I'm afraid such special treats are all too rare these days.'

His finger was moving deep inside her, creating a sensation that was both pleasant and slightly uncomfortable. She was still not at all sure she wanted to be taken in this way and considered asking him not to do it, but then decided she was being silly. If she was to spend an entire month at the Playground, she could hardly expect her bottom to remain out of bounds.

Sir Terence kept his finger in her bottom for several

minutes, gradually relaxing her instinctively tense sphincter muscle. At the same time he slipped his cock between the wet lips of her sex and slid it slowly back and forth, oiling it with her juices. She stiffened when he withdrew again, nibbling her lower lip in anxious readiness for the possible discomfort to come.

'Relax, my dear,' he coaxed gently, pushing his lubricated erection against the puckered entrance to her bottom.

Constance gripped the sheet beneath her with both hands. A small cry issued from her throat as her clenched muscles yielded to the greater power of his rigid cock. A sharp bolt of pain lanced through her tummy, gradually giving way to an unexpected sensation of the purest pleasure that brought back teenage memories of when she had lost her virginity. In a matter of minutes she was responding eagerly to the thrusts of her master's cock into her ultra-tight rectum, thrusting her hips back to meet every deep stroke. The pain spreading out from her belly and infusing her already aching buttocks stopped just the right side of exquisite.

'I knew you'd love it, my dear,' Sir Terence panted, his strokes becoming more agitated. 'You must always remember, your master knows best.'

Chapter Nineteen

Constance felt like a conquering queen when she returned to the Playground a fortnight later. The black-windowed limousine had once again been sent to deliver her, so she remained ignorant of the precise location of the place.

KT had visited her the previous week, to finalise the details of her contract and answer any queries about her duties. She had had another meeting with Sir Terence in his suite at the King Charles and, once again, the experience had proved a pleasurable revelation. He had suggested she might pierce her nipples before taking up her new post. Constance had already been contemplating just that and was happy to comply with his wishes. Of Jonathan Covington, she had heard nothing. She still yearned for him, but expected they would almost certainly become reacquainted during her month at the Playground.

For her second visit she was allowed to bring one small suitcase, but the clothes required for her duties would be provided. KT showed her to her quarters, a comfortable suite on the third floor of the guesthouse. Each room, including the bathroom, was equipped with a closed circuit TV camera and there were no locks on the doors. Though she might be technically in charge, Constance would not be allowed to forget that she was, first and foremost, a slave. There would always be a master nearby to ensure she was punished whenever she deserved it.

Her duties, beyond those of a sexual nature, were relatively undemanding. She would welcome new guests, both masters and slaves, and see to it that every desire of the former was satisfied. It did not take her long to realise that the real running of the resort was still in the hands of her masters.

Though she was officially KT's replacement, Constance would not be allowed to discipline her subordinate slaves. Any disobedience was to be reported to a master, who would mete out the appropriate punishment. She was, in fact, little more than a symbol of authority for the masters who would enjoy nothing more than putting a pushy woman in her place. This suited her perfectly. Not only was she being given a whole month in which to explore her fantasies further, she was also being handsomely paid for the privilege.

Her duty uniform reflected her position perfectly. A crisp white blouse buttoned to the throat, with cutouts for her breasts and a magenta coloured silk jacket with a gold tag on the right lapel that read, *CB – Senior Slave*. Her matching ankle-length skirt was cut high at the back, leaving half-moons of her buttocks on view. Black seamed silk stockings, suspenders and high heels completed her ensemble. Underwear was strictly forbidden. Off-duty, she would go naked.

KT left as soon as she had been thoroughly familiarised with her duties and she began her new role as senior slave. Strutting through the hotel in her over-dressed state, head held high, she immediately attracted the attention of masters and slaves alike. She had already made up her mind to maintain the self-assured air of Constance Brooking, successful businesswoman. Meekness would appear contrived and it would be so much more enjoyable for the masters to take her down a peg or two. Each man who caught her eye was offered a smile that could be interpreted as encouragement or defiance. It was all part of the game she was immersing herself in.

She did not recognise any of the slaves from her previous visit and none of the masters looked familiar either. She wondered how Jon would react to seeing her strutting around as though she owned the place. He would certainly not hesitate to bring her back down to earth, and how she would enjoy that...

'Senior slave. My word!'

Constance turned in the direction of the voice. The man was lying on his stomach by the swimming pool, a naked and very pretty blonde in her early twenties on her knees beside him, massaging his shoulders. Constance thought his face looked familiar, but could not recall where she might have seen him before. It had certainly not been on her previous visit to the Playground.

She smiled. 'Yes, master.'

'Come here,' he told her. 'Closer. Okay, turn round again. I think I prefer the rear view. You have a fine arse, senior slave. Or am I allowed to pass such sexist comments to one in your position?'

'Of course you are, master,' she replied.

'I wasn't sure,' he said. 'You look rather – formal. You must be something really special to be prancing around here fully dressed, when all the other slaves are naked as the day they were born. Well, Miss High and Mighty, what makes you so different?'

Constance smiled. Her image was working to perfection. There was genuine resentment in the voice of the master and now he would surely feel obliged to assert his authority. 'I'm just a slave in uniform,' she replied. 'I'm filling in for KT, while he's on holiday.'

'A slave filling in for a master?' he exclaimed. 'Now that is an innovation. You are, of course, required to attend to the needs of your guests?'

'Of course, master.'

'Very well. I would like you to bring one of those chairs over here and sit in front of me with your legs wide apart. Hurry up, chop chop! Now, play with yourself. Let your fingers do the walking.'

His young slave giggled, obviously enjoying Constance's humiliation as much as he seemed to be.

Adopting a suitably shamed expression, Constance pushed her split skirt to one side, exposing her neatly groomed sex to his prying eyes. She ran both hands up her stockinged thighs, then slipped two fingers of each in between. Her quim was already hot and soaking and her fingers slid in with ease. She kept her head bowed as she vigorously frigged herself, moaning softly. It took her only a few moments to reach climax, but she continued fingering herself until the master directed her to stop.

'Enough of that,' he barked. 'I know what you really need. Meet me in the gymnasium at seven. You won't be needing your uniform.'

Constance was only too eager to keep her appointment and the master did not disappoint her. Having warmed her up with ten minutes on the exercise bicycle, spurred on by regular slashes of the cane to her buttocks, he chained her to the bench press and vigorously punished her with his cock in both ends, watched by his slave and several masters. When he was finished with her he forced her to crawl on her hands and knees from the gymnasium. It was a fitting start to her new role as an 'authority' figure.

It quickly became clear that her decision to play the confident lady of the manor had been an inspired one. She proved irresistible to the men, who had taken for granted that the slaves at the Playground were all grovelling creatures who walked around naked, constantly advertising their availability to their masters. Constance represented a challenge to their authority. She walked as though trying to intimidate them, daring them to assert themselves with her. That might be all very well in the world outside, but here in the Playground the haughty bitch would have to be taught the meaning of subservience.

While on duty she was frequently caned, spanked and strapped, for the sheer sadistic pleasure of stern masters. Every night found her satisfying a different man, or sometimes several at once. On one unforgettable occasion she was roped to her bed by a trio of masters, who then simultaneously screwed her. Another time she was forced to wear black leather briefs lined with pointed metal studs, while she knelt to fellate a number of men, one after the other, with her wrists handcuffed behind her back.

The first fortnight passed in a blur of lustful excess, which left her aching and more satisfied than she had ever dreamt possible. Constance began to fantasise that she could indeed spend the rest of her life like this, in total devotion to hedonistic gratification. Her boutique, her nice house, her friends and business acquaintances seemed like memories from a distant past. She was like a convert to the most perfect religion on earth, convinced she was ready to give up everything for the sins of the flesh.

Then Sir Terence paid an unexpected visit, cruising regally up the driveway in a gleaming black Rover. Constance greeted him and, along with two staff slaves, escorted him to his private suite at the very rear of the guesthouse. She sincerely hoped she would be chosen to spend the night with him.

'You seem to have settled in quite well,' he said as soon as they were alone. 'Any problems I should know about?'

'No master,' she replied. 'Everything is just fine. This place is like paradise on earth. I've never felt so… fulfilled.'

He smiled. 'I'm glad to hear it. It's been some time since I've visited. I intend staying for a couple of days and I'd like you as my personal slave while I'm here.'

Constance was overjoyed. There were over thirty attractive young women Sir Terence could have chosen from, but he had not hesitated to select her. He had even brought with him the clothes he wanted her to wear.

The slave uniform comprised of crotchless red rubber tights, matching high heels and a creation of studded black leather straps bound tightly around her upper body. A silver chain was clipped to the gold rings in her nipples. This would serve as her leash. For the next few days she would walk with even greater pride, revelling in her part as property of Sir Terence.

His arrival provided the perfect excuse for a banquet, followed by the kind of after-dinner entertainment unique to the Playground. Two naked slaves volunteered to perform a pussy tug-of-war in the centre of the games room, with the assembled masters betting on the outcome. Each girl was handcuffed and two pairs of steel clamps, joined together by a chain, attached to her labia. They then began pulling in opposite directions, whiplashes stinging their buttocks. Either one could bring the game to an end whenever the pain became too unbearable. It lasted for almost ten minutes, until one girl slumped to her knees, sobbing for mercy, tears streaming down her cheeks.

The next game involved two teams of three girls holding a cake fight on the lawn, whilst masturbating themselves with dildoes. When they were thoroughly covered in the gooey mess they licked one another clean, while the masters whipped them indiscriminately.

'Choose a slave, Constance,' Sir Terence said, some time later.

'Master?'

'I said choose a slave. There are plenty still available. Make sure it's one you really like. You and she will be sharing my bed tonight.'

She would have preferred him to choose, but he was the master and she would obey his wishes. She studied the slaves that had still not been claimed for the night by masters, her gaze eventually coming to rest on a slender and elegant woman in her early thirties.

Constance took a deep breath, then approached her. 'Sir Terence would like us to entertain him tonight.'

The woman smiled.

Fifteen minutes later the three of them were naked on Sir Terence's bed. The woman, whose name was Miriam, needed no persuasion to begin playing lesbian games with Constance. She found herself responding instinctively, recalling the pleasure she had experienced with her previous female partners. The pair kissed passionately, hands exploring one another. Sir Terence was content to watch until they moved into a sixty-nine, tongues greedily feasting on lust-slicked pussies. He then got into position behind Constance. Miriam instinctively knew what he intended. She moistened his cock with her mouth, then gripped it in her fist and helped him to ease into his favourite slave.

For the second night of his stay Sir Terence kept Constance for himself. The threesome had been a highly erotic experience, but she was still glad to have her master to herself once again.

Before leaving, Sir Terence complimented her once more on the excellent job she was doing at the Playground. As soon as he had gone she was back in her uniform and once more shamelessly baiting the men with her self-confident poise. Rest was not one of the perks of her job.

The following Saturday she received another pleasant surprise in the form of Jonathan Covington. The instant she saw him her heart beat faster and all the feelings he had previously stirred within her returned. As far as Constance was concerned they had some unfinished business to attend to. She had to check an impulsive urge to throw herself at his feet. If he shared her sense of lustful urgency, he managed to keep his feelings well hidden.

'So, how are you enjoying the role of the Playground's chief slave?' he enquired when she had escorted him to his suite. 'I like the nipple rings.'

'Thank you, master,' she smiled. 'I'm loving it so much, it doesn't seem right to be getting paid as well.'

'Spoken most unlike an ambitious businesswoman,'

he replied, reaching for her with both hands.

She shuddered as he teased her nipples and caressed her breasts, studying her recently caned bottom in the full-length mirror behind her. His hands moved inside her blouse. His touch was electrifying. She moved closer to him, glancing towards the bed, mentally begging him to throw her onto it and ravish her. As though reading her mind he suddenly ripped open her blouse, grabbed her hands and pressed them to the bulge in his leather trousers.

'Oh master, I'm yours,' she gasped, squeezing the throbbing outline of his cock.

'I want you to do something for me,' he said.

'Anything, master. Anything you want.'

He pushed her hands away. 'I want you to go downstairs and fetch me a slave. Young and pretty – preferably blonde. That is part of your job, I presume.'

'Uh, yes, master... of course,' she stammered, feeling hurt and confused.

'Then do it,' he barked. 'And in the meantime I shall take a shower.'

She did not bother to change out of her ripped blouse before hurrying downstairs, choking back tears of humiliation. Why was he treating her like this – making her want him, then cruelly rejecting her? Had he wanted to whip her, or debase her in a thousand other perverse ways, she would have understood and welcomed it. But his particular form of sadism struck her as depraved beyond belief.

She found a young blonde slave by the swimming pool who looked like she would fit the bill perfectly. The buxom girl was happy to accompany her to Covington's suite. He had finished showering and was lying on the bed, his erection forming a tent in the towel around his waist.

'What's your name?' he asked the blonde as she nervously approached the bed.

'Laura... master.'

He smiled. 'It's a pleasure to meet you, Laura. We're going to have a pleasant afternoon together, if that's all right with you.'

'I'm at your service, master,' she answered. She glanced at Constance, who was standing by the door, her tattered blouse still hanging open.

'Senior slave won't be staying,' he assured the girl. 'Fix me a gin and tonic, CB. Then you may go.'

By the time Constance handed him the cold drink he had already handcuffed Laura to the bed.

Constance spent the remainder of the day alternately cursing him and aching for him. It was bad enough that he should reject her, but ordering her to bring him another girl had added insult to humiliation. If only she could reject him. The fact that she couldn't had little to do with her duties as a slave.

He might have subjected her to further torment that night, had two masters not won her in a poker game. She had no time to think about him for the remainder of the night as the two men exhausted themselves by using and thoroughly abusing her, in the manner to which she had become accustomed.

But Covington's particular game was far from finished. The following afternoon she was once again summoned to his suite. She thought she was prepared for anything, but instead of the expected teasing and tormenting, he took her to his bed, lovingly stripped her, covered her from head to toe with silken kisses, then made love to her with a passion that was bone-crushing. He gave his magnificent stallion cock to her in each and every

237

possible way, not once denying her the complete pleasure she craved. When their passion was finally spent she dozed blissfully, wrapped like a true lover in his arms.

Her romantic illusions were somewhat shattered that night when he brought her back to his suite, for what she assumed would be a continuation of their afternoon delight. He laid her out on the bed, bound her hand and foot with silk scarves, then switched on the TV. He flicked through the channels until he came to room nineteen, where a diminutive redhead in white ankle socks and tennis shoes reclined provocatively on her bed studying a pornographic magazine and half-heartedly masturbating.

'I believe her name is Annabel,' he told Constance. 'I shall be spending the next couple of hours with her. I'll release you when I come back. Enjoy the show.'

He left the following afternoon without making love to Constance again. She was left wanting him more intensely than ever, which she suspected was exactly his intention. She wanted to scream, to throw herself onto the bonnet of his car and force him to take her with him. Instead, she calmly watched him depart, consoling herself with the certainty that she would eventually see him again. If only she could be so certain of his intentions towards her.

Though there was no question of forgetting him, or even putting him temporarily from her mind, she was determined to make the best of the remainder of her stay at the Playground. In five days she would be back in the real world and facing the more mundane demands of her own business. It might be some time before she was able to return to her earthly paradise.

The following Saturday night she returned to her post as *Slave in the Hot Seat* on S/M-FM. Half an hour into the broadcast there was a loud crashing noise from downstairs.

'What was that?' Constance cried, forgetting the man on the other end of the telephone line, who was lovingly detailing his favourite method of disciplining a female slave.

KT rushed from the attic to investigate. Wearing only a black lace bra and red rubber shorts, Constance was still on air a few moments later when the first of the policemen who had broken down her front door reached the top of the ladder.

Chapter Twenty

'With these rings, I make thee my slave.'

So saying, Constance's master took the gold rings from their box and ran them carefully through her freshly pierced labia. The initial nerve-numbing pain of the needle spearing her flesh was already being replaced by a near-pleasant throbbing.

'Now, we come to the anointing of the slave,' the presiding master announced.

Constance was taken by surprise, having thought that her piercing heralded the end of the ceremony. The bridesmaids helped her to her feet, freed her from her bondage and stripped her of everything but her veil. She was then ordered to lie on the altar with her head on the cushion, her arms spread and her legs raised with her feet pointing up at the arched ceiling.

Her master climbed onto the altar and strapped a wooden spreader pole to her ankles to keep her legs splayed. While he was doing this, the master of ceremonies placed a longer pole under her neck and lashed either end to her wrists. The bridesmaids hooked a leather leash to both rings in her labia, then eased them in opposite directions, peeling open the damp petals. Constance whimpered in anticipation.

'You will keep your legs up straight until I give you permission to lower them,' her master directed, emphasising his words with several taps of his riding crop on her tensed belly. 'Is that understood?'

Constance nodded.

'The slave is now ready to be anointed with fire,' announced the master of ceremonies.

As eight of the slave guests lined up, each holding a thick black candle, it became horrifyingly clear to Constance exactly what he meant. He lit each candle in turn, then the slaves gathered around her.

'Master, no!' she shrieked.

'Quiet,' he ordered calmly, scoring the backs of her thighs with an effortlessly savage lash of the riding crop. 'When have you ever been afraid of a little pain? Keep those legs up, else you'll really have something to complain about.'

He signalled to the eight slaves, who tilted their flickering candles over her. She shrieked piteously as scalding wax dripped onto her breasts, belly and thighs. Another crack of her master's crop reminded her to keep her legs still. Her bridesmaids stood to either side, nobly contributing to her torment by maintaining an excruciating pull on her pussy rings.

The anointing by fire seemed as though it would never end. The slaves holding the candles watched impassively, none of them strangers to similar erotic tortures. Finally, when Constance was almost covered in tiny mushrooms of hardened wax and breathlessly begging for mercy, her master decided she had had enough.

The slaves stepped aside as he mounted the altar once more and positioned himself between the shapely thighs of his slave bride. Constance raised her head, a small moan of delight issuing from beneath her veil when she saw that he was unzipping his trousers. Suddenly, the fires of hell seemed worth every drop of candle wax.

'What do you say, slave?' he demanded, brushing her stretched labia with the distended crown of his stiff cock.

'Take me, master,' she responded urgently. 'Please take me... I'm *begging* you.'

For Constance, the audience gathered around the altar no longer existed. She and her master were alone and she wanted nothing but him. Gripping the pole between her ankles in both fists, he eased his gnarled erection into her slippery sex, with a slowness that was almost unbearable.

'Give it to me, *please* master,' she gasped.

His shaft half-buried between her thighs, he glanced at the master of ceremonies. 'She did say give it to her, didn't she?'

The thin whip in the other man's fist whistled and slashed across her breasts, dislodging several lumps of wax.

'Owwwwww...!' she yelped.

'Make sure those two don't give her any slack,' her master barked, glaring at the bridesmaids.

The master of ceremonies obligingly ensured they attended fully to their sadistic duties with several cracks of his whip to their bare bottoms. The tug on Constance's labia grew ever more excruciating. But when the full length of her master's cock was finally inside her, the acute pain became virtually indistinguishable from the accompanying pleasure.

Hovering only feet from the action, the camcorder captured every forceful thrust of his cock into her, every ecstatic cry that escaped her throat. She climaxed twice before eventually receiving the welcome flood of his hot cream.

The bride having been thrashed, tortured, screwed and fully humiliated, the ceremony was finally over. As the other watching masters stepped up to shake her master's hand and offer their congratulations, the bridesmaids released Constance and helped her from the altar.

'Beautiful, isn't it?' Barbara smiled, holding a mirror between her thighs.

Constance gazed down at the reflection of her own sex. Gingerly touching her glittering labia rings, she had to agree that it looked most appealing.

As with a traditional wedding, the ceremony was followed by a feast. Constance's master sat at the head of the banquet table. She crouched at his feet, now naked but for her thigh boots. Her food was served up in silver bowls, her fingers taking the place of cutlery. In between courses she licked his highly polished boots, much to the delight of the guests. At the end of the meal he rose to his feet and an expectant hush fell over the room.

'Masters and slaves, I would like to thank you all for coming here this evening,' he began. 'Taking Constance as my wife was a great honour, but taking her as my slave is indeed the icing on the cake. As I am sure many of the men present this evening are already aware, she is not a woman who is hampered by inhibitions. I have no doubt that she will keep her promise to make me the most satisfied man on earth. She'd better!' He picked up his riding crop and whacked the table top to a murmur of approval from the watching gathering. 'However, while we praise Constance for her beauty and dedication to her calling, we mustn't forget a very good friend who cannot be with us today. Kenton Turley has been condemned to spend the next two years behind bars, for the crime of running a late-night pirate radio station that did no harm to anyone. Let us raise our glasses to KT and wish him the best of luck with his appeal.'

Constance cast her eyes downwards. Mention of the man who had introduced her to the dangerous delights of bondage and submission brought back unwelcome memories of being dragged handcuffed and half-naked through her front door and bundled into the back of a police van. Released on bail forty-eight hours later, she had found herself transformed from a reputable businesswoman into a criminal celebrity. A beautiful blonde and a pornographic pirate radio operation was the stuff of tabloid wet dreams.

For the first time in her life, Constance was completely powerless over the events that were affecting her. Her reputation was quickly ruined beyond redemption. It seemed as if her business was about to follow. The gutter press laid siege to the boutique, scaring away staff and customers alike. Hack journalists dogged her every move and telephoned her at all hours of the day and night, desperately seeking an exclusive on the woman they had christened 'the Queen of Porn FM'. When she refused to co-operate, one of the tabloids found a 'former lover' who was only too glad to cash in.

Lurid tales of sadomasochistic orgies and other 'even more shocking' activities indulged in by Constance and her perverted friends were splashed like a royal scandal over the pages of the papers. Tapes of some of her broadcasts on S/M-FM and a copy of the *Slave in the Hot Seat* video were produced as yet further evidence of a criminally irresponsible libido. Her tabloid CV was completed with the revelation of her 'close friendship' with the notorious Mistress Amber.

As she surveyed the ruins of her life, in near despair, Sir Terence DeMille unexpectedly came forward as her saviour. Her dignity was beyond salvation, but he could still save her from financial ruin. Even if she was eventually found innocent of all the offences she had been charged with, she knew her business would never recover. Sir Terence invited her to lunch and made her the proverbial offer she couldn't refuse. As well as paying her an exceptional price for the boutique, he would ensure she was defended at her trial by the best barrister money could buy.

The price eventually paid by the Queen of Porn FM was a fine of eighty thousand pounds and a one-year suspended prison sentence. She emerged from the courthouse in the company of her master, who hustled her through the throng of waiting reporters and into his car. The registry office was booked for that afternoon. She did not even have time for a change of clothes.

Constance's master concluded his after-dinner speech by announcing that, as a thank you to all the masters who had attended the ceremony, his slave would be at their complete disposal for the next few hours. The men around the huge table cheered and applauded enthusiastically, leaving her in no doubt that all would be only too glad to partake of his generosity. She looked up at her master with a grateful smile. What better wedding present could he possibly bestow upon her?

The master who had presided over the slave-taking ceremony was awarded the honour of enjoying her first. He preferred to enjoy her in private, but assured the others that she would be returned to them as soon as he was finished. Then taking her hand, he led her away from the party and out into the garden.

'Lovely night, isn't it?' he remarked, slipping an arm around her waist.

'The most perfect night there's ever been,' Constance replied sincerely.

'No regrets?'

'Only about what happened to KT,' she answered. 'I

still can't believe they sent him to prison. It makes me feel like I got off lightly.'

'You lost your business and your reputation,' he reminded her. 'A high enough price to pay for the crime of pleasure.'

'But I have my freedom.' She laughed as soon as she had uttered the words. 'I mean, I'm not locked up. S/M-FM has landed KT in jail and me with a whole new career.'

He smiled. 'So you've signed the contract with that satellite TV company?'

She nodded. 'And one with the Sunday Exclusive. Imagine me, a soft porn TV presenter and agony aunt! I've barely had time to catch my breath since the court case ended.'

'At least now you can be successful and be yourself at the same time,' he said. 'It's just a pity you won't have so much time to devote to the Playground from now on.'

'I'll always have time for the Playground, Sir Terence,' she assured him. 'Actually, I'm glad I have this chance to show you just how grateful I am for all you've done for me.'

Falling to her knees in the damp grass, she unzipped the older man's trousers. Sir Terence leant back against a tree and stroked her hair as she withdrew his cock and eagerly applied her lips and tongue to coax it to full stiffness.

'Oh God, Constance, I should have married you myself,' he groaned.

With his cock nudging the back of her throat, all she could manage in reply was a soft moan. She sucked him for several minutes, then rose to her feet again. Wrapping her arms around the thick trunk of the tree she crouched down and thrust out her hindquarters invitingly.

'Are you sure?' he asked, caressing her goose-pimpled and reddened buttocks.

'Of course I'm sure, Sir Terence,' she replied. 'It is your favourite indulgence, isn't it?'

Presented with such a token of her esteem he was not about to argue. He moistened a finger in her sex, then pushed it gently into her delightfully tight bottom.

'Ohhh, that feels so nice,' she purred. 'Put your cock in my bottom, master. I'm ready.'

Trembling with excitement, he positioned the bulbous crown at the puckered rim of her anus. Her ecstatic cry rent the cool night air as inch after inch of his thick shaft stretched and filled her. He paused when she cried out again, concerned that he was hurting her.

'Don't stop, please – I love it,' she moaned, thrusting back against him, urging him deeper. His balls brushed the cold steel of her labia rings as his cock sank to the hilt in her warm and welcoming snugness. He cupped her aching buttocks with both hands, withdrew slowly, then penetrated her fully again. With each careful stroke he built up a deep thrusting rhythm that sent Constance into sensual rapture. She wished the camcorder was present to record the event. She would enjoy seeing herself bent over against a tree, a slut at one with nature, enjoying a master's cock in the most basic manner imaginable.

Twenty minutes later, his passion satisfied, Sir Terence returned her to her master. Jonathan Covington led her to another room at the rear of the house, where the rest of his guests were gathered expectantly. They had passed the time while they waited for her by preparing the other slaves for the orgy. The naked women, including

Constance's bridesmaids, were lined up side by side, bent double over a horizontal timber beam that ran across the entire span of the room. Their wrists were roped together, palms flat against the polished wooden floor. The left ankle of each slave was roped to the right ankle of her neighbour. With their legs splayed and rear quarters upthrust invitingly, they presented a mouth-watering display for the assembled masters. However, the instant the star of the occasion appeared all eyes turned to her. Constance felt weak with excitement at the sight of the men waiting to ravish her.

'She's all yours, my friends,' Covington told them. 'Let the real fun commence!'

'Aren't you going to tie me up too, master?' she enquired.

In reply, he gave her bottom a sharp smack and pushed her in the direction of the waiting men. Two of them grabbed her arms and dragged her into the centre of the room. For the moment, at least, tying her up was the last thing on their minds. A strong master seized her from behind and pulled her down on top of him. Holding her around the waist with one arm, as though fearing she might try to escape, he unzipped his trousers. Constance reached blindly between her thighs. Her fist closed around his stiff cock and she guided it into the deep valley between her tender buttocks. She closed her eyes dreamily and heard the rasp of zippers from all around. In no time she was presented with an array of eager erections. As the master beneath her slid slowly up into her bottom, another crouched between her thighs and entered her with one smooth lunge. Fingers twisted in her hair. Her head was turned sideways and another pulsing column of flesh stretched her lips wide and slipped deep into her mouth, choking off her cry of pleasure. Two more filled her outstretched hands. Another man squatted over her belly, slid his thick cock into the valley between her breasts, and then moulded their softness around it as he fucked her there.

Covington watched intently, standing in front of another slave, his hips grinding as he thrust between her full red lips. There was a camera in his hands and a satisfied smile on his face. Banishing all his misgivings about Constance's suitability as a wife and slave had taken some time, but he was now certain that marrying her had been the right decision. With her undoubted talent, beauty and complete lack of inhibition, coupled with his skills as her agent, there was nothing they could not accomplish together. He felt no jealousy as he watched her writhe beneath the heaving mass of male bodies. She deserved a reward, both for all she was doing, and all he knew she would do in the future for him – her master.

More exciting titles available from Chimera

All **Chimera** titles are available from your local bookshop or newsagent, or direct from our mail order department. Please send your order with your credit card details, a cheque or postal order (made payable to *Chimera Publishing Ltd*) to: **Chimera Publishing Ltd., Readers' Services, PO Box 152, Waterlooville, Hants, PO8 9FS**. Or call our **24 hour telephone/fax credit card hotline: +44 (0)23 92 646062** (Visa, Mastercard, Switch, JCB and Solo only).

UK & BFPO - Aimed delivery within three working days.
- A delivery charge of £3.00.
- An item charge of £0.20 per item, up to a maximum of five items.

For example, a customer ordering two items from the site for delivery within the UK will be charged £3.00 delivery + £0.40 items charge, totalling a delivery charge of £3.40. The maximum delivery cost for a UK customer is £4.00. Therefore if you order more than five items for delivery within the UK you will not be charged more than a total of £4.00 for delivery.

Western Europe - Aimed delivery within five to ten working days.
- A delivery charge of £3.00.
- An item charge of £1.25 per item.

For example, a customer ordering two items from the site for delivery to W. Europe, will be charged £3.00 delivery + £2.50 items charge, totalling a delivery charge of £5.50.

USA - Aimed delivery within twelve to fifteen working days.
- A delivery charge of £3.00.
- An item charge of £2.00 per item.

For example, a customer ordering two items from the site for delivery to the USA, will be charged £3.00 delivery + £4.00 item charge, totalling a delivery charge of £7.00.

Rest of the World - Aimed delivery within fifteen to twenty-two working days.
- A delivery charge of £3.00.
- An item charge of £2.75 per item.

For example, a customer ordering two items from the site for delivery to the ROW, will be charged £3.00 delivery + £5.50 item charge, totalling a delivery charge of £8.50.

Chimera Publishing Ltd

PO Box 152
Waterlooville
Hants
PO8 9FS

www.chimerabooks.co.uk

info@chimerabooks.co.uk

www.chimera-freedating.com

***

Sales and Distribution in the USA and Canada

Client Distribution Services, Inc
193 Edwards Drive
Jackson
TN 38301
USA

***

Sales and Distribution in Australia

Dennis Jones & Associates Pty Ltd
19a Michellan Ct
Bayswater
Victoria
Australia 3153